A Bride's
DILEMMA

IN FRIENDSHIP, TENNESEE

A Bride's
DILEMMA

IN FRIENDSHIP, TENNESSEE

DIANA LESIRE BRANDMEYER

BARBOUR
PUBLISHING

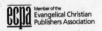

Dedication

God has placed amazing women in my life to help me on my journey.

Barbara Schlapkohl, Barb Friederich, Luanne Burkholder, Brenda Singleton, Terry Stretch, Debbie Wright, Patty Wiesner, and Marty Lintvedt—thank you for carrying me in prayer. Jennifer Tiszai, without you this book wouldn't be.

Prologue

Travis Logan leaned over the deck railing and watched the river swirl and froth as the steamboat shoved its way through the muddy Mississippi. An older gentleman stood next to him. Travis hadn't seen him on board before. "Nice out here on the water."

"Better than down below." The man swayed.

"Are you feeling okay, sir?" Travis reached over and steadied him while he grasped the railing.

"Must be the motion. It's the first trip I've taken on a big ship." The man's knuckles were white.

The man did look a bit green. Some people couldn't handle the rhythm of the ship. "The fresh air should help." Travis relaxed. Other than suggesting a piece of ginger to settle the man's stomach, there was little he could do for seasickness as a doctor. And he'd left that life behind. Now a horse claimed his thoughts and his future. He walked a few paces away and then stopped. He should offer the man some assistance, maybe collect a family member? He turned back to ask, "Can I get someone for you?"

The man released the rail and dropped to the steamboat deck with a thud.

Travis's physician training kicked his future out of the way. He automatically knelt and felt for a pulse. It was there. Weak, but there.

"Sir, can you hear me?"

No response came from the man. Sweat beads swelled on his forehead and dripped down his neck. Either the man had succumbed to heatstroke, or worse, had some kind of fever. Pricks of fear stabbed Travis's neck. He'd been at the bedside of too many men who succumbed to a fever during the War Between the States. And he couldn't prevent their deaths.

Feet shuffled around him as a small crowd of passengers gathered in a half circle to gawk and whisper.

"Someone go after the ship's doctor." He didn't mind giving that order. It would be best for the man and Travis.

"Doctor got off at the last stop in Cairo, Illinois. We're picking up the new one in St. Louis," a deckhand propping himself up with a mop called from behind the crowd.

Travis's jaw tightened. "Anyone know this man's name? Where his cabin is?" He searched faces for some indication of recognition and saw none.

There were mumbles as the man's identity was discussed, but no clear response came other than he'd been seen boarding the ship in Memphis alone.

A flock of seagulls squawked as they flew overhead, casting shadows that flittered across the unconscious man's face.

"Is there an infirmary at least? Perhaps the captain can look in on him." Travis didn't want to announce he was a doctor. If he did, he'd likely be pressed into service until St. Louis.

"There's a room he used a few floors below deck."

"Let's take him there then. I'll help you get him there." He hoped the captain would take charge of the patient, leaving Travis to go back to planning his life as a horse breeder.

The deckhand propped his mop between a brass spittoon and the rail. The wooden handle clunked against the brass.

Travis draped the older man's arm around his shoulder and waited for the deckhand to do the same. Then they lifted him.

"Where we going?" The man rallied for a moment. "I don't feel so good."

"We're taking you to the infirmary, sir. What's your name?" Travis hoped for details, but none came.

After a while, the man woke. During his short lucid periods, Travis learned his name was Caleb Wharton from Friendship, Tennessee. More importantly, before dying, Caleb Wharton had given Travis the deed to his land and offered him heaven.

Chapter 1

With a short piece of cinder, eighteen-year-old Heaven Wharton scratched another vertical line between the logs across the rough chinking. According to the marks, Pa had been gone now for almost ninety days. She set the cinder on the protruding edge of the log just over the marks and out of reach of her little sister, Angel's, hands.

"Angel, it's time to get up." Quiet from her parents' bedroom seeped into the kitchen.

Gathering the hem of her work apron, she wiped the cinder from her fingertips. She let the smudged fabric fall and settle against her black skirt. She hadn't heard from Pa since he left. Their supplies were running low, and it was four weeks until Christmas. If he didn't send for them soon, she'd have to go into town. She hated going there without Pa. She didn't have his friendly way about her when it came to Angel. He could make a stranger change his tune about treating Angel like a broken doll. And the stranger would be friends with Pa before he moved on. Heaven just got mad, and angry words sparked from her tongue in defense of her sister. No, she didn't look forward to going into town without Pa.

Soft footsteps shuffled behind her. She felt her face tighten. This wasn't the life she'd been brought up to live. "Go back and put on your shoes, please." Her sister's stockings would be filthy.

"I'm sorry. I forgot." Footsteps thudded against the plank floor as Angel went back for her shoes.

Heaven's fingers gripped into fists. That was Angel's last clean pair of socks. They'd have to wash this morning, even though it wasn't wash day, so she would have dry ones by tonight.

Angel returned with her feet covered. "Do you think we'll hear from Pa today?" Her eleven-year-old sister had asked that question every day since their father had left.

"I hope so, Angel. We'll keep praying for him, just like we do every night before bedtime." Pa had left them behind in Tennessee and gone to look for work at the new Union Stock Yard and Transit Company in Chicago. He promised to send money so they could join him. So far he hadn't even sent a letter.

"I wish Ma were still alive. Then we wouldn't be by ourselves." Angel's blond curls were a tangled mess, and her unfocused blue eyes still held the sleepy morning look.

Heaven stooped and gathered the small girl into her arms, attempting to hug her own sadness away with Angel's. "Me, too. But she's not, so we're going to be strong, right? The Wharton women are capable, that's what Pa says, and that's what we are—Wharton women." Heaven wished for the same confidence she'd used in her tone. Instead, her stomach looped into a knot and pulled tight. If Pa didn't come home soon, she wasn't quite sure what she would do. Thankfully, it wasn't spring, so she didn't have to worry about plowing, and her great-uncle seemed to have had an affinity for green beans. There had to be a hundred jars of them in the cellar, but without Pa around, they hadn't been able to get fresh meat. She'd tried shooting rabbits, but she always missed. There were a few pieces of smoked beef and ham in the spring cellar that would take them through another month. After that, Heaven realized she'd have to leave Angel in the cabin while she went out to hunt something bigger and slower.

And what will I do when I kill it?

Her parents had sold their beautiful home and moved into this little two-room cabin in Friendship because Pa had been fearful the battle might reach Nashville. At least that was the story they told their daughters, but Heaven found out it was because her pa had lost the house in a game of cards. Turned out moving from Nashville kept them from being killed in the war. And Heaven and Angel were safe, but not her mother. Her parents should have taken the offer of Heaven's friend, Annabelle. Annabelle's father offered to let them live in their carriage house. Her father was too proud to do that, Ma said. At least there she knew what to do and suspected she would still have her ma.

Now Heaven had been left in charge without the knowledge she needed to run a home without help. They had been to the only church in town a few times, not often enough to make any friends, at least not any close friends like she had in Nashville.

In Nashville they had floors that gleamed from wax. Here the floor was made of rough wood planks, and crawling creatures had made their way into the cabin all summer. Now that it was cold, it was the mice they had to worry about.

In Nashville, before the war, she only had to worry about small things. Would she be able to get to the Sunday social if it rained? Would Jake like her new hair ribbon?

At the thought of Jake, molasses-thick sadness filled her soul. Things would have been different if he'd returned from the war. But that was before. She had to remember that life was over because of that awful war, and she had to set it behind her.

Now they were farmers. "We are starting a new life," Ma had said as they packed a wagon a year ago with the belongings they hadn't sold. "Be thankful your great-uncle Neal left us his farm when he died, and we have a place to live."

"If Wharton women are strong, how come Ma died from typhoid last spring?" Angel tugged her fingers through her tangled curls.

"Sometimes things don't make sense." Like now. Heaven, at eighteen, should be married to Jake and living in her own home, maybe with a baby on the way and one on her knee. Instead, the war had taken her intended, the fever had taken her ma, and now it looked like Chicago had taken her pa. Her hand fluttered to her neck and she caressed the lorgnette her mother used to wear. "Did you fold up your nightdress and put it under the pillow?"

Angel shook her head no.

"Please see to it then."

While Angel did as asked, Heaven stood in front of the cookstove, thankful to her great-uncle that she didn't have to cook over an open fire, and gave their breakfast a quick stir. It would be ready soon. She gave the spoon a sharp tap on the edge of the pan to clean it and then set it to the side on a small plate that rested on the warming shelf.

"All done. I don't know why we have to be so neat about things." Angel plopped her hands on her hips. "We don't have any visitors."

"It wouldn't do to have a messy house. Proper ladies keep their houses in order in case someone should drop by for a visit." She plucked Angel's cap off the branch their mother had hung on the wall next to the stove to hold their hats and wet things. "We need to gather the eggs, and when we come back in, the porridge will be ready." She placed the scratchy, black wool cap in her sister's hand.

With a sigh, Angel set it on top of her head and yanked on the sides. "I could do the chickens myself, you know."

"Soon."

"You say that every day." Angel's lips drew into a pout.

"And I mean it." Heaven helped her sister with her coat and wrapped a black knitted scarf around her throat. She wouldn't take a chance that Angel would get ill. Then she slipped on her own coat and looped the egg basket over her arm.

The cold end-of-November rain that threatened earlier when Heaven went to milk their cow made good on its promise. Big plops of water pelted them as the girls stepped off the porch.

Angel stretched out her hand and waited for Heaven to grasp it.

The chicken coop wasn't far, but there was still enough distance for the rain to trickle down Heaven's neck and make a trail between her shoulder blades. She shivered and wished she'd wound a scarf around her own neck even if it was that awful black. She loved her ma, but she was tired of wearing mourning clothes.

Reaching the slanted door of the chicken coop, Heaven let go of Angel's hand to yank the metal handle on the ill-fitting door. The wood, swollen from the rain, held tight to its frame. It took several strong pulls before it gave way. Inside, the small structure held little heat, and the missing chinking between some of the logs let in the only light. The wind blew rain through the doorway. A few of the chickens were on their nests clucking, still getting ready to lay eggs.

The rain intensified, pinging against the tin roof. The chickens that weren't laying scurried around Heaven's feet, pecking at her ankles, reminding her they wanted to be fed.

Angel felt along the side walls where the chickens roosted on shelves. As her hand touched fluffed feathers, a loud squawk sounded.

"I'd say she has an egg for us today. Be quick or she'll peck you." Heaven tossed dried corn kernels onto the straw-covered floor. The chickens pecked and bickered with each other as they searched for the grain. The black rooster flapped his wings and crowed and pushed aside a hen to collect his breakfast.

Her sister slid her hand under a speckled hen, pulled out an egg without getting pecked, and held it up. "Is it a golden egg?"

"Not on the outside. It's a brown one."

"Do you think we'll ever find a golden egg?"

Heaven winced. If only it were possible for that to happen. "I don't think so, Angel. Our riches come from God, remember?" Heaven nudged the handwoven gathering basket into Angel's arm.

"Then I'm going to ask him to send us a golden egg so we can get our steamboat tickets and go where Pa is." Angel's mouth twisted while she worked her free hand through the air, finding the rim of the basket. She traced the edge then nestled the egg inside before turning back to search for more eggs.

"I don't like November. Do you, Heaven?"

"Hadn't thought about it much. I guess it's not my favorite month since the sky always seems gray and the leaves have dropped to the ground. I like October when the sun hits the leaves and they look like they're on fire."

"Ouch!" Angel's hand came away from the hen with the egg. "Got it anyway, you old meanie. Jake said your hair looks like that when the sunshine sometimes lands on it."

"You remember that?" Heaven touched her strawberry blond waves, remembering how, when the sun brought out the red, Jake would call it his special fire that warmed his heart.

"I remember lots of things."

Heaven knew her sister would soon want to talk about memories too painful to discuss if she didn't change the direction of the conversation. "What's your favorite month, Angel? I bet it's a summer one, because you like to get in the creek with a bar of fancy soap."

"No, it's not. It's December. I know that's when baby Jesus was born, but I like it 'cause we always get a stick of candy and a little gift." Angel's brow furrowed. "Is that bad, Heaven? Would Ma be mad at me for saying that?"

Heaven bent over and kissed the top of her sister's head,

inhaling the scent of the woodstove that snuggled in her hair. "No, I think Ma would understand." She handed the egg basket to Angel to carry back. "This is your chore, remember?"

"I know."

The wind whistled through the cracks in the coop. Heaven shivered. Winter was pressing down on them. "I think we should go to town today. It's only going to get colder, and we need to stock up on a few things just in case Pa isn't able to send for us before Christmas."

"I like going into Friendship. Are we going to take the wagon?"

Heaven laughed. "No, I don't think we will be purchasing that much today. We'll take our basket and walk."

"We can't even ride Charlie into town? Even though it's raining?" Angel begged. "Please?"

Heaven sucked in a breath. What had she been thinking? It was raining, and Angel could catch a cold, which could lead to something more serious. "Maybe we should wait until tomorrow when the sun might be out, and it would be a more pleasant journey."

"No! Let's go today. We can take Charlie, and it's not raining that hard. We can drape Great-Uncle Neal's old overcoat on top of us to stay dry. Please, Heaven." Angel folded her hands into prayer hands, her fingertips touching her chin. "It's been forever since we've seen a single person besides ourselves."

"What if we stayed home and baked a cake instead?" Heaven was sure that bribe would work. They hadn't made a cake in a long time, and now that she'd offered to do it, she regretted it. There probably wasn't enough flour to make one since the mice had discovered it.

"I want to go to town. Please, can we go? Please!"

Heaven wished she hadn't suggested it, but once you let a horse out of a barn without a lead, it is hard to rein back inside. "We'll leave after breakfast unless—" She paused. "Unless it starts raining hard."

Angel jumped up and down with her hands clasped tight to the basket. Her blond hair floated like a cloud around her head while the eggs clacked against each other in the basket.

"Angel! The eggs!"

The spring went out of her legs. "I can't wait! I'm going to eat really fast." The small girl stepped out of the chicken coop, not waiting for her sister.

"Wait for me, Angel Claire. Remember, there is a hole in the path to the cabin. You don't want to smash those eggs. They almost didn't survive your excitement about going into town."

Angel stopped. "Are you ever going to put the rope up so I can come out here by myself?"

Heaven's body tensed. She had to let her sister do things for herself, she knew that, but it didn't mean she couldn't watch Angel's every step.

"Do you think there will be enough to make me a jump rope, too?"

"There might be a piece left. I'll string it later today. If it stops raining."

"It's a good day. I get a rope line, a jump rope, and we get to go to town!"

Heaven didn't share her sister's excitement. Too many

things could go wrong. Still, she needed to go to Friendship, and if she went today, she wouldn't have to think about making the trip again.

Unless Pa didn't send for them soon.

Travis Logan passed another swamp where bald cypress trees stretched out the bottom of their trunks and dug in their roots to make their homes. He slowed his horse, Pride and Joy, to a gentle walk to cool him as he approached the town of Friendship, Tennessee. Early in the morning it drizzled, leaving the last leg of his journey damp and uncomfortable for both him and his horse. He was in search of Caleb Wharton's place and knew he was close. Still, he considered it right smart to head into the general store for clearer directions before going any further, maybe even warm up a bit.

Friendship appeared to be a good-sized town. He passed a general store, post office, and livery stable. A man wouldn't have to go far to get what he needed. Right in the middle of the main street sat a public well. With a quick pull on the reins, he halted his horse and dismounted. He looped the leather reins around the saddle horn. His boots squished in the muddy street as he led his companion to the water-filled troughs to drink. The town was quiet, only a few people on the sidewalks. He figured the earlier rain may have kept some folks home. A stagecoach pulled away from the hotel, its wheels sucking mud. The driver tipped his hat at Travis then flipped the reins to increase the speed of his team of horses.

While Pride and Joy drank his fill, Travis scratched the

black's neck and looked over the other half of town. There was a second general store doing business at the end of the street. If you couldn't get what you needed at one place, you could probably get it at the other. Gathering the lead line in one hand, he walked the horse to the front of the Peacock & Co. General Store and then tethered him to the hitching post. He adjusted his black hat with a finger, raising the brim so he could see better.

Across the street, stood a boarding house with a sign swinging from a post in the yard, MISS EDNA'S PLACE OF REST. Sounded like a funeral parlor. Might be cheaper to stay a week there than at the hotel if he couldn't move into Caleb's place right away. He didn't know if Caleb had left it vacant or hired a caretaker. He didn't intend to show up unannounced and take over the farm. A person needed time to pack up his belongings and find another place to stay. Not too much time though. He wanted to get started making the place his own. His mare would be arriving in Dryersville next month.

The horse bumped his velvety muzzle against Travis's shoulder. The blue eyes, signifying the horse was a true black, seemed to question him. Travis reached up and scratched Pride and Joy's forehead. "Won't be in there long, buddy."

Three wide, worn wooden steps led to the covered sidewalk under the Peacock & Co. sign. Travis noted the toy wagon and kitchenware display in the front glass windows. He paused long enough to wonder if he'd ever have a wife and child to treat some Christmas. Maybe Friendship had a woman who would steal his heart the way his mother had stolen his father's. He wanted a marriage like theirs, built on trust and

companionship. It had taken him awhile, but now he knew Mary couldn't be the one to give him that.

The wood and glass door yawned onto the porch, spilling out a blond-headed woman holding on to a younger girl's hand. At that moment, the sunlight decided to break apart the clouds, and with its touch, turned the woman's hair the color of gold and fire.

An older woman with a gray bonnet tied tightly around her plump chin blew through the door after them. "Now, don't forget we'd like to see you in church on Sunday."

"We'll keep that in mind, Mrs. Reynolds." The golden-haired beauty didn't stop. It looked more as if she sped up her pace trying to get free of Mrs. Reynolds. "Don't imagine with the winter weather we'll make it too often."

"We will look forward to seeing you when you do come." Mrs. Reynolds turned back to enter the store and stopped the moment she spotted him. Her eyes leaped from his to the scar on his cheek.

He tipped his hat to her.

She offered a "Welcome to town, stranger," smile and then stepped back into the store.

The rustle of the pretty woman's skirt brought his attention back to her. Travis couldn't remove his eyes from the two females. Was the golden-fire-haired one married? Since she wore black, she might be a widow. The younger one was most likely a sister, too old to be the woman's child. Something didn't seem right about the younger girl. The woman had a tight grasp on the child's hand even though she was old enough to navigate the stairs on her own. He listened as she said "now" each time they stepped down.

Golden Fire Hair carried a woven basket on her arm, which she removed and placed in the younger girl's hand. She untied the horse on the opposite side of the stairs where he'd tied Pride and Joy. It was a nice-looking gelding. He was appraising its value and mentally measuring how many hands the horse stood when he realized the woman had noticed him staring. He tipped his hat, "Howdy, ma'am. Nice horse you have there."

Her face flushed, and her thank-you came out more like a warning growl.

"His name is Charlie," the younger girl said.

"Shh. Don't say anything." The woman turned back to face him, despite the scowl she wore. He sensed the hedge of protection she placed around the child. "We must be going."

He removed his hat and held it low, shielding his chest. "Be seein' you." He watched her help the child onto the horse, climb on behind her, and ride away before turning the knob and entering the store.

The warmth from the box stove sitting in the middle of the store sucked him in like a bug to a flame. The heat seeped through his damp overcoat into his skin and melted the tightness from his ride out of his shoulders and back.

He felt bad for Pride and Joy having ridden in the same cold rain. He'd order extra oats tonight if he stayed in town.

The quietness of the store settled on the back of his neck. Sure enough, he drew stares from the woman named Mrs. Reynolds and another woman holding a bolt of checked fabric. Their chatter halted as he walked past, and his hand went to the white line on his face. His scarred cheek gave him the appearance of a man with a reputation—one not well earned. He ignored the women. Walking past the barrel set up for a game of checkers, he headed straight for the counter. Once those in the store seemed to deem him no threat, several quiet conversations began behind him.

"Name's Henry. Looks like you were caught in the rain this morning."

"Travis Logan. Yes, it was a miserable ride."

"Haven't seen you in here before. Are you here to stay or just passing through?" Henry stroked his graying black whiskers with his rough hand.

"I'm looking for directions to Caleb Wharton's place." He placed his hand on the glass counter next to a jar holding stick candy and wondered about the little girl he'd just seen. Did her sister buy her one of these for the trip home? He hoped so. As a kid, he'd liked the peppermint ones.

"What do you need with Caleb?" Henry stood straighter as he lowered his hands under the counter, a move Travis knew would make it easy to draw out a rifle in case of trouble.

He withdrew his hands from the counter and took a half step back. "Caleb's passed on and left his farm to me. I thought I'd take a look to see if it will work as a place to raise horses."

"Horses?" The clerk dragged the stool next to him closer and perched. "That right? What happened to Caleb?"

"Caught something that couldn't be cured on the Mississippi."

"And he left you his place?" Henry smoothed his rough linen work apron at the chest with his hairy hand.

"Yes sir. Made me promise to come here. Said it was heaven and I'd love it."

"Sounds like Caleb." Henry tugged on his earlobe then spat in the spittoon behind the counter. "Well, ain't that something. Heaven, huh? You're not far, about a mile down the road you rode in on. There's a broken wheel half buried on the corner of his land. The lane's growed up a bit, but you can see it if you look for it. You'll find the cabin around the bend."

"I'll need a few supplies. I imagine I'll be back in town later for more, once I know what I need."

"I'll be glad to help you, but I imagine you won't be needing much as there is a. . ." Henry coughed. "Caleb's had someone looking after the place." He reached in his apron pocket and withdrew a pad of paper. He set it on the counter and pulled a pencil from behind his ear, ready to take Travis's order. "Caleb brought the missus and his family here in early spring. The place was in pretty good shape. It belonged to his wife's uncle—odd old coot, he was. Surprised us when Caleb decided to head north to look for work, but he wasn't quite the same after his wife died."

"He didn't say much about that. All he talked about was this place, so he might have changed his mind about working up north." Tension that had been riding his shoulder blades left. This must be a sign that giving up doctoring was the right thing to do. He could use a break, and a homestead in good shape with milking cows, chickens, and a nice barn seemed to be in his future. "Then I guess I'll just head out that way now, since it sounds like all I need is already there, just like Caleb said." As Travis walked out the door, Henry laughed, and Travis thought he heard him say, "I hope he has a gun."

Chapter 2

As they rode Charlie home, the warm noon sun stroked its fingers down Heaven's back, rubbing away the angst Mrs. Reynolds had caused. The horse's feet squished in the mud, making a sucking sound with each pull from the road. It wasn't a long way back to the cabin, but it was slow-going with the muddy road. She didn't want to rush Charlie and take a chance on him twisting his leg. She didn't need a lame horse, or worse, one with a broken leg. Once back in Memphis, she had wanted to surprise her pa with a picture she'd drawn and instead ended up witnessing her pa put down a sick horse. Her stomach soured at the remembrance. No, slow and steady would be best.

The horse trod past the cotton-stubble-filled pasture. Disturbed by the noise, a flock of blackbirds took to the sky and veered to the south.

"Who was that man at the store?" Angel's light voice added to the rhythm of the creaking leather of the saddle.

"I've never seen him before. That's why I didn't want you to talk to him. We don't want anyone else knowing we're out here alone." Last month three men on horseback had stopped to see if she needed any help chopping wood. They didn't want to help. They wanted her home and quite possibly her as well. She sent them back down the road with a few rounds from the shotgun and then prayed they wouldn't return. So far they hadn't been back, so she guessed they'd moved on. She probably should have mentioned it to Preacher Reynolds, but she didn't want to be beholden to anyone. He would have made her and Angel move to town and live with them. That would have left their home unprotected. She couldn't do that. She'd promised Pa she'd take care of the place and keep it nice so they could sell it.

Heaven's disappointment in not receiving any news at the post office from her pa turned to worry. What if he was hurt and couldn't get a letter to them? Or maybe he thought it unnecessary to let them know he arrived safely and was saving every penny so he could send for them. Her free hand went to the strand of hair hanging in front of her ear and began to twist the wayward lock.

Or had something even more awful happened to him? Her lungs shriveled, and she found it difficult to breathe. She knew these were the times that were supposed to bring her closer to God, but mostly she wanted to yell at Him for the way things were turning out in her life.

"Heaven, are you twisting your hair?" Angel tipped her head back onto her sister's chest, smashing her mother's lorgnette into her skin.

She dropped the strand of hair from her fingers and moved the small magnifying glass. "Why?"

" 'Cause Ma always said you twist your hair when you're

worried. I think you're worrying about Pa. Are you?"

Her sister's perception of things unseen had grown in the last month.

"I'm not twisting it right now." She wasn't since she'd let it drop the second Angel mentioned her habit. She couldn't have Angel's brain sizzling with worry, too. "Pa is fine. I'm sure of it." She wasn't positive about that either, but she didn't need Angel thinking about what might be wrong. "Besides, we're doing fine without him." She wasn't so sure of that either, since there wasn't anything but that small amount of salted meat left. But eleven-year-old Angel didn't need to be thinking about where the next meal was coming from.

"I miss his stories."

"I'll read to you tonight, or maybe we can make up a story together. We could try and piece a few of Pa's together and make a new one." Truth be told, even if she was too old for Pa's stories, she never tired of hearing him spin one.

"It won't be as good as sitting next to Pa while he tells it."

"I can't do anything about that, Angel. You will have to make do with me until he sends for us." Angel's back went board hard against Heaven's chest. Yes, she could try and protect her sister from as much as she could, but some things could only be fixed by a father.

From the movement of the leather strips, Angel could picture Charlie's powerful neck bobbing as he walked. She relaxed against her sister's chest, holding the reins. She knew she was only allowed to hold them because he knew the way home.

Heaven wouldn't have let her take them otherwise. No one would ever have to lead Charlie back to the barn where he knew he'd be fed when he arrived. If anything, he had to be held back from running the entire way.

She had to find some way to make Heaven let her do things. The only thing she couldn't do was see, but Heaven kept her in the cabin like she was a drooling idiot not fit for public gatherings. "Mrs. Reynolds said we should come back to church soon."

"Uh-huh."

"Mrs. Reynolds said they are having a Sunday school Christmas play, and there is still time for me to be a part of it, but I need to go to Sunday school."

"Uh-huh."

"Mrs. Reynolds said. . ."

"I know. Angel, I was right there with you." Heaven's voice had that stone-sharp edge to it that Angel recognized as warning her that she had *almost* gone too far. Her ma had that same tone. She guessed that was where Heaven learned to use it.

"I know." She would have to approach this problem another way, because she wanted to be an angel in the play. After all, it was her name, so she should have the part. "Don't you miss seeing other people, Heaven? If we went to church more often, we could make new friends."

Heaven didn't say anything for so long, Angel thought she might have fallen asleep, which meant she drove the horse by herself. She lifted Charlie's reins higher. Her heart expanded with excitement then deflated when she felt her sister stir behind her.

"I miss my best friend, Annabelle, very much," Heaven finally replied. Heaven didn't know it, but Angel saw her sister's words as teardrops.

Angel missed her school friends in Nashville, too. They didn't even know she was blind and didn't have to go to school anymore. Wouldn't they be surprised to know that she missed learning, too? Right now she'd even be happy to see Fred Thompson, and she didn't like him, not since he tied her braids together last fall.

Friendship didn't even have a school. How would she ever make any friends if Heaven didn't take her to church?

The fire crackled in the fireplace, sucking the dampness of the day out the chimney with its smoke. Heaven gently rocked in the old blue rocking chair they'd brought with them from Nashville. The chair had sat on the back porch for as long as Heaven could remember. She and Annabelle often climbed in it together when they were small and munched lemon drop cookies the cook gave them.

Did Annabelle like being married? The wedding was set for last June, and Heaven was sick about not being able to be there, even if she didn't much care for the man her friend was marrying. Had they moved in with Annabelle's father, or were they able to move into a place of their own? Annabelle might even be with child by now. Heaven hoped for the best for her friend but wished she and her childhood friend could climb in the bed and have a night of talking like they did before Heaven's family moved.

The last few golden moments of sunlight slipped through the windowpanes and cast the cabin in a cheery glow. She needed to stop soon if she wanted to get to the barn and feed Charlie and the other animals before dark. She liked this part of the day, putting the animals to bed. Even that tiresome goat, Mr. Jackson, was worn out by then and would leave her skirt alone.

Her knitting needles slid across each other, adding a background rhythm to the tune Angel hummed while washing her stockings. Heaven hoped that by having to wash on a day that wasn't washing day, Angel would remember to put her shoes on instead of racing across the floor that never seemed clean.

Heaven squinted in the dim light, not wanting to light the lamp until she came back from the barn. There was still time to knit a few more rows before the last bit of red faded from the sky. The scarf was a Christmas present for Pa. The one he'd taken up north was thin with wear. She'd unraveled her mother's blue wool sweater. There was enough to make two scarves for Christmas gifts. This one was for Pa. Then she'd make one for Angel. A few more inches and Pa's would be completed.

Then what? The rocker creaked faster against the plank floor. She didn't have an address to send it. She would continue to pray they would hear something soon. Just because there wasn't a letter at the post office today didn't mean they wouldn't be in St. Louis or Chicago to celebrate the Savior's birth. Not likely though. She knew how long it had taken them to travel to Friendship from Nashville, even though they came by wagon and not a train. She could only imagine how long it would take to get to one of those northern cities, especially on a steamboat. It was time to realize they would still be living in this cabin come Christmas.

Heaven's shoulders sagged. She lowered the knitting to her lap and rubbed her forehead with her fingers. She would have to go hunting soon or go into town hanging her head and asking for help. She couldn't do that, wouldn't do that. She was a Wharton, and Whartons made their own way no matter what life planted in their path. Pa had made that clear. Whartons weren't moochers.

She longed to have her pa back in control. No longer would she have to worry about Angel's health and safety. At least she wouldn't have to do it all alone.

Maybe she ought to consider taking Angel to Sunday school. Mrs. Reynolds had said something about a Christmas social, too. Not that there were a great deal of men around here to marry, but maybe she would meet someone. Someone who wouldn't mind that her sister would have to be included in any future plans.

Maybe the man at the store today?

She had pretended to ignore him, but when he took off his hat, she couldn't escape the desire to pat those wavy dark brown curls into submission. The scar on his cheek looked fresh, but so many men these days wore scars visible and invisible from the war. Maybe he'd be at the social. They'd be properly introduced and fall in love, and then she wouldn't be alone.

Humph! Now she was dreaming. She was awful close to the age of being considered a spinster. Her chances of finding love would be better up north—if Pa would just send for them.

She picked up her knitting, the needles clicked faster and no longer accompanied Angel's tune. There wasn't one.

Angel had stopped humming.

Heaven slowed the rocker. She set her knitting aside and glanced over to see what had caused the cessation of the happy tune.

Angel stood with a back stiff at their ironing board. One hand held a dripping stocking as her head cocked to the left, listening.

Heaven's heart quickened. She dropped her knitting into the basket sitting next to the rocker. "What do you hear, Angel?"

"Pa's home!" Angel squealed. "His horse is coming down the lane!" She let the stocking she'd rinsed fall back into the bucket. Hands held in front of her, she bolted across the cabin floor toward the door.

Springing from the rocker, Heaven caught Angel by her mutton sleeve as she raced past. She pulled her to a stop and encircled her arms around her. "Wait. Let's make sure it's Pa before we go telling someone we're here alone."

With quick steps, she reached the corner where they kept the rifle. Pa told her to leave it there so she'd always know where to find it. She picked up the heavy weapon, cradling the barrel in her arms. She'd get Angel settled before getting in her shooting position. "Get up in the loft and stay there. I'll call you out if it's Pa."

Angel whirled around and faced Heaven with her hands curled into fists.

"Go, Angel!"

Her lower lip curled into a pout, but she turned and headed for the loft. She counted off each of her steps like a nail driven by a hammer until she reached the stairs.

At every number, Heaven flinched. It was Angel's way of expressing her anger. She wanted to be independent, but Heaven knew Angel wasn't ready. When her sister's feet cleared the last step on the loft ladder, Heaven turned back to the door. She cracked open the wooden door and shoved the Spencer's barrel through the narrow opening. Her hands shook, and her mouth lost all its moisture.

She stepped onto the covered porch, aiming the rifle. One rider came trotting around the bend. One rider. Her shoulders felt lighter. Maybe Angel was right. Maybe it was Pa! She shielded her eyes from the setting sun.

Then her heart broke into chunks. It couldn't be him. This man sat taller on a horse than Pa. He wore a hat down low over his eyes, but she could see enough of his face to know it wasn't someone she knew. His clothing resembled what the man outside the store this morning wore. Someone must have told him about her being alone up here, probably Mrs. Reynolds. She didn't care how good-looking she thought he was when he tipped his hat to her. He was just another one of those marauders trying to take their place. Where grief had settled in her heart, anger now planted its boots. This time she wouldn't bother to warn the rider. No need to waste the words—they didn't seem to change any of their minds. By accident she'd learned that if she fired in the air, they turned around and left.

She set her feet like Pa trained her and brought the butt of the gun above her shoulder, aimed above the man's hat, and fired. The rifle kicked. She stumbled two steps back and slammed her elbow against the cabin door frame. She tumbled sideways, dropping the gun to the porch. The shot echoed in her ears. Then horror blossomed in her throat as the man slid from his horse to the muddy ground.

She'd killed him. Now Angel would be alone, because she was sure once the sheriff found out Heaven had murdered the man, she would hang.

Chapter 3

The rumble of stagecoaches, the blare of a train whistle, and the din of shopkeepers calling out their wares on the Nashville street pelted Jake Miles as he rode in his enclosed carriage. He kept his focus on the horses' twitching ears as they pulled the carriage. They weren't immune to the bustling noises, but they didn't flinch the way the man holding the reins did.

The team's iron shoes clanked against the cobblestone, scraping against the stone sideways as they hit a sunken place in need of repair. His raw nerves reacted, tightening each muscle like knots on a ship's rope. He concentrated on keeping the panic inside of himself. *You're home. You're safe.*

Glimpses of stores he'd frequented before the war snagged the edge of his vision. He narrowed his lids to tunnel his line of sight, not wanting to see the harsh marks etched on his city by the Union Army or the face of anyone who might know him. He didn't want to be singled out, called a hero, or asked if he had news of others who were still missing.

He had nothing to offer any of them.

After his unexpected arrival two nights ago, he had hidden

in his boyhood bedroom at his parents' home. He extracted promises from them and the house staff not to let news of his return be told to anyone. He was too broken to be seen. Broken on the inside where it counted. Once again he wished for a missing limb or eye. If he had something broken to show on the outside, then maybe he wouldn't feel so much weighty guilt.

Today he'd ventured out among the living, knowing after all this time that he must release his fiancée from her promise to wait for him. She needed someone whole, not the shell of a man he had become. He pictured her golden hair and blue eyes tearing the moment she saw him. She, like the others, thought he was dead. Maybe she hadn't even waited for him. His stomach reached for his heart, and they twisted together. He hadn't thought of that possibility. His parents hadn't heard from her since the false news of his death had been confirmed. She'd been beyond consoling, they told him, hiding away in her home grieving. His own parents hadn't even lived their lives. Instead, they'd quit all aspects of societal life, including attending church. They'd turned into hermits, facilitated by the help of servants who saw to their needs for food and clothing. He found that disturbing and hoped that would change now that they knew he wasn't dead.

It would be for the best if Heaven had married someone else. Still he needed to talk to her, see her, and touch her soft hands one last time. Make sure she was all right. Then he could let her go and could get out of Tennessee. Head for the West where a man could leave behind the coward and find something decent within him. If there was any to be found.

If he hadn't run into Bradford Pickens at a market in

Knoxville, he wouldn't have returned at all. Pickens kept going on and on about Jake being a hero and getting out of the war alive. Jake wanted to punch him in the mouth to stop his lies. Then Pickens said he was heading back to Nashville, and he would let the others know he'd seen Jake.

He knew he had to get back before Pickens did and tell his family he'd survived the war. And Heaven. He wanted at least that small bit of respectability left to his name.

A man waved at him from the sidewalk, and Jake fought the urge to turn the carriage about and return to his parents' home. He kept going, his last bit of courage growing smaller. His mother made him promise he would see Heaven today. Jake wished he was off to see the place and not the woman. It would be much easier to face the Almighty than the woman he was about to disappoint.

The redbrick two-story house didn't have the same appearance. The drive was overgrown, but there were fresh buggy tracks. He parked his father's carriage in front of Heaven's home, fighting the instinct to turn and run.

The big tree that had graced the yard still stood. A shaft of sunlight reflected off of something in the bark, and he walked over to inspect it. Bullets were lodged in its majestic trunk.

"Yankees shot the tree and the house, inside and out."

Jake looked up to see who was speaking. A man, one he didn't know and several years his senior, had stepped out onto the porch. Had Heaven married after all?

Jake said to the man, "They left their mark on a lot things around here." *Including me.* "Were you here then?" Maybe Heaven had been spared living through the Battle of Nashville.

"No, the other family was. They were anxious to sell and leave those memories behind. What brings you by the place?" He hung his thumbs on his overall straps.

The other family. Did that mean the Whartons had experienced what he had not? The dark feeling of guilt swirled thick around him. "I was looking for an old friend, Heaven Wharton."

"They don't live here anymore. I heard her father lost this house in a poker game to the man I purchased it from. They were gone by the time the Yankees got here."

Relief snapped the band of tension around his chest, and he relaxed. She was safe and not married, at least not to this man. He was grateful she hadn't married an old codger. "Do you know where they moved to?"

"Heard tell they moved out west somewhere." The man's cheeks sucked in as he pursed his mouth and then spit a wad of tobacco off the porch into Mrs. Wharton's once-prized rose bushes. "Hope you find your woman."

Jake slid his hand across the rough tree bark. The last time he'd been here, he'd kissed his girl good-bye and made her a promise. She'd worn a blue dress the color of a stormy sky that brought out the jewels in her eyes. The tears in them made them sparkle. His gut clenched. If only he still deserved her, he'd have run home the moment they set him free. But he didn't, and that's what he had to remember.

"Me, too, sir. I've some things to say to her."

Heaven scrambled to retrieve the fallen rifle. She held it and aimed at the man on the ground in case he was fooling her and sprang to his feet. She waited, but he didn't move. She lowered the rifle to her side, unsure of what to do next. The world seemed to have gone silent. Maybe God had taken her hearing for this awful act of murdering a man.

Angel appeared in front of her, tugging at her sleeve. "Did you kill him? I didn't hear the horse run off, and I don't hear a voice. Shouldn't we go see if he's dead?"

Sounds of the farm joined her sister's questions. The chickens were cackling, and the rooster crowed. Heaven let out the breath that had clogged her throat. "I—I guess we'd better see. I hit him, Angel. I never hit anything."

"Where did the bullet get him? Could you tell?" Her sister's eyes were wide, and Heaven worried the images she was envisioning were more vivid than the reality.

"I aimed in the air like always and pulled the trigger. Then his hat lifted off like a blackbird in flight, and the reins slid from his hands. Without making a single sound, he slipped off his horse and hit the ground." Heaven stepped off the porch. "I'm sure I killed him."

Angel grabbed Heaven's arm. "I'm going with you."

"Stay here, Angel."

"No. I'm coming, too. If he's dead, he ain't going to hurt me."

Heaven's fingers felt numb, and her legs were as heavy as that rifle in her hand had been. She vowed she'd never shoot that thing again, at least as long as that man lying in the mud wasn't dead. Maybe she'd gone too far. Maybe she couldn't handle taking care of Angel and the farm. Maybe it was time to go to town and throw herself on the mercy of the good preacher and his wife—if the man wasn't dead. "Stay close just in case he's foolin' us."

"What are we going to do with him if he ain't dead yet?" Angel asked.

"I hope he's wounded and not badly." Heaven walked a bit faster, pulling her sister along by the hand at a pace she'd never before used. "We'll have to tend to his injuries."

"Then he'll tell the sheriff you shot him. If he is dead, we can bury him in the back field. That way no one will ever know. We'll be long gone and living with Pa before anyone finds him."

The casualness of Angel's voice sent shivers of dread through Heaven. Had they suffered so much loss that life had become trivial to her sister? She stopped, and with her free hand, she pulled her sister closer, looking into eyes that couldn't see. "Angel, I was wrong to shoot that man. I didn't even know why he was coming here. I acted out of fear, and that gets me and a lot of people in trouble. We will try and save him, and if he isn't saveable, well then, we'll just have to think of a way to save me without burying the poor man where no one will find him. He might have a family, and they'll want to know what happened to him. Think about us. We haven't heard from Pa in a long time, and that causes us concern, does it not?" *Please, God, if he is dead, don't let him have a family waiting for him the way we wait for Pa.* She took her sister's hand in hers and squeezed it. "I know you mean well, little one, but we have to live right. Come on, let's see what we can do for this fella."

Annabelle Singleton's special order for wool had come in

this morning. She waited for it to be brought to the counter, excited to get it. She had plans to start her stock of fine knitted accessories. When she had enough made, she would somehow open a shop in Memphis, no matter what her father said. It had to be that far away, where her father couldn't interfere with her ideas and try to take over, keeping her his little girl. And far enough away that no one would know about her embarrassment.

She'd waited out the war for her fiancé to return, not once even casting a longing look at another man. She'd rolled bandages and thought of William, made sewing kits and wondered if one of them would get to him. She did it all, holding the love of William in her heart. Then he'd broken hers. He didn't even have the decency to tell her in person. Instead, he'd sent a letter about how sorry he was to hurt her, but you can't help love, he'd said. When it comes, it comes.

Apparently it had come in the form of a Yankee woman who now bore his name.

She'd decided then and there she would become an independent woman of means and, thanks to her grandmother leaving her some gold, the opportunity glistened in front of her.

"Here you go, Miss Singleton." The clerk placed the wool on the counter for her to inspect.

She brushed her fingers over the strands. Its softness would be perfect for her project. "Thank you. Can you wrap that for me, please?"

"Of course." The clerk drew out some brown paper and placed her precious bundle inside.

"Mrs. Kirby, I'll be right with you."

Annabelle went cold. She hadn't faced William's mother since the letter. She bit her lower lip. How could she smile and be graceful to her when her son had broken Annabelle's heart?

"That's all right. You all take your time. I'm in no hurry."

Annabelle sucked in air at the unfamiliar voice. Could *she* be here? Annabelle angled her body slightly, wanting to see the woman that attracted William enough to jilt her. Had William even mentioned Annabelle? Both Mrs. Kirbys stood behind her. The younger one offered a smile so sweet Annabelle felt like she'd eaten too much Fourth of July ice cream. William's mother ignored her.

"Miss Singleton?"

"Yes?" Did her voice shake? She'd wanted William's wife to be ugly, thinking—hoping—maybe he'd felt sorry for her and that's why he married her. But that wasn't it; the dark-haired beauty with porcelain skin could have been a china doll. Everything Annabelle wasn't.

The clerk pushed the package tied with twine across the counter. "Would there be anything else you'll be needing?"

"Not today, thank you." The package crinkled in her hand, and she clutched it tightly. Her face felt hot. She had to get out of the store away from the fiancé stealer. With a quick step, she turned and brushed past the two Mrs. Kirbys without a word, making a beeline to the door.

She had to get out of this town. Running into that woman was an impossible situation, one she couldn't have happen again. It was too painful. William had been a good catch before the war, and he returned from the war with all his limbs intact. Now there were few available men, unless she wanted to marry someone ancient.

And she didn't.

Taking care of her father had been enough of a warning of what it would be like to be married to someone his age. Hosting parties for old couples, endless dinners, and no children. No, she didn't want that kind of life. She'd rather make it on her own.

"Watch out!" A carriage went past her in a blur, coming within a horse hair of running over her.

"Whoa!" The man on the carriage bench yanked back on the reins. The horses slowed and settled with a whinny.

Annabelle, numbed and shaken by her near death, thought she had to be seeing things, because the man on the carriage seat looked just like Jake Miles, and everyone knew he was dead.

"Annabelle?"

Odd, he sounded like him, too. "Jake?"

He climbed down from the carriage. "Are you hurt?"

"Aren't you dead?" What a silly thing to ask when the man stood right in front of her. But she was so sure he was dead.

"No, that was a mistake. I'm alive."

"A mistake that you're alive?" Befuddled, that's what her brain was. Surely he didn't mean a mistake to be alive.

"Sometimes I feel that way." He looked away from her.

"Did you just get back? This is big news, and no one has mentioned it to me. What happened to you?" Had he been a deserter reported as dead? She hoped not. The Jake she knew before the war had starch.

"Been here a few days."

She waited for a buggy to rumble by. "Does Heaven know?" She wanted to be happy for her friend but found it difficult.

She'd found comfort these last few weeks in knowing Heaven was unmarried, too. She'd even considered asking her to set up shop with her since it appeared they would be spinsters.

"No. I'll be telling her as soon as I can find her. I went to her house, but she's not there."

"No, her family moved to Friendship in January."

"Heaven, too? Did she marry someone?"

"No, she waited for you." And here he was, back like he said he would be, and looking for Heaven. Jake was a much better man than William.

"I'll need to get a train ticket then."

Train ticket. That's all she heard. Could this be her chance to get out of this town? "When are you leaving? I'd like to go with you. I haven't seen Heaven in so long."

"No. I need to see her alone, and I'm not planning on returning to Nashville. I'm leaving as soon as I can. Tomorrow afternoon at the latest."

"Then I'd like to send a few things with you for Heaven and Angel."

"I don't imagine I'll have time to wait for you to pack up a box of pretties for them." Jake edged toward the carriage. "If you're all right, then I need to get back home. I promised Mother I'd have lunch with her."

"I'm fine. Please give your mother my regards." A plan began to formulate in her mind. With her father away on business, she would be able to pull off her escape sooner than she thought. She wouldn't be able to ask his permission. He wouldn't let her visit Heaven. She'd asked him hundreds of times since that awful letter came, crushing her heart and her dreams. Surely he would understand she had to get away now that William and his bride had returned to Nashville.

It hurt that Heaven's dream of being married was about to be resurrected, but she soothed the pain with the knowledge her new dream was about to begin.

Chapter 4

Heaven scooped up the black hat from the drive and approached the man lying still, face down in the mud. She dropped the hat next to him as she kneeled, grimacing as her black skirt sunk in the mud. He seemed to stretch out to the next county in length, and she hoped his weight was in his legs, or she didn't stand a chance of moving him. She had to turn him before he suffocated in the mud. Sticking her hands between him and the earth, she lifted, hoping to get him high enough that he'd fall the rest of the way, landing on his back.

Her arm muscles strained against his weight. She almost had him. . .if she had a little more strength. "Angel, quick bend down here next to me."

Angel touched Heaven's head and then brushed against her side until she knelt in the muck.

"Stick your hands straight out, and you'll feel his chest." It wasn't proper having her sister touch a stranger in such an inappropriate manner, but then she ought not be touching him either. Mrs. Reynolds wouldn't approve. Then again, she wouldn't have approved of Heaven shooting this man either.

She almost laughed and would have if the situation hadn't been troublesome.

"His chest is as hard as dirt." Angel wiggled her shoulders, knocking into Heaven's. "Now what?"

"On three we push as hard as we can. One, two, three!" The man seemed to stall halfway then rolled to his back, taking them with him.

"Whoa!" Angel seemed to fly as she somersaulted over the man's body and landed with a thud.

Heaven's hands were stretched out in front of her. Her stomach lay across the man's chest. Heat flooded Heaven's face. This wasn't proper at all. She pushed off the ground and scooted on to her feet, thankful no one was there to see her sprawled across this man.

"Angel, are you okay?"

Her sister stood, brushed her hands on her skirt, and laughed. "That was fun. I'm fine. I told you I could help." Angel smirked. "So, is he dead or alive, and where did the bullet hit?"

The man on the ground moaned.

Heaven screamed. Her hands covered her mouth as she backed away.

"Guess we don't need to bury him," Angel said. "It's a good thing, too, because I don't think we could have drug him around back. We'd have had to pile dirt on him right here, and that would've looked suspicious."

"Angel, watch what you're saying!" Heaven bent over the man. "Can you tell me where you're hurt?" The brownest eyes she'd ever seen looked into hers. Her breath caught as recognition dawned. "You're the man from the store this morning."

"Hurts. Heard a gunshot. Did my horse spook and toss me?" His hand moved to the side of his head, exposing a white jagged line where there must have been dark curly hair.

Then Heaven noticed the river of blood pouring through his fingers. Her vision wavered into semidarkness. *God help me. There's blood, and lots of it.* She steadied her mind. She didn't have the luxury of being a Nashville lady right now. "We'll figure that out later. Do you think you can stand and walk into the cabin?"

Angel gasped. "We're taking him inside?"

"We can't very well leave him out here bleeding, Angel Claire. That wouldn't be polite."

"He's bleeding? So you did hit him?"

At times like this, she wished she could stare her sister quiet. "Shh." There might still be time to cover this up if Angel didn't blurt out the truth. Maybe he could be led to believe it was a stray shot from a hunter.

The man struggled to push into a sitting position. He held his head, "Dizzy, but I think I can make it. My horse— needs—"

She glanced over at the horse that seemed content to watch them while snatching bits of dried grass. "He'll be fine. I'll get him in the barn right after we get you settled and fixed up. Try standing now. Hold on to me in case you get so dizzy you start to fall." Heaven offered her hand to help steady him. Once he was upright, Heaven had a feeling that if they didn't hurry to the house, he'd be on the ground again. "Angel, take two steps to your right, and you'll be next to him. I need your help to support him. Now grab his arm and sling it around your neck.

I'll do the same."

Heaven staggered under the weight as the man's knees buckled. "Hold on, Angel! Don't you dare fall, mister, or we'll leave you where you land this time."

"Do my best, ma'am."

"I appreciate that." She didn't want to talk. All of her energy went into bearing his weight. She had no idea men were so heavy.

"It's getting dark."

"Yes it is." Heaven hoped he meant the sky and not what was going on inside his head. A few more paces and they'd be at the porch steps. "We're almost there, sir. Angel, once we get him up the steps, I want you to open the door so I can get him inside."

"Where you going to put him?"

"I think Pa's bed would be best."

"Why not a chair?"

"Because I think a bed's the best place."

"I don't. I think a chair is best. He ought not be in a bed in our cabin—not without Pa being here."

Sometimes Heaven wanted to treat her sister like a turkey and wring the common sense right out of her. "You're right, but Pa isn't here, and I am. So we're going to do what I say."

"I still don't know why we can't stick him in the rocker and work on him there."

"Steps, Angel. One, two, three." Angel made it to the porch deck, skittered to the door, flung it open, and rested against the door frame.

The man moaned and grew shorter as his knees buckled.

His weight pressed against Heaven's shoulder. "Can't stand much longer."

"Angel, help! We can't let him fall. Help me get him to the bed." It wasn't far, but it seemed as if they were trying to reach Nashville by foot. As they gained momentum, the man's weight became unwieldy, and it was all Heaven could do to steer him toward the bed. She pretty much aimed his fall rather than eased him gently down.

He sat on the bed and then fell over on his side with a thump, his feet still planted on the floor.

"Now is he dead?" Angel asked.

"No, just out cold, which is good. The wound needs to be cleaned and maybe even stitched tight. Better to do that while he's out." She didn't look forward to drawing a thread through the man's scalp. Last November, when they first came to live at Great-Uncle Neal's cabin, Pa tore his arm open on a tree branch. Ma had tried to show Heaven how to stitch his skin together, but one look at that needle going through skin had sent her crashing to the floor. Now she would have to do it, because there wasn't anyone else. It wasn't right that Pa had left them. Once again her anger flared. That was at least twice today, wasn't it? Well, it wasn't fair. He should have taken them along or at least sent word to them by now. Didn't he know she was sick with worry? And now she had to sew skin together!

"What about his horse? Can I take him to the barn?"

That reminded her of her promise to hang the rope between the barn and the house. She'd convinced Angel to wait until tomorrow. *"Never put off till tomorrow what you can do today."*

She heard Ma's voice as clear as summer springwater in her head.

"No, not by yourself. It's dark, and you might lose your way back."

Angel clutched her hips with hands of iron, and she stood taller. "Dark? Heaven, it's always dark for me. I have a better chance of getting back than you ever will."

"You can't leave me alone with this man. It isn't proper."

"Maybe you should have thought of that before you dragged him into Pa's bed."

"Angel!"

"It's true, and you know it. Besides, one of us has to get that horse in the barn before he runs off. Do you want me to stay with him?"

She glanced back at the man on the bed. How long would he be unconscious? He was bleeding a lot, a steady trickle running down the side of his face onto his arm. He'd landed in a way to make it easy for her to patch up. The bleeding had to be stopped now. But Angel outside alone terrified her.

"Heaven?" Angel grasped her arm. "I can do this. You have to take care of him. He's too heavy to drag out of here if he dies."

"Go. Hurry. Don't dawdle. Just stick the horse in the stall and get back here. I'll feed everyone later."

"I will."

"Watch out for that hole. Remember, it's thirty-six steps from the porch, and then step to the left. . . ."

"I know. You've been making me count it now for weeks." She turned and headed for the door faster than Heaven had seen her move in months.

Freedom, sweet freedom. Angel hated that her sister shot that man, but she almost couldn't contain her joy at the unexpected gift his injury had brought. A chance to do something on her own. She couldn't mess this up. If she did, it would be forever before Heaven let her venture out alone. At the count of thirty-six, she stepped left and continued counting in her mind. It was so easy to count and think of other things now. Like how to find the horse. She stopped short. Good thing Heaven hadn't thought of that, or she wouldn't have let Angel out of the house. Still she had to figure out how to find him.

Come on, Angel, you're smart enough to figure this out. Think it through. She cocked her head and listened. The wind blew leaves to her left. That's where the horse had been. She took two steps in that direction and listened again. She could hear tree branches swaying and clicking into each other. No horse sounds, no pawing the ground or heavy breathing through the nose. She puckered her lips and made a kissing noise.

Horse lips ruffled together in response.

Satisfaction filled her posture. She knew where that horse stood. Now all she had to do was to get his reins and lead him into the barn.

Annabelle returned to her father's home, clutching her embroidered handbag containing her freedom, a train ticket for tomorrow morning, close to her chest. With freedom less than a day away and a foolproof plan of escape in place, her heart warred with her stomach. She'd never been so daring. Did it show on her face? In her walk? She needed to appear normal and not flushed with the thrill of what was to come.

"Good afternoon, Miss Singleton." John, their manservant, helped her out of her coat.

"John, I've made arrangements to have some things I won't need shipped to Heaven Wharton and her little sister. A porter will be here later today to pick them up."

"Will there be a large or small package, Miss Singleton?"

Annabelle attempted to appear thoughtful as if she weren't quite sure. She didn't want John to suspect anything. "It might be best to pack it all in one of those old trunks. That way everything will arrive intact. Don't you think, John?"

His eyebrows rose slightly.

Annabelle fiddled inside her purse. Did he suspect she was planning on leaving? Distraction might be a good idea. "My wool came in today. I want to get that trunk packed quickly so I can start working with it."

From her peripheral vision, she saw his eyebrows settle back into place. Good, he didn't suspect anything.

"Would you be needing any help with the packing, Miss Singleton?"

"No. No, thank you." Did her voice just squeak? She faked a cough. "I do hope I'm not catching a cold. I best hurry. I know what I want to send to Heaven. I do believe I'll ask Cook for some of that jam Angel likes so well. I'll wrap it to keep the jar from breaking. Thank you, John. I'll let you know when the trunk is ready to be brought downstairs."

"Yes Miss Singleton. And I do believe Cook would be

happy to send the little one some jam. I'll request it on my way to collect the trunk you'll need upstairs to pack."

"Thank you." Annabelle scurried to the stairs. First thing she needed to do was collect her mother's wedding ring out of the box in her father's room. She'd planned on wearing it when she married last June, so if she tilted the truth a tiny bit, the ring already belonged to her.

But would it keep her safe? The trains were dangerous to ride on alone, but Jake would be with her. But what if he changed his mind and didn't board at the last minute. Maybe she should take someone along. But who? And she'd have to find them a way back to Nashville, unless they wouldn't mind going all the way to Memphis and never coming back.

Chapter 5

Heaven wrapped a cloth around the pot handle and lifted it from the stove plate. The cabin door opened, and Angel stepped in wearing a smile that had been missing for months. "Where have you been?" Heaven hauled the heated water across the room to her pa's bed. "Why did it take you so long?"

Angel's smile slipped from her face, and Heaven knew she'd wounded her sister.

"I had to find the horse, and then I took off his saddle. I fed everyone, too."

Heaven stopped abruptly, and the hot water sloshed across her chest. "Ouch!" The pot in her hand swayed from its cloth-covered handle. She tightened her grip. "You did?" Angel was outside in the dark where just last week a wolf stole a few chickens when they'd forgotten to shut the door to the coop. Fear gripped her, twisting her stomach so much she almost doubled over.

"Heaven, nothing happened. I'm okay. I didn't get eaten or attacked by anything except that dumb goat, Mr. Jackson." She tugged at her skirt. "I think he took a bite out of my skirt. I think I heard it rip."

"But how? How did you find your way to do all of that?

I never put up the ropes for you." She set the pot on the floor next to the bed. She took the cloth from the handle and dipped it into the hot water, wincing from the heat. Too late now to keep Angel contained. She'd expect to be allowed outside all the time. But she couldn't think about that now. A bigger problem lay in her pa's bed.

"You taught me how to listen and count, and that's what I did. He didn't die while I was out there, did he?" Angel rubbed her hands together to warm them. "If he did, I figured we could tie a rope to his legs and let his horse drag him out of here. It would be easier than us trying to move him since he'd be deadweight."

"He's still breathing and hasn't woken up yet. I'm praying we won't have to try your method, although it's an interesting solution." She wrung out the cloth, and the water ran into the pan. Heaven held her breath. It was just a wound. All she had to do was wash it and see if he needed stitches. *Please, God, if I have to sew him up, keep him knocked out.*

Angel tiptoed across the floor and stood next to her sister. "Sure hope he doesn't wake up and start yelling like a girl."

Heaven bit her lip. "So pray, Angel. Pray that he doesn't wake up until we have him all fixed and bandaged. God have mercy on him, 'cause if he wakes up while I have a needle in his skin, I'll most likely end up sticking it in his eye."

"As long as he still has the one eye, he'd be better off than me." Angel breathed over Heaven's shoulder.

A tidal wave of guilt rushed over her, trying to suck her under. She didn't have time for self-pity right now. "If you aren't going to commence praying, then please go retrieve Ma's sewing basket."

"I'll pray while I'm getting it. I can do two things at once just like you." Angel stepped away, "Heavenly Father, Heaven done shot that man. . . ."

"Angel, God knows what I've done. You don't need to confess my sins to Him. I'll do that later. Just pray for what I asked, please." She dabbed at the wound. The blood wasn't coming out as fast now. She glanced at the stranger's face and touched the scar, tracing it with her finger. It didn't detract the least from his handsome face. His cheekbones were chiseled, and yet the scar seemed to soften his look rather than harden it. It was still pink, so it must have happened only a short time ago. She didn't feel so bad now about shooting him. He must be a troublemaker. Someone else stitched him up not long ago. Wonder what he was after then?

Angel continued praying, "And that's all we are asking, God—keep Heaven out of jail, and make this man go away."

She should have been listening to Angel. Who knew what she'd requested from God?

"Here's the basket." Angel set the basket on the floor. A log in the fire sizzled and then popped. "Want me to thread the needle?"

Heaven's head popped up before she could stop it. Hope coursed through her. Had her prayers been answered?

Angel flashed a toothy grin. "Got you."

Heaven gritted her teeth and choked back a sob. She dropped the cloth back into the water, wiped her hand on her apron, and then picked up the basket.

"Are you mad at me, Heaven?"

"No, I just wish you could see, and for a moment, I thought you could." *Where was that silk string Ma used?* "Ouch. Found the needle."

"So you're going to stitch him up?"

"There isn't anyone else, is there?" Her fingertips brushed against the spool of silk thread. She grasped it. Now what? She tried to think. Ma had done something with the needle before she'd started to sew her pa's torn skin. What was it? "Angel, what did Ma do to the needle?"

"She stuck it in the fire."

"That's right." Heaven stood and hurried to the fireplace. She bent down where the coals were hot and placed the needle as close as she could without getting burned. The fire was hot, and she couldn't hold it there long. She just hoped it was long enough.

Her hands shook as she tried to wiggle the thread through the eye of the needle. Outside Pete the rooster crowed. He should be locked in the chicken coop away from the wolves. She couldn't think about him now. She squinted, holding the needle up to the firelight, and shoved the thread at the hole for the third time. This time it glided through.

Bending over her patient, she aimed the needle at his skin. Bile rose in her throat. She swallowed. She'd have to get closer. Her arm wasn't long enough, and it was dark. She backed away. "I need to light the lamp and bring it over here. I should have thought of that sooner."

"I could do it without a light. I make good stitches. That's what you told me—nice and small." Angel grasped her sister's elbow.

Heaven yanked her arm away. "No. I can't let you touch an unmarried man that way. You're too young." She spun around and took a few steps to the kitchen table where the oil lamp stood. She pushed the needle through the top of her apron and then lifted the chimney from the lamp and turned up the wick. She struck a match, touched it to the wick, and up shot a flame. She blew out the match and then lowered the wick and replaced the chimney.

She set it on the stool next to the bed where its graceful flame danced across the wall. She knelt on the floor and withdrew the needle from her apron. It was time. She would have to touch his face and again was grateful he wasn't awake. This was hard enough without having the man stare at her. Her palm rested against his face. Rough whiskers poked her skin. With caution she leaned over the wounded area and squeezed the skin between her thumb and index finger as tightly as she could. "Angel, sing something. Help me get my mind off what I'm doing."

"Swing low, sweet chariot, comin' for to carry me home. . . ." Angel belted out the words.

Heaven cringed. "Never mind, Angel."

"It's a good song, and it might comfort him if he can hear us."

"I think I'll do better without the song. So don't sing it." She held the needle poised to stick it through her patient's skin.

Angel continued to hum the tune.

Dear Lord, let this man remain ignorant to what went on here tonight. She plunged the needle through the skin and forced herself to think of quilting.

"Mary!"

The sound of thrashing and mumbling startled Heaven, waking her. Disoriented she shoved the blanket she had wrapped over her to the floor. Why was she in the rocking chair?

"Mary!"

Her patient. He was awake. She took a step and stumbled, falling to the floor, her feet entangled in the blanket. Righting herself, she hurried to the man's bedside. "Shh! Shh!" She tried to soothe him while feeling his brow.

His arm shot around her, pulling her close to him. Her face was within kissing distance of his. "Mary." He mumbled. "Why?"

Heaven untangled her neck from his arm. He was burning up. A fever. And Heaven knew he was as good as dead, just like her ma.

Heaven hollered up the ladder. "Angel, I need you."

She ran to the reservoir attached to the stove and ladled the lukewarm water into a bowl. She swiped a clean cloth from the shelf and hurried back to her patient. She set the bowl on the floor and dipped in the rag. She washed his face, hoping to take away the heat. Not wanting him to get chilled, she retrieved the blanket she had been using and covered him with it.

Angel clattered down the ladder. "What's wrong?"

"He's got a fever." She hoped the panic was only in her body and not in her voice.

Angel came over next to her sister. "What do you want me to do?"

"I need you to keep washing his face with this rag." She put it into her sister's hand. "I am going to get the willow bark tea brewing."

"But he ain't awake. How is he going to drink it?" Angel asked.

Heaven stopped in her tracks. How would she get him to drink it? "I'll think of something." Or at least she hoped she would.

She lit a lamp and placed it at the end of the table where the light would shine onto the cabinet. She whipped the curtain covering the lower half to the side, exposing their supplies. She pushed things aside until she uncovered the medicinal basket. She picked through the herbs and medicines her ma had brought along and grabbed the dried willow bark. Her mother's graceful handwriting danced across the brown package.

She needed to heat the water for the teakettle. While the water warmed, she crossed the cabin floor to the bedside of the man. Angel clearly had done what she could, as there were water drips blossoming across the quilt. She put her palm on his forehead. Still hot.

He thrashed in the bed again. "Mary, why?"

Who was Mary? Heaven faltered. Maybe he did have a wife. If he did, she wanted to make sure he lived.

"Is it working?" Angel nudged her elbow.

"I don't think so. He's still hot."

The teakettle whistled.

Back at the stove, she poured the hot water into a mug and placed a palm full of dried leaves into it. It would have to steep for at least a quarter of an hour. She collected a clean kitchen cloth. She would dunk it into the liquid and moisten his lips. Maybe she could squeeze drops into his mouth if he called for Mary again.

She thought it had steeped long enough; she didn't know for sure. She strained the tea into another mug to remove the bits and pieces of willow bark. Collecting the cloth and the tea, she went to her patient.

"Did you add honey?" Angel's face scrunched. "It tastes awful without it."

"No, I don't imagine he'll notice the bitterness."

"That stuff's awful. I'd notice even if I was near death."

"You were near death. Do you remember what it tasted like?" She moistened her patient's lips.

"No. I can't remember." Angel looked disappointed. "I don't remember anything about being sick. Only when I woke up, I couldn't see, and Ma was dead."

"I'm thankful you're here, Angel, or I'd be all alone trying to take care of him."

"Mary?" His eyes fluttered open.

"She's not here, sir. You need to drink this."

He closed his eyes and moaned. "Mary?"

Heaven seized the opportunity and squeezed the cloth into his mouth and prayed the willow bark would bring down the fever and that he wouldn't choke on the liquid.

He spat it out.

"Oh!" Heaven jumped back and wiped her face with the hem of her apron.

"What happened?" Angel's voice was edged in fear.

"He spit it out, and it landed on my face."

Angel snorted a donkey laugh. "Told you to put honey in it."

"I didn't think he would taste it." She stared at him. His eyes were closed. He wasn't aware of her at all.

"Guess I'd better add the honey."

"I'll get it and a spoon." Angel hopped off the stool. "Be right back."

Heaven sighed. It was going to be a long night.

Travis didn't want to open his eyes if the sunlight hurt his head this much with them closed. What he couldn't figure out is why his head hurt. Slowly he cracked them open. A finger of sunshine stabbed him in the eye. He covered his eyes with his arm against the assault. His head throbbed, or rather, one side of his head did, not both. What happened to him?

He wasn't lying on the ground, and he was warm and dry. In a bed. *In a bed?* He'd been on his way to Caleb's place. After that he couldn't remember.

Before slamming his eyelids closed, the brief glimpse of the room he'd seen had offered a view of a chinked wall and a daguerreotype on a dresser of two people he didn't recognize.

Pieces of images came to him—angels, heaven, and a choir. Had he left this earth and then returned? No, that didn't happen. It could have been a strange dream, but if felt real, and the pain in his head wasn't his imagination either.

"Sir, are you awake?" A soft hand brushed against his arm. "You had a fever, but it's gone now."

Slowly he dragged his arm away from his eyes. The sunlight kissed the hair of the woman standing next to him. The woman from the store. Holding a rifle. His heart pumped blood through his veins faster than water out of a bucket full of holes. He struggled to sit up. He had to get away from this crazy woman.

"I'm not sure you should do that yet. You have a pretty ugly head wound." She hoisted the gun, resting it on her shoulder.

He sank his head back into the pillow. He'd try it her way, at least until he was strong enough to wrestle that rifle away from her. "How'd I get that?"

Her face paled, and her stunning blue eyes rounded. "I was aiming over your head."

"You shot me?"

"I was trying to scare you away. You must be taller than the others. I'm sorry—unless you're coming here wasn't honorable." Her finger snaked into the trigger hole. "Then I won't be sorry at all."

"I was on my way to Caleb Wharton's home."

"Well, you found it, but why were you coming here? Did someone tell you we were all alone out here?" Her grip on the barrel tightened.

"Caleb told me to come here."

She withdrew her finger from the trigger and lowered the gun. "Pa? Pa sent you? Did he send passage money with you? Where is he? Did he send a letter with you? Is he okay?" Her face flushed with excitement, making her blue eyes shimmer like sapphires.

Travis had a feeling Caleb had been less than forthcoming. Considering his feverish state, he guessed he could excuse the man. "I'll tell you everything I know as soon as you put that gun over in the corner."

She spun around and headed to the corner, seemingly assured he wouldn't be a danger to her since he brought word of her father. Travis was glad she did as he asked. He didn't want her holding that gun when he told her about Caleb.

"What's your name anyway?"

She turned back and smiled. "Heaven Wharton."

In a flash, he understood what Caleb had done.

Travis wanted her far away from the corner before he gave her any information about her father. He watched her almost float across the floor with a Christmas-morning smile. Beautiful. And he was about to hand her a stocking full of nothing. That smile would disappear, and most likely, giving her the news about her father would keep that smile locked away for a long time. He hated to be the one to cause that.

"You didn't tell me your name." She stood further from the bed than before. Now that he was awake, he figured she wanted to maintain propriety.

"Travis Logan."

"Are you from around here, Mr. Logan?" She gathered the side edge of her apron, twisting it between her fingers.

"No I'm not. My family resides in the eastern part of the state in Knoxville." He could see the impatience in the jiggle of her foot. Still she seemed determined to be the gracious southern hostess.

"What county would that be, Mr. Logan? We're originally from Davidson County. Nashville."

"It's Knox County, Miss Wharton." His throat was dry. "Could I trouble you for a drink of water before I tell you about your father? I have such a bitter taste in my mouth."

"That's from the willow bark. I'll get you some water."

"Why did you give me willow bark?"

"You seemed feverish, thrashing about in the bed, and I knew that's what my ma would have done for you if she were here."

"That was a good idea. It must not have been a high fever since I'm better this morning. Except for this." He touched the side of his head and winced.

"That's going to take some time to heal. I tried stitching you up, but it's a lot different to pull a needle through skin than through cloth. My stitches aren't as pretty." She glanced away, but not before he saw her face scrunch.

"It's a bit different, that's true. Have you done that before?"

"No, I tried to watch Ma stitch my father, but I fainted. So it's a miracle from God that I was able to close your wound."

Travis knew about miracles, but that he'd been on the receiving end didn't seem fitting. God should have chosen to save Caleb, not him.

Annabelle finished with the note she'd penned for her father on her last piece of fine foolscap and blew on the ink to dry it. She hadn't written that she didn't plan to return to his home, only how much she had to get away, especially after her encounter with William's wife.

William's wife.

It galled her to write that, and it showed with the blobs of ink she'd left on the paper. Satisfied she'd given him enough information, she placed the pen back in the crystal holder. Her plan was set in motion now, the trunk sat at the station waiting, and she'd found a reliable, perfect, and unexpected chaperone.

She sipped the chamomile tea and nibbled at the small piece of toast she'd brought upstairs with her. She'd been too excited, nervous about the trip to eat her dinner. The tea had cooled and no longer held any appeal. The toast was too dry to consume. She dropped it onto the flowered china plate and pushed her chair back.

Had she forgotten anything? The few things she'd knitted, three dresses, a dress for Heaven, and the jam for Angel were at the top of the list. She'd filled in the trunk with things she needed to start her new life and some that would remind her of home—an embroidered pillowcase her mother had made and one of father's cigars so she could conjure him in her mind with a sniff.

Anticipation instead of sleep filled her thoughts as she wandered around her bedroom memorizing it, because if her plan worked, she wouldn't be returning. She stopped at her dressing table and picked up the framed daguerreotype of her mother. It might fit in her reticule. She wanted to bring it with her, but no, if she did, her father would immediately know she had no plans to return. She hoped someday he would send it to her. She hugged the frame to her chest. "I miss you, Ma."

Chapter 6

The cup Heaven carried shook against its saucer as she walked across the cabin. It was as if her body knew something wasn't right and didn't want her asking questions. She couldn't believe she'd stood there acting like a debutant, asking everyday questions, while all she wanted to do was shout like a little girl, "Where's my Pa?" Her black skirt rustled as she crossed the floor, as if whispering warnings of unpleasantness to come. She hated that skirt.

"Here you are, Mr. Logan. Do you need help, or do you feel confident that you can hold the cup?" She avoided looking at the stitched side of his head, preferring to concentrate on the curly dark hair mussed from a rough night.

He reached for the cup, brushing his fingers against hers. It caused a tingle to rush through her. How strange. That had never happened when Jake touched her hand. The tremor caused the cup and saucer to tip until it almost slid out of her grip, but she found the strength to hang on until he had a firm grasp on it. She stood at the foot of the bed while he drank. It seemed it took a lifetime for him to drink the contents. When he finished, he didn't offer her the empty cup.

She held out her hand to take it from him when small taps echoed under the window as something walked across the porch.

"Mr. Jackson! That troublesome goat is walking on my porch again!" Her hands curled into fists. She wanted him off of there. He was always chewing on the posts. She took a step toward the door and stopped. Mr. Jackson could wait. He'd just come back again anyway. She didn't want to delay any longer. She spun around, "You were going to tell me about Pa?"

He pointed to the stool next to the bed. "It would be best if you sit, as it's a long story."

His tone made her knees weak, but she made it to the stool without embarrassing herself by tripping and landing on his chest. She took time to arrange her skirt, making sure her ankles were covered. She looked and found him staring at her. His brown eyes were warm and caring. Mary, whoever she was, should consider herself blessed.

"Who else lives here?"

"My sister, Angel, is asleep in the loft." Her sister had helped last night in ways Heaven wouldn't have thought possible. The two of them worked in harmony like a pair of well-trained horses.

"I met your father on the steamboat, not long after we left Memphis."

"You know where he is! You've brought our passage money?" She scooted to the edge of the stool. She had so much to do—lists to make, things to pack—and she needed to find someone to buy this place. Then she realized Mr. Logan hadn't answered her question. In fact, he stared at her in a sad sort of way. "You don't have the money? Were you robbed?"

"Please, Miss Wharton. Let me finish."

The bad feeling slid on like a strained pelisse. "Go ahead. I'll listen."

"While we were on the deck observing the water, your father fell. . . ."

"He went overboard? He drowned!" She sprung to her feet. Her hand caressed the back of her neck while she paced the length of the bed. "I knew he shouldn't have gone on that boat. He should have taken us with him and traveled by land. If we'd gone with him, he wouldn't have. . ." She hiccupped a sob.

"Miss Wharton. He didn't drown. Please sit down."

She sat but didn't want to. The small, dark cabin closed in on her. She forced herself to look him in the eye. "Tell me."

"He didn't drown, but he isn't alive."

Numbness crept from the roots of her hair to her toes. She worked her lips, trying to form words. A guttural sound escaped before her vocal cords could shake free of the shock. "Not alive? Dead? Pa's dead?" Her mind flew into action. She was left to take care of Angel. What would she do now? How would they survive the winter? There was no family left to run to. Maybe Annabelle's father would let them stay, but she would have to get there, and the train fare. . . And Angel! What would she tell her? Her mind pushed and pulsed against the sides of her head. She feared her skull would burst.

"Miss Wharton,"—he touched her shoulder—"I can see lots of things are worrying you. Would you like me to tell you the rest of what happened later?"

"No. No, I have to know now so I can tell my. . ." A sob escaped. "My sister." They were alone now, just the two of them. The realization found purchase and settled into her shoulders. It was an enormous burden she wasn't sure she could carry. She dabbed her eyes with the hem of her apron. "Go ahead, tell me."

"I did everything I knew how to do, but nothing worked. I tried to save him. I couldn't. He died on September 27 from a high fever."

Fever. Icy cold formed layers around her heart, and she fought to take a breath. It wasn't possible—no not at all. Not Pa, too. The man had to be mistaken. "September?" That wasn't long after he'd left. That's why they hadn't heard from him in all these months. "What took you so long to come and tell us?"

He seemed uncomfortable, wiggling in the bed away from her, and turned his head. "I wasn't aware there was anyone to tell."

Her mouth slacked open, and she gasped. Surely Pa had mentioned them, unless he'd been too sick.

"Then how did you know to come here?" Suspicion marched into her mind. He was here because he thought the place was abandoned.

She was right about shooting him after all.

Annabelle greeted her companion with a conspiratorial smile as she climbed into the closed buggy. She'd scooted out of the house with a cheery good-bye wave to John, even though leaving without saying a proper forever farewell to him left a small knot of sadness hanging in her throat.

"Good morning, Mrs. Miles." She slid under the edge of the wool carriage blanket Mrs. Miles held up for her. A waft of attar of roses hugged her. Annabelle's own mother used to wear that fragrance. "Isn't it a great day to ride a train?"

"Isn't it though, even if it's a bit chilly? Now we must stay out of Jake's sight so he doesn't make us disembark before we've even left the station." The older woman smoothed the blanket over her lap.

"He's going to be surprised to see us, isn't he?" Annabelle hoped Jake wouldn't be furious at her for asking his mother to be her chaperone. Mrs. Miles had agreed readily, stating she'd enjoy spending time with her son. She had told Annabelle how much she had missed him. On the train he wouldn't be able to hide in his room the way he did at home, and Mrs. Miles said she had a lot she wanted to say to him.

Mrs. Miles's striking green eyes glimmered as she patted Annabelle's gloved hand. "I do hope to see him marry Heaven while we're there, too. I've been praying he'll come to his senses once he sees her and forgets that nonsense about not being good enough for her."

"That would be nice." If Jake did marry Heaven, then Mrs. Miles would have to travel back alone. Annabelle hadn't thought about that situation. Even though she'd made the decision to travel to Memphis on her own, that was her worry, one that Jake's mother shouldn't have. She'd simply convince Heaven not to get married without Jake's father present. She tugged the edge of the blanket under her hip and settled in to take in her last views of the city she'd called home.

"Pa's dead? What happened?" A young girl's voice shrieked from above.

Heaven's eyes widened. "That's my sister, Angel. Apparently she is eavesdropping. I have to go to her."

Travis tugged the blanket under his chin. "Before we continue this conversation, do you think I could—could use the, um. . . ?"

Her face flushed a delightful rose color as she understood his request. He hadn't meant to embarrass her, but he really needed a trip outside.

"Of course. Do you think you can make it alone, or. . . ?" Her throat bobbed as she swallowed. "Should I bring you a chamber pot?"

Now her face was past rose, more of a blood-red color. Come to think of it, his face was feeling a bit warm. "I'll be fine. I'll take my time getting up so the room steadies. If you'll just bring me my clothes."

"You don't need any. We didn't remove anything. That wouldn't have been proper."

Proper? Where did she think she was, in a big city where women took notes of every uncovered sneeze? "My boots?"

"Still on your feet."

"On my feet." He wiggled his toes. They bumped into leather. He peaked under the quilt. He was fully clothed right down to his muddy boots. "Guess your sheets are going to need washing."

"They were going to need it anyway after you bled all

over them." She stepped away. "I'll see to Angel while you're outside."

After she'd left him alone, he stood. His head pounded, and the room dipped and swayed. It didn't matter how weak his legs were; he would make it outside to the privy. Alone.

When he came back inside, he found Heaven next to the fireplace in a rocking chair holding her sister and stroking her golden hair. Heaven briefly raised her red-rimmed eyes and met his then rested her head against the top of her sister's. The fire had nearly died. Only a few winking embers remained.

He didn't say anything but let them grieve, knowing there was more to come. The chill of the cabin wrapped around him, sending goose bumps down his arm, and he hoped it was that and not the return of the fever. His fever must have been high for him not to remember what had occurred the night before. Gathering a few small logs from the pile next to the fireplace he knelt and placed them on the embers. With a squeeze from the bellows, air whooshed across the bed of embers. Orange and then blue flames jumped and then licked the logs until they tasted the bark. Satisfied the fire would burn, he stood, unsure of what to do next.

Heaven lifted her face. The peach tone had faded, leaving her pale. "I'll make breakfast."

Angel grabbed her sister's neck. "Not yet."

"That's okay. Can I do something?" He felt out of place. He'd seen a lot of death but hadn't experienced the womenfolk's side of it.

"There is nothing for you to do, no one to send a telegram to. It's just the two of us now." Heaven lowered her eyes and kissed the part on her sister's head.

"You have a preacher I can get for you?" He shifted his weight. "I could ride back into town."

"No!" Angel hopped off her sister's lap and slapped her hands on her hips.

Travis backed up.

"You can't tell anyone. They'll take Heaven away and lock her up." Her arms folded around her chest, and she rocked on her heels. "If that happens, I won't have anyone."

Heaven reached out her arms and encircled her sister. She pulled Angel back onto her lap, all the while glaring at him.

Travis looked at the door. He should leave and come back later when they'd had time to calm down. Then he would tell them the rest. But he couldn't. He had never been able to shrug off his need to rescue animals and humans. These two were scared and feeling hopeless. He wouldn't abandon them. "They won't lock her up. I promise. If anyone asks, I'll tell them it was an accident."

Travis found himself in the kitchen. What did he plan to do in here? He wasn't sure, but at least he was away from the scary girl who seemed even fiercer than her sister. He picked up a toy-sized china cup. It looked as if it would hold only a thimbleful of coffee, as his father would say. "Can I get anyone a cup of coffee?"

Heaven released her sister and wiggled out of the rocker, leaving Angel. "Forgive me, Mr. Logan. I've forgotten my manners of hospitality." She wiped her eyes with her hands and appeared to pull a smile from out of nowhere and apply it across her face. "I'll make you some breakfast."

"That would be nice." He didn't want to eat; he wasn't hungry. But he wasn't about to mess with her hospitality manners, as they seemed important to her. He stood back and watched her work in silence while Angel huddled in the rocker in front of the fire.

"Sit down, Mr. Logan. Angel, come try and eat something."

"I don't want to." Angel's voice sounded dull and flat to Travis. He tried but couldn't imagine the pain the little miss felt.

"Angel, you need to come eat, too. We aren't wasting these eggs." Heaven turned from the stove and pointed a spatula at her sister. "Now."

Travis waited for Angel to find a place at the table, afraid he might take her seat and cause another outbreak of anger. "Is the chair at the end of the table all right for me to sit in?"

"It's Pa's chair, but I guess he won't be needin' it, so you can sit there." Angel scooted closer to the table.

Heaven plunked a plate on the table in front of him. Travis sat and stared at his plate of scrambled yellers. His stomach flipped and did a twist. Perhaps he wasn't quite ready for heavy food, or maybe it was the untold details of why he was at the Wharton's home. He picked up a piece of perfectly browned toast. With a knife, he shaved off a sliver of butter. "Did you make the butter here on the farm?"

"Miss Bessie did." Angel spooned a hunk of eggs into her mouth. "Heaven just churns it into butter."

"Angel, please act like a lady at the table. Don't talk with your mouth full, and take smaller bites." Heaven filled a china cup with coffee nestled in a saucer. It rattled as she set it in front of Travis.

His finger wouldn't fit through the handle of the tiny cup. He picked it up and rested it in the palm of his hand like an egg, afraid it would crack. "Thank you for the breakfast. It seems I'm not that hungry though."

"Does it hurt much? I'm sorry I don't have anything to dull your pain. We don't keep spirits in the house."

His hand went to the wounded area and touched it without consideration of the possible contact pain. He winced. He'd have to cover that after he talked to Heaven about her father's wishes. "It's not too bad. I have some pain medication in my saddlebag. If it gets to feeling worse, I'll take some. I don't like to use it though. I've seen soldiers get to where they want more and more of it long after their pain should have been gone."

"Are you a doctor?" Angel asked.

His eyes shifted to the toast on his plate. Eating would buy him time before having to answer. He picked it up. He was unsure what to say to Angel's question. He was a doctor, still, but he didn't want to be. He no longer wanted to wake up regretting a mistake he might or might not have made that caused a man to die. "I was. During the war." No longer hungry, he dropped the toast on the plate. Crumbs broke off, scattering on the worn tabletop.

"We could have used you last night, since we didn't know what we were doing when we patched you up." Angel spider-walked her fingers across the tabletop to the right of her plate where her glass of milk sat.

Travis, sure she would knock it over, grabbed her hand and placed it on the glass.

"Stop it! Don't help me!" Angel pushed back from the table. "I can do things. I can do lots of things if people would just let me."

Travis was taken aback by the display of anger. Then it occurred to him that Angel hadn't been blind since birth. He'd seen this same behavior in some of the soldiers with head wounds that caused them to go blind.

"How long has it been since you could see, Angel?"

"Angel, finish your breakfast. There's too much talking going on, and it's going to get cold." Heaven scrambled out of her chair. "*Dr.* Logan, I imagine that your coffee could be warmed up a bit."

Why did Heaven want to avoid his question? It seemed odd to him, or maybe they were one of those families that ignored such things.

"That would be nice." He held up his cup. "Then I need to see to my horse." He noticed the dried mud on his jacket sleeve. "I need to get a set of fresh clothes, too, one less distressing to look at."

She topped off the cup with the dark liquid. "I fed your horse when I milked the cow this morning. I fed the chickens, too, Angel. After last night, I thought you might like to sleep a little later."

"That's okay—just for today."

Heaven began to clear the table. Since it had been a small breakfast, it didn't take long to accomplish the task.

"Before you get your shirt, I want to know everything about how Pa died and why you were the one chosen to tell us."

Travis cleared his throat and ran his hand against his

scruffy chin. He needed a shave. "I don't know if you want Angel to hear all the details."

Angel wrapped her arms around her chest. "I want to know."

"You can talk in front of her. He's her pa, too."

Travis felt his shoulders tighten. "You're stubborn women. But I'll answer your questions after I get my clean clothes." Because when they found out what he had to say, he was sure Heaven would go for that rifle and usher him out of the cabin.

"Your clothes can wait. We can't." Heaven plopped in the chair across from him, next to Angel. She grasped her sister's hand. "Go on now. Tell us about our pa."

"Caleb, your father. . ."

"Quit stalling," Angel said.

He cleared his throat. "He caught something in Memphis is my best guess, and when he fell on the deck, he was sweating and feverish."

Heaven paled, and her eyes widened at the word "feverish." He wondered why.

"Did he say anything about Angel and me before. . . ?" Her eyes glistened. "Before he passed?"

Angel pulled her hand out of Heaven's. "That's all? He caught a fever and died? That's why you've been stalling? Lots of people get a fever and die. That's what happened to Ma. Might as well get him his clothes and send him back to town. He's told us what he came to say, and he promised he would tell people that you shot him by accident."

Travis glanced at the corner where the rifle seemed to sparkle. "There's a bit more."

Heaven's eyes narrowed. "More?"

Could he get to that gun before her? He scooted his chair back and angled his body toward the door. "Before your father died, he had the ship's captain write his will." His legs tensed, readying to spring from the chair. "He left me this farm."

Heaven stood so fast her chair fell, banging on the floor.

Travis was a second behind her, ready to run for the gun.

"Why would our pa give you our home?" Heaven's lips narrowed, and her lips rolled in tight.

"I don't know. We'd been talking in between his bouts of fever about where the best place to raise horses would be. He insisted it was here." The peach had returned to her cheeks, but not the sweet blush color, more the overripe, ready-to-explode-with-juice color.

"I'll get your clothes, Dr. Logan, and then I want you out of here and on your way back to that Mary you were calling for." Heaven's frostbitten words stopped him from telling her what else her father had given him.

Chapter 7

All concern about being prim and proper fled Heaven's mind as she gathered the hem of her skirt and stormed off to the barn. She sidestepped the hole, realizing she no longer had a need to fix it. Not if what Dr. Logan said was true. He would have to take care of this place now.

Inside the barn, sunshine poked its long fingers between the boards, lighting the tack corner, making it easier to see.

Mr. Jackson butted against her thigh, smearing mud on her fresh white apron. She pushed his head. "Go away, goat."

He stepped back and then reached down to nip at her hem.

"Stop it!" Mr. Jackson irritated her on a good day. Today she looked at him and saw stew meat.

She unbuckled a saddlebag. It wasn't proper to be going through a man's personal belongings without being married. Unsettled, she rushed the chore. Her fingers touched cotton, and she pulled out a shirt. A paper fluttered to the ground.

Mr. Jackson made a dive for it.

She snatched it up. "Not for you." She was thankful she retrieved it before him and that the barn floor was dry so there wouldn't be telltale wet marks. It wouldn't do if Dr. Logan thought she'd been sneaking through his private papers.

Holding the paper with great care, she slung his clean shirt over her shoulder, wishing she didn't notice the scent of leather mixed with the smell of spice. It smelled just like him, making her feel warm and safe, and how could that be when he was taking their home from them? *Can't trust your nose, goose.* She planned to put the paper back, hoping he wouldn't notice it had been moved. Silly, really, since he would know she might have seen it, since he'd let her retrieve his shirt.

As she moved closer to the saddlebag, a ray of light snaked through the barn wall, illuminating a name she knew, and knew well. Her pa's perfect penmanship caught her unaware. She traced his name with her fingertip. He'd touched this paper. It was the last thing that she knew for sure he had written. With this new loss, her grief weighed heavier, and this one final contact with her pa overcame her good manners.

Before she knew what she was doing, she'd read the document from beginning to end.

Bile rose and burned her throat. She swallowed the thick spit. She wouldn't let her father get away with this. Not this. Anything but this. Unconcerned about how much her mother would have chastised her for unladylike behavior, she bent and gathered a large amount of her dreadful black skirt into her hand, hiking it higher than her ankles. With the other, she grasped tight the disturbing paper she'd discovered. With her head down, she charged toward the cabin.

Blinking back angry tears, she shoved the paper in her apron pocket as she ran over the bumpy ground. She was going to send Dr. Logan packing, and she didn't care if she had to shoot him again. This time she'd aim for his heart, and his Mary could wonder what happened to him forever for all Heaven cared. Angel would be amenable to helping bury him out where Pa had planned to pen the pigs last spring.

The fingers of the earth snagged her foot. In her hurry, she'd forgotten about the hole in the path. On her way to the ground, she heard an awful popping noise and felt a lightning bolt of pain. Right before she hit the dirt, she grasped the paper tighter. Then her mind took a nap.

Heaven opened her eyes. Her face felt sticky. Touching it, she found it covered in mud. Why was she on the ground? She braced herself with one hand and pulled her leg a fragment closer. Pain landed like a mule kick in her chest, taking away her breath and sending it to the Mississippi. "Why, God? Why?" As soon as life around her began to sour, it went on to curdle soon after.

She smacked the ground with a fist. "How much more pain are You planning to send my way, God? I can't take it anymore!" How would she manage now? Because she'd surely broken her leg. Could it get any worse? She'd shot a man, caused her sister to go blind, and now she'd messed up her own body.

"Angel!" Her sister's hearing had improved since losing her sight. Heaven hoped to reap the benefit. She shivered, causing waves of pain to roll through her leg.

"Angel!"

Nothing.

Maybe she should shout for Dr. Logan. No, she wouldn't ask him for anything.

"Angel! Help me! Please help!"

What was taking the woman so long to get his shirt? He paced the floor of the cabin, wondering how he was going to explain Heaven's father's will. Standing up straight in a pile of goose poop would be easier than telling her he only wanted—

Angel bumped into him, or did he bump into her? "Dr. Logan! Heaven's calling. She cried, 'Help!' Can you see what's happening?"

"I didn't hear her, but I'll go see." Apparently Angel had no intention of letting him go alone, he discovered as he followed her to the door. Stepping out on the porch, he didn't see anything, but he heard a moan. "Miss Wharton?"

"She's by the barn. I can tell." Angel headed to the steps. "Come on, she needs us."

"I'm right behind you. I see her. She's lying in a heap on the ground."

"I bet she fell in that hole she keeps telling me to watch out for."

"It looks like she did." Travis looked to the sky for a moment. *Why, God?* He couldn't seem to escape people who needed doctoring.

Angel squatted next to her sister. "Heaven, you fell in the hole, didn't you? Good thing Dr. Logan and I are here to save you."

Travis bent over. His head wound thumped. "Do you think you can walk?"

"No, I can't get up at all." Heaven's forehead was drawn tight with the pain.

"Guess I'll have to carry you inside then." He slid his arms under her and lifted.

She screamed and went limp.

Travis was thankful she didn't weigh much, since he wasn't feeling quite as strong as he did yesterday. Yesterday he'd been in good health on his way to his new life. Today he had a hole in his head and a beautiful woman in his arms. Now that she was captive, he took the chance to observe her without fear of being shot. Her face, missing the angry hue of this morning, was alabaster white. And holding her close, he noticed the tiny speck at the corner of her eye wasn't dirt but a birthmark in the shape of a teardrop.

"Angel, can you get the door?"

"Are we by the hole?"

"About two steps in front of it." He waited to see if she would cling to him or head out on her own.

"Then I'll start at three." She took a step and started counting. When she reached ten she stopped. "Will you tell me if I count wrong? I don't want to trip on the step."

"I will." He followed behind her as she made quick time across the yard.

"Seventeen. I should be at the step. Am I?" Angel looked over her shoulder. Her gaze hit his chest.

"Yes you are, and there are three. . ."

"I know. Three steps." Confidence showed in her stance as she flew up the stairs and made it to the cabin door. "Stick her on Pa's bed, I guess."

Travis's stitches pulled as he lowered Heaven. As the blood rushed to his cut, his head throbbed.

She opened her eyes and cried out with pain. "It hurts! Did I break it? My leg, is it broken?"

"I'm not sure yet, since I haven't had a chance to inspect the damage. It might be a bad sprain. I'll have to take off your boot so I can look at it."

"Angel can do that." Her face was no longer white but red.

"She could, but can she tell if your leg is broken or if it's a sprained ankle?"

He could see the waves of indecision on her face. "I'm a doctor. I've seen a lot of ankles."

"Ladies' ankles?" Horror showed in her widened eyes.

"No ma'am, just soldiers' ankles. Will you let me look at it?" She nodded.

He unlaced her boot and pulled at the heel to remove it. She screamed.

He stopped. "I'm going to have to cut this off of your foot."

"You can't." Her voice wavered. "Please. It's my only pair."

And she wouldn't have the money to buy another pair he guessed. "It has to come off, Miss Wharton, and if I have to pull it off, it's going to hurt so much you'll wish you could shoot me twenty more times."

"No, wait. Please. We have laudanum in the kitchen. Angel, can you show him where we keep the medical basket? I can't stand this pain."

"You have laudanum? Why didn't you use it when you were stitching me up last night?" If she had, maybe they wouldn't have had this conversation this morning. He might still be sleeping, and she wouldn't have stepped in that hole.

"I forgot we had it."

"Forgot it? Or didn't want to offer it?" Travis shook his head in disbelief.

"Please?"

"I'll get it." He chastised himself for making her think he wouldn't give it to her. Angel collected the basket while he found the medicine and grabbed a spoon. He hesitated giving it to her, having seen others take even a small amount and not be able to stop once the pain was gone. Still, he didn't think he could treat her like a soldier and set her leg without the pain being deadened. His shoulders tensed as images of the battlefield slammed against each other in his mind. Here he was taking care of someone—again. All he'd wanted to do was raise horses, and now everything was complicated. He had to treat her; he couldn't just walk out of the house and leave her there.

Soldiering forth, he sat on the stool next to the bed. He poured the liquid into the spoon. "Open up and swallow fast. This won't taste good."

He gave her the large dose and waited for the telltale haze to slide across her eyes, signaling the power of the drug. She smiled at him and then winked. Startled, he withdrew his eyes from hers while wondering if he'd given her too much. She was quite small, not like the men he'd treated. Even the youngest were larger than she was.

"Angel, I need you here, too, or rather, I would feel better if you stood close by while I treated your sister. I noticed your sister prides herself on propriety."

Angel nodded, her lips screwed up as if she were considering saying something.

"Is there something on your mind, Little Miss?"

"It's just that if something improper happened, I wouldn't see it. So how can I protect Heaven?"

He sighed. From what he'd quickly learned about the Wharton women, they were all about protecting each other from harm. "No, I suppose you can't see me, so you'll have to trust me. I'll tell you everything I'm doing as I do it so you'll be able to hear my voice and know where I am."

"Guess that's all I can do." Angel rushed past him and scooted him off the stool. "You stay by her foot. No way am I letting you kiss her, not when you've been calling for Mary."

Mary. He felt like he'd been gut shot. How had Angel known about her? He must have said her name last night while under the influence of the fever. It wasn't likely he'd ever be kissing her again. Just another failure in his life. No matter that others said, it was better this way. He didn't think so then, but now that he was looking at the beautiful woman in front of him, the pain of betrayal was beginning to fade. But he brought it back to the front and filled in the diminishing colors. He wouldn't be blinded again by a pretty face, no matter how sweet that teardrop by her eye looked or how the softness of her skin tweaked a long-forgotten feeling of wanting to be responsible for someone. No, he wouldn't be dazzled by such things. He'd take care of her long enough to see her back on her feet, and then he'd leave.

Leave? But the farm was his, wasn't it? It was a dilemma. If he left, someone else would eventually take it from Heaven and Angel. Or worse, Heaven would actually kill the next man who rode down her drive. That had to be why Caleb had given him both the farm and Heaven. As if you could give a daughter away without her knowledge. He had some cogitating to do.

"Dr. Logan." Heaven's voice was thick as honey.

Her eyes were glazing, and Travis knew the medicine was working. "Yes, Miss Wharton?"

"I don't. . ." She blinked or more like closed her eyes and opened them slowly. " 'Tis not working—the medicine."

"Yes it is, Miss Wharton. I do believe it's about time for me to slip off that boot."

"Dr. Logan. You are a beautiful man." Heaven's eyes lowered, and she stroked his hand with a finger. "You have such capable-looking hands."

His hand felt as hot as a poker just out of the fire where Heaven's finger had mapped its way across the back of his hand. He jerked it back. This was not something he'd ever experienced in the battlefield.

Angel snickered. "Maybe we should keep him, Heaven, if you like him so much."

Travis wiggled the boot free.

Heaven whimpered. "Stop. Please stop!"

"It's off now." He slowly rolled down her stocking to see if the skin had broken. He hoped not, because that would mean months of recovery.

"I'd like to keep Dr. Logan." Heaven's voice seemed thicker. He liked the way it sounded.

"Dr. Logan?" Her eyebrows couldn't seem to settle in one place as she attempted to focus on him.

"Yes, Miss Wharton?" Travis wondered how he would splint the ankle.

"I think I could love you. Could you love me, too?"

Heat crept up his face as Angel put her hand in front of her mouth to hold back the laughter. He was glad she couldn't see him, because she would likely tease him mercilessly. He wasn't a stranger to that, not with having older sisters.

"I'm sure I could, Miss Wharton. You are a mighty desirable woman." If she knew what else her pa had given him besides the land, would she still be saying that? He'd have to figure out what to do with these two soon. His plans hadn't included a wife, much less one with a precocious sister.

"Then I think we should get married soon, Dr. Logan. Pa's right. And I'm so tired of being alone. If we were married, I'd not be alone anymore."

She stared right at him; shimmering sapphires with feathery lashes pierced his heart in the lonely place, making a hole where she entered like a thief in the night. She'd make someone a beautiful wife, but not him. Then her eyes closed, and her head fell back on the pillow. From the way she was snoring, he knew she would be out for a while.

Her ankle was sprained, not broken. The tightness in Travis's neck released. Heaven's treatment wouldn't be pleasant, but not as unpleasant as it would be if she had broken a bone. She'd have to soak her foot in a bucket of cold water several times a day. He shivered again. As cold as this cabin was this morning, he wondered if a layer of ice would form across the top before she could plunk her foot into it. He felt sorry for her, but it was better than a broken ankle. The last time he'd treated a broken bone, an infection turned the foot green. He shuddered at the memory of sawing off that man's foot. At least this time the patient should retain all of her parts.

"Angel, I need some old clothes that I can cut into strips. I have to bind your sister's ankle. Do you think you could find me something to use? Something Heaven won't be angry about us taking scissors to?"

Angel stood. "I suppose we could use one of Ma's crinolines. Heaven won't be happy about that though." She twisted a curl in her fingers.

No, she probably needed her mother's things to make new clothes for her and Angel. "What about a shirt of your father's?" Caleb wouldn't be needing those anymore. A man's shirt didn't have enough fabric to make anything useful for the remaining Whartons.

"Pa left a shirt and a pair of pants behind. Sometimes Heaven wears the pants though, to clean out the barn."

Since the barn belonged to him now, he knew Heaven wouldn't need to muck it out. "I'll take the pants. They'll make long and strong strips. If Heaven complains, I'll find a way to calm her down. Can you bring me the scissors from your sister's sewing basket, too?"

Angel took a step forward and touched Heaven's arm. "Heaven? He wants me to get the scissors. I know I'm not supposed to, but if you don't wake up and tell me not to, then I'm going to do it."

Heaven remained still.

"Guess that means it's okay."

Angel's toothy grin lightened his mood, and then the dangers of a blind child handling sharp scissors occurred to him. "I imagine this one time it will be okay to break your sister's rule. Just point the sharp end to the ground. Don't run or skip on your way back here."

"I can do that. Pa's pants are hangin' on the wall peg behind you."

Light on her feet, Angel took off, seeming to forget her vow of never leaving Travis alone with her sister. He shook his head. That poor girl needed to be able to do more things on her own. He would tell Heaven about the soldiers he had worked with and how their attitudes about life got better when they were treated normally. Not that Angel acted like a spoiled invalid. Far from it, she was as sharp as a razor just run over a strap. It seemed to him Angel's problem was her sister. Maybe he could work with Heaven on that while he was here waiting for her to get strong enough to go. . .to go where? It seemed she and Angel didn't have a place to go.

Angel brought him the scissors. "Heaven never lets me touch these. I told her I could, and I would be careful. Can I cut the strips out of Pa's pants?"

Travis wanted to say yes. "If there was another pair, I would say yes. But since we only have the one, I probably need to cut them so we get straight strips."

Disappointment flashed over her face, and her little body seemed to grow smaller as he hunkered down on the stool. "I understand."

"I think you could do it, darlin', but one wrong cut, and we'd have to get into your mama's petticoats. I would rather Heaven be mad at me than at you if a mistake is made."

Angel lifted her face and beamed. "So it's not because I can't see?"

"No, Little Miss, I don't want to get your sister's ire up.

She's already shot me once this week."

Angel giggled. "That she did, Dr. Logan."

Annabelle grasped the edge of a chair as the dining car rounded a curve, sending her off balance. She would have landed on the floor if not for the gentleman who caught her.

He steadied her. "Are you all right? These trains often take you on a ride you didn't purchase a ticket for."

She touched her chignon, checking that her hair hadn't escaped its silver net. "I'm fine, sir. Thank you kindly for assisting me."

"My pleasure. Thaddeus Kincaid at your service anytime, Miss. . . ?"

"Singleton. Thank you again, Mr. Kincaid." She noticed the clipped speech and harsh ending consonants. Mr. Kincaid was not a southern man.

"Annabelle?" Mrs. Miles tapped her on the shoulder.

She turned slightly, trying to avoid knocking anything from the table they stood next to.

"Are you okay, dear?" Mrs. Miles patted Annabelle's cheek. "I saw you almost take that dreadful fall."

"Mr. Kincaid rescued me, Mrs. Miles. I'm quite all right." The dining car door opened from the other end, and Jake stepped into the aisle. He stopped and tilted his head as if to make sure he was seeing correctly. They'd been found out a little earlier than Annabelle had hoped.

"Mother? Annabelle?" Jake hovered behind Mr. Kincaid. "What are you doing here?"

Mr. Kincaid stepped aside.

Annabelle scooted past him and grasped Jake's arm. "Surprise! Your mother and I thought it would be wonderfully fun to go with you to visit Heaven."

He scowled at her. "You did, did you?"

Annabelle dropped her hand to her side. She hadn't expected him to be happy, and he wasn't. He resembled Mrs. Cooper's growling terrier that used to plague her and Heaven when they walked to school. She backed up a few steps, letting his mother get closer.

"Jake, when she asked me to escort her, I couldn't think of a better thing to do. I've not had a chance to visit with you since you came back, and now I'll get to see Heaven as well." Mrs. Miles tugged at her son's sleeve. "Have you eaten? Annabelle and I were getting ready to have lunch. Of course you haven't. That's why you're in the dining car."

"Mother. . ."

"Now Jake, don't be angry at us. We girls need a little adventure in our lives. So come, sit and dine with us. Then you can tell us how you're going to catch Heaven when she faints at the shock of seeing you."

"Mother, I told you. . ."

"I know, Jake. You think you're going to break that girl's heart again and tell her you can't marry her. I think when you see that lovely girl again, you're going to change your mind." Mrs. Miles stopped at a table and waited for her son to pull out her chair. "Annabelle, come, sit by me."

"Yes Annabelle, please sit by my mother. It's quite kind of you to accompany her on this unsafe journey." His face said otherwise, lips drawn in a straight line and no hint of friendliness in his eyes.

So that was why he was angry. He thought she'd endangered his mother. She hadn't. So far everyone had been kind and helpful. "I knew we'd be safe once we found you. And that didn't take long." *Just long enough to keep you from making us leave the train.*

A server placed steaming bowls of tomato soup in front of each of them. Annabelle bowed her head and silently gave thanks, pushing back the nagging feeling she shouldn't have left home without talking to her father one more time. She would have though, if he'd been home. She was right to take this opportunity, since her father wouldn't be home for two more weeks. Waiting that long wasn't possible. Not with that northern, fiancé-stealing woman in town.

Annabelle observed Jake as Mrs. Miles engaged her son in a stilted conversation in which he gave one-word responses. The Jake she knew always wore a smile, suggesting something fun was about to happen. His blond hair hung shabbily around his ears, and his face held a sharpness that wasn't there when he left. What had happened to him while he was away? Everyone said he was a hero, the only man in his regiment to make it out alive from the Battle of Shiloh. Most southern men wouldn't brag about that but would wear it like a suit of fine clothes everywhere they went.

". . .luggage, Annabelle?" Jake stared at her. "Mother said you brought luggage. How many bags?"

Around them dinner plates were kissed with the sounds of silver. The dining car steward walked the aisles refilling glasses.

"I have a trunk filled with things for Heaven." *And what I need when I leave Heaven's.* No need to fill him in on that plan just yet. For now she'd keep that secret tied up in her heart.

"With Mother's things, I'll need to arrange transportation to Friendship. I had planned to rent a horse."

"How far is it from the station to Heaven's?" She hadn't considered getting the trunk delivered.

"We'll disembark in Jackson. The rail line doesn't stretch to Friendship."

"Stagecoach then? Or can we rent a buggy?" She wondered how much extra that would cost. She had to be careful with her money if she wanted to succeed on her own.

"Something. We'll have to wait and see what's available." Jake picked up his glass and drained it. "Now if you'll excuse me, I'm going to the smoking car."

"Jacob, I had hoped we could talk more after dinner." Mrs. Miles's shoulders sagged.

"Not tonight, Mother." Jake stood and nodded at Annabelle. "Pleasant dreams, ladies."

He'd grown ungrateful as well. Annabelle reached over and squeezed Mrs. Miles's hand. She wished her mother were still alive. Jake should be more thankful. "We'll have a nice time without him. I brought a new book along, and we can take turns reading to each other."

Mrs. Miles's lips rose up gently. "I'd like that."

Chapter 8

Travis set the bucket of cold water he'd collected from the pond on the floor next to the bed. "She's going to wake up when her toes hit that water. It's likely she'll be fightin' mad. Angel, I want you to step back so she doesn't land a solid hit on you if she starts swinging her fists. Might be right nice if you'd pray she doesn't hit me."

Angel backed up against the cabin wall.

With great gentleness, Travis slid one arm under Heaven's head. Using the other hand, he maneuvered her into a sitting position.

"What are you doing? I hear the blankets moving, and I can't see you!"

"I apologize. I did say I would tell you everything. Your sister needs to be in a sitting position, so I slid her up against the wall close to the edge of the bed. That way I can dangle her leg over the edge into the bucket."

"Heaven's not going to like this—you sliding her on the bed and touching her leg, not being married. No, she won't like this at all. It's not proper, not proper at all."

"No, not for anyone, unless they are a doctor. Don't you

forget that only a doctor can do this sort of procedure, and that makes it proper." God forgive him, he had no idea if the ladies of society would ever forgive Heaven for this, but they would never find out. He didn't have a choice, or at least not one that wouldn't put Angel in danger of getting hurt.

Heaven's eyes slid open one at a time. "Please, Dr. Logan, say you're going to marry me." Then, just as quickly as her plea expanded into the room, her eyes closed.

Angel was still praying when Travis heard her say, "If Heaven wants to marry Dr. Logan, that's okay with me, too. . ."

He had to get out of this house. Too many marrying-minded women for him to be around. Heaven's head lolled to one side, and then her shoulders began to follow. He bent over her and placed his hands under her arms to level her.

Heaven reached out and grabbed him with both hands and pulled him close. "Dr. Logan, you have my permission to kiss me, but just this once."

He was sorely tempted to do just that to those rose-colored lips. He grunted. It had been a long time since he'd kissed anyone. Mary had been the last. "Maybe another time, Miss Wharton, when you're not drugged. Angel, I'm propping your sister against the wall, and then I'm stuffing a blanket around her so she doesn't slide down again." After he was satisfied she wouldn't be moving, he stooped, grabbed her foot, and plunged it into the cold water.

Her shriek pierced his ears. Her fist landed on his cheek mere inches from his wound.

"Leave it there!" Travis barked. "It's sprained, and if you don't leave it, your foot will swell like a watermelon." He held her ankle with one hand and fended off her fists with the other. "Be still, please, Miss Wharton. I'll let you remove it in a few minutes."

"What happened?"

Heaven's fingers were still curled into tight fists, but at least they weren't flying at his head anymore.

"You tripped in that hole you're always warning me about." Angel sat on the bed next to her sister. "You done swinging your fists at him?"

Heaven groaned. "I did? I told you it was dangerous. Did I hit my head, too?" She ran her fingers through her hair. "Why is my mouth filled with cotton?"

"The laudanum you had stored but didn't remember to use on me? I gave you some. It makes you thirsty, gives you a headache, and does a few other things." He thought better of telling her the drug made her talk out of her head and say things she didn't mean. There wasn't a need to embarrass her. He looked at Angel and wondered if she would tell her sister about the marriage proposal. Right now she was stroking her sister's hand. Maybe she realized her sister wasn't in her right mind when she said those crazy things.

The cabin was getting colder. The fire had feasted on the logs he'd put in earlier. He'd tend to it and then wrap her ankle.

"Angel, can you get your sister a cloth to dry her foot? I'm going to throw another log on the fire." He turned back to Heaven. "Keep your foot in there until I get back."

"Just make that fire roar. The water is so cold. I have goose bumps."

Travis took a quilt from the end of the bed and wrapped it

around her shoulders. "Maybe that will help."

She tugged the quilt tight around her shoulders. "Hurry back. I don't know how much longer I can keep my foot in here."

Travis added several more logs to the fire. Angel waited by her sister and held out the cloth to him.

"This will be fine, Angel." With his fingers, he tilted Heaven's chin, trying to ignore how soft it felt. He inspected her eyes, looking for signs of too much of the painkiller. They didn't seem overly glazed or dull. He was reluctant to give her more, but if she fought him too much, he would. "I don't want to give you any more laudanum, so this is going to hurt a bit. You can scream if you want to. Angel and I won't judge you for it."

"What are you going to do to me that will make me scream?" Her voice wavered.

He knew she wasn't as sure as she wanted to sound. She probably didn't want to cause any distress for Angel. "First, I'm going to take your foot out of the water and dry it. I don't want you to try and help me support it. If you do, it will hurt more. Let me do all the work, and the pain will be less."

Heaven nodded and sucked in her breath and held it.

Either she would yell really loud or pass out. He hoped for the latter.

Travis lifted Heaven's foot from the water. Water drops plunked back into the bucket. He resisted the urge to rub her icy foot with the towel to get the blood circulating. Instead, he gently patted the cloth over her diminutive foot. A foot he wouldn't normally ever see unless he was married to her.

Especially since he had given up doctoring. "You all right?"

She let out a ragged breath. "Maybe there's still some drug working to keep the pain away."

"Maybe." He was feeling his own injury now and was a bit tired and shaky. "Angel, can you scoot the stool over here for me? I need to sit while I do this part."

Angel did as he asked and then climbed on the bed next to her sister.

He rested Heaven's foot on his lap.

She gasped and brushed the quilt from her shoulders. "Dr. Logan!"

"Does it hurt now?"

"No, it's just my foot"—her face was flushed—"is in your lap."

"Excuse the impropriety, Miss Wharton. It's the only way I can wrap it tightly. My head is hurting, or I'd try and do this another way."

Her head lowered, and her hair fell over her face, hiding it from him. "Much obliged, Dr. Logan."

Angel couldn't see the two of them, but she found the exchange interesting. With Heaven declaring her love for Dr. Logan and him taking such good care of Heaven, Angel was thinking of possibilities. She liked Dr. Logan, and Pa had given him their home. If Dr. Logan liked Heaven, they would have a place to live.

She heard carriage wheels rambling down the lane. "Someone's coming. I'll find out who it is." She slid off the bed and headed for the door before her sister had a chance to respond.

Stepping out on the porch, she could hear voices in the distance. She grinned. God must agree with her plan, because those were the voices of Preacher and Mrs. Reynolds. She couldn't wait to bring them inside to meet Dr. Logan, who at this very moment had his hands on her sister's leg.

A rooster bickered with another one out in the yard as the buggy creaked to a stop. Angel listened to the huff of the horses' breath and the creak of the springs on the carriage as someone stepped out. Preacher Reynolds probably, since the man always got out first and helped his lady out. Angel had no idea why that was so important. She didn't need help getting out of a carriage. Maybe that changed when you got as old as Mrs. Reynolds.

She waited, not yelling a hello as she normally would. She was practicing her lady skills just as Heaven would want her to. No shouting at the company. Company should come to the door and be asked in immediately. Company should be offered something to eat and drink. That's what she would do, with one little bend in the rules. She'd wait until they were on the porch before saying anything to Heaven about their guests.

"Come on in. We are so glad you stopped by. Heaven will be thrilled to see you. She's in here." Angel maneuvered them to the bedroom doorway. "Look who's here, Heaven. Preacher and Mrs. Reynolds came by to say hello."

Horrified couldn't be the best word to describe how Mrs. Reynolds looked, but it would have to do. She stood there with her mouth forming an O, taking in Heaven's exposed leg draped across Dr. Logan's lap. And him—he looked frightful. Still in his clothes from yesterday and the bandage around his head.

"What's the meaning of this?" Preacher Reynolds pushed past his wife. "Why is there dried blood on the sheets? Who is this man? What's he doing here?"

Heaven's mouth refused to work. Her tongue stuck to the roof of her mouth.

"I'm Travis Logan—Dr. Logan." He offered his hand to Preacher Reynolds, who stared at it and then smiled and offered his own back.

"Dr. Logan. We hadn't heard about you setting up an office in Friendship. Welcome to our town."

Heaven relaxed a bit.

"Thank you, sir. I haven't set up an office yet. Not sure I will. I planned on raising horses on what I thought was a vacant farm."

"Now why would you think that it was uninhabited?"

"He galloped down the drive like he was going to steal everything we owned. And that's when Heaven. . ." Angel stood behind the Reynolds, who seemed to be frozen between the two rooms.

"Heaven thought she and Angel were in danger yesterday, and she shot in the air to warn me away. Except she missed. That's why there's blood on my clothing and the bed." Travis finished Angel's sentence.

Mrs. Reynolds rushed into the room. Tears welled in her eyes. "Heaven, Angel, I'm so sorry. This has been an awful year for you. I'm so glad we came to see you. Preacher Reynolds heard about a man coming out here, and we wanted to check on you. It's a good idea we did. Why didn't you come and get help after you shot him?"

Heaven wanted to scream. Why wasn't that an obvious answer? "I couldn't send Angel, and I didn't want to leave her here with him. If I took her along, the man might have bled to death before we returned."

"It's not good to be this far out of town when you're alone. I don't know what your father was thinking when he left you."

Heaven forced her brain to pay attention. She was walking on marshy ground. Soon it wouldn't only be marauders she had to worry about, but the good church people wanting to help her. She wouldn't mind some assistance, but not the kind they would want to give to her and Angel.

"Now you're hurt. I don't think you should be living out here alone. We need to find a place for you to stay."

Yes, that was the kind of help they would offer. "We have a place." Heaven flashed a quick look at Dr. Logan. *Please don't tell her, not yet.* She moved her leg, and the pain in her ankle caused her to yell.

"Heaven took a misstep on her way back from the barn and sprained her ankle. Right now I'm wrapping it. I'm grateful you're here, Mrs. Reynolds. Angel was chaperoning, but with her unable to see, it's questionable if she's suitable."

"I am suitable." Angel stormed into the tiny room overflowed with people. "You told me everything you were doing so it would be as proper as it could be. It wasn't like I could go for help."

"Humph." Mrs. Reynolds moved closer to Heaven. "Very questionable situation. Are you saying this man slept here overnight with the two of you?"

Heaven did her best to follow the conversation—the one said aloud and the unspoken one. Was the woman suggesting that she and Angel climbed under the quilts with Dr. Logan? "Not with us, Mrs. Reynolds. He was here, Angel was in the loft, and when I wasn't checking on him, I was sleeping in the rocking chair or reading my Bible."

"So your sister wasn't even downstairs? Preacher, we need to plan a wedding this weekend." Mrs. Reynolds patted Heaven's hand. "Now don't you worry. We won't let anyone know about this indiscretion. It will stay right here in this cabin, but we've got to make it right with the Lord."

"But. . ." Heaven tried to think of a response.

"It's okay. Heaven already asked him to marry her." Angel beamed brighter than the afternoon sun.

"Marry?" Heaven glared at Travis. When had she asked him to marry her? It was the last thing she wanted to do. Marry the man who stole her family farm? There was another reason she was mad, too, but her mind seemed to be loosely wrapped in cloth, allowing only a few thoughts to slip through.

"Sir, nothing improper happened here." Travis stood chest to chest with the preacher. "It was two people needing immediate care, is all. There's no need for forcing a marriage."

"I see." Preacher Reynolds didn't look like he understood, but at least he wasn't insisting on marrying her off right away.

"Would you mind stoking the fire, Preacher, while I tend to Miss Wharton?"

"Not at all. Seems like you have plenty of women now to properly chaperone."

Heaven watched as the preacher left the room. Why didn't

Dr. Logan want to marry her? *Mary.* Maybe he was already married to Mary. She stifled a giggle. But what if he wasn't? He wasn't wearing a wedding ring. The laughter died in her throat. He didn't want to marry her. Why did that hurt?

Another rejection—this time brought on by a man and not caused by a bullet. *Jake.* If he were here, he would marry her, and he wouldn't wait until the weekend. She didn't even know Dr. Logan, not like she knew Jake. Even if Dr. Logan looked good enough to sop up with a biscuit, that didn't mean she wanted to marry him. He wanted her home, but not her and Angel. This marriage business must have been Angel's solution. She would give that girl a detailed lecture on why that was not only improper but disrespectful to make up such a lie.

Dr. Logan returned to the stool and picked up her foot. "I need to get this bound. Would you like some more laudanum? I'm afraid what I gave you earlier has worn off by now."

Why did his eyes have to look so kind, comforting even? His calm manner and easy touch with her ankle even made her feel secure.

"No, I don't want any more. I still don't feel normal, so perhaps there is still some residue?"

"You are looking a bit peaked. It'd be better not to take it if you can handle the pain from the movement." He unwrapped the cloth that he'd started before the interruption of company. "I have to start over. This must be wound tightly or it won't give you enough support."

Mrs. Reynolds peered over Dr. Logan's shoulder.

"Ma'am, if you could move to the bed, I believe I could do a better job of this. If you'd hold Heaven's hand, she can squeeze it when she hurts. Then she might not have to scream, scaring all of us and keeping me from having to do this again."

Her brown hair, twisted into curls around her face, didn't correspond with her expression, which was anything but lovely, since it was screwed up with displeasure. "Yes Dr. Logan. I can see where that would be helpful." The thick material of Mrs. Reynolds's dress rustled, unlike the soft cotton his sisters wore.

Mrs. Reynolds perched on the edge of the bed. "Give me your hand, dear."

Heaven placed her hand in the open palm. She wasn't sure if she hoped she had to squeeze hard enough to make Mrs. Reynolds squeal or not. She'd like to, but that would be just like cutting off her nose to spite someone else, as Pa would say. As if anyone would cut off their own nose. She sniffled. She missed him, missed him badly.

Dr. Logan lifted Heaven's ankle, and pain spiked straight up through to her hip. She wrapped her fingers tight around Sister Reynolds's.

"Oh my, but you have a good grip." Mrs. Reynolds peeled Heaven's fingers from hers.

Heaven wanted to smack her. Maybe she should scream next time. That would no doubt be considered the proper thing decorum necessitated, rather than being too strong.

"Are you almost done, Dr. Logan?" She would like to watch his hands wrapping her ankle so she could do it herself. Doing so would likely send Mrs. Reynolds back to the marriage discussion. Instead, she tried to imagine how those lovely locks of hair would feel in her hand. She felt the fabric of her skirt being arranged across her toes.

"Yes ma'am. I'm finished now. Mrs. Reynolds, perhaps you could get clean sheets on the bed for Heaven. I think the girls might want to sleep together tonight. Rest assured I'll be sleeping in the barn."

Clean sheets? Heaven hoped the ones in the trunk were decent. She'd been washing Pa's sheets and putting them back on the bed as soon as they dried. At least there was another set. Heaven glanced at Mrs. Reynolds. "I'd be grateful to you, ma'am. Angel can help you."

"You do look plum tuckered out. I'll do that, but I reckon you should come back home with us." Mrs. Reynolds patted Heaven's arm. "You can't stay here alone."

"I'm not alone. Angel's here."

"She can come, too, of course."

"My animals need taking care of." She wasn't leaving her cabin. Enough people and things had been taken away from her, and she wouldn't stand to lose one more. If she moved out, it was as good as giving up.

"I'll stay on awhile. They're going to need help," Travis said. "I can sleep in the barn and take care of the animals while Miss Wharton's an—. While she heals. She'll be up and around in about a week."

Why didn't he tell them he owned the land now, that Pa had given it to him, and that Pa was dead? Could he be reconsidering taking it from them? If that were true, she wouldn't leave, because if she did, she had a feeling she'd never be coming back. Once it was known her pa was dead, she and Angel would be taken care of. The church family would flock to her aid, insisting she wasn't capable of taking care of the small homestead and Angel. Then someone would find an old toothless man that could still stand and insist they marry. She didn't want a husband if it wasn't Jake—and that was impossible even for God.

"If Dr. Logan will stay in the barn for a few days, I wouldn't have to trouble anyone to help take care of my animals. Considering how he ended up with a head wound, it would be handy to have a man about the place until I can hold a gun steady." She might as well become 'that eccentric spinster' sooner rather than later.

Mrs. Reynolds stood up, all starch in her veins and her nose slightly in the air. "We'll ask Preacher Reynolds about what to do. You all keep this door cracked while I'm gone." Without waiting for a reply, head high she left the tiny room.

Angel followed the motherly Mrs. Reynolds.

"Why didn't you tell them about Pa and his will?"

"It's not for me to tell, Miss Wharton. I figured you'd let everyone know when the time is right. Now, if they'd have asked me why I was here, I would have told them, but they didn't." Dr. Logan smiled. "That might be considered lying, but in this case, I consider it a chance for you to handle your grief the way you want to."

Weariness of the day smothered her. She was tired and worried about the future, and this kind man had offered her a gift—a time to recover before her world fell like bird feathers from a cat's mouth.

Mrs. Reynolds rushed in the room, tears dripping from her eyes. "You poor soul. Angel told us about your father."

"I'm sure it was this laudanum that kept her from speaking

out, and I didn't feel it my place to inform you." Dr. Logan held Heaven's eyes with his, making her feel all warm inside. "I believe they need some time alone to take in the loss."

"Dr. Logan, I mean no disrespect, but these girls need to be comforted with a woman's touch, and leaving them alone will not accomplish that."

"None taken, Mrs. Reynolds; however, it has been my experience the family needs time to grieve amongst themselves before they have to put on a brave face for others. With this recent loss, I would expect that to be most important. If they want to come into town tomorrow, I'll be happy to bring them."

"We'll need to have a service for Mr. Wharton soon. Even though there's no body, the family needs to do something to honor the dead," Preacher Reynolds said from behind his wife. "Perhaps it would be best to plan on that rather than a wedding?"

Angel buried her head in Heaven's shoulder and hiccupped a sob. Heaven gathered her closer. The poor child had been through more than enough tragedy this year. Both of them had. How would she ever help her sister to feel secure again?

"If you think that best, Preacher."

"I do, and this man is a healer, so it will be fine for him to sleep in the barn. And, Mrs. Reynolds, I know your proclivity for helping people, but I think tonight it would be best not to mention this to the other ladies in town."

"I do not gossip. I'm very careful with my choice of words, sir. I don't appreciate you disparaging my character in front of these fine people, especially the doctor." Mrs. Reynolds put a hand to her chest. "Is that what you want, Heaven? To be alone tonight? I could stay here, I suppose." She glanced around the room. "There doesn't seem to be a place for me to sleep."

"Don't make us go. I don't want to go, Heaven." Angel's muffled voice sounded far away to Heaven. Right now nothing seemed real to her.

"Yes ma'am. I want to stay in my home. Angel and I would feel closer to our pa here, and I'm tuckered out. I can't imagine a ride into town with my ankle. We'll be fine, especially with Dr. Logan out in the barn."

"Then I'll put some dinner together for you and tidy up before we leave. Preacher, since Dr. Logan is wounded as well, you can help me by tending the animals and fixing a bed for him out in the barn."

"There's no need to fix dinner for us, Mrs. Reynolds. We have a nice stew left from yesterday that can be reheated."

"At least let me get the biscuits rolled out for you. I wish I'd have brought along one of the pies I made today. We were in such a rush, I forgot about them. We could ride back to the house and get it, maybe bring back a few other things to eat as well so we could join you for supper."

"No, really, you've done enough." Heaven was glad the woman didn't ask what she'd done other than cause Heaven distress. "I'm not hungry. Are you, Angel? Doctor?"

Dr. Logan shook his head. "I'm ready to rest more than eat."

"Not hungry," Angel said, but her face at the mention of pie had said otherwise.

Heaven wondered if Angel thought the Reynolds's might change their minds about them staying at the cabin if they had time to ride to town and back.

Preacher Reynolds carried Heaven to the rocker in front of the fire. Heaven figured it was so she could visit with Mrs. Reynolds as she worked. Heaven would rather have been stuck in the chicken coop or out in the barn with Mr. Jackson. "There, now you're settled. Dr. Logan, why don't you come with me to the barn, and we'll scout out a place for your bedroll."

Dr. Logan nodded. "I'd like to check on my horse."

"I'm coming, too." Angel bolted for the door.

"Angel." Heaven wanted Angel to stay. She didn't want to be left alone with Mrs. Reynolds. Besides, would those men be capable of watching out for her sister?

Angel halted. "Please? I want to pet Dr. Logan's horse, and Mr. Jackson needs petting."

"Be careful."

"I will."

Mrs. Reynolds came up from the root cellar with a jar of green beans and set them on the table. "I looked at your stew, and I think some of these"—she held up the jar—"would be a nice addition, and it looks like you have a lot of them to use up."

"That we do. Great-Uncle Neal apparently had a great fondness for the vegetable." Heaven hoped the woman hadn't taken the time to inspect the lack of any other kind of vegetables in the cellar.

Mrs. Reynolds took a bowl from the kitchen shelf and placed it on the table. She started adding flour, lard, and water to make the biscuits. "You're almost out of flour. Should I bring some up from the cellar?"

"No. We'll get it when it's needed." Heaven didn't want her to know there was none left.

"Your great-uncle was an interesting man, you know. He worked at the cotton gin and never missed a Sunday service. Shame he never found a good woman to marry."

"Maybe so, but if he had, we wouldn't be living here."

"The good Lord has interesting ways of carrying out a plan, doesn't He?" Mrs. Reynolds flopped the dough on the floured tabletop and rolled it with a pin. "Why don't you close your eyes and rest while you have a chance, dear?"

"Thank you, ma'am." Heaven closed her eyes. At least this way she wouldn't have to keep up her end of the conversation.

After the rumble of the Reynolds's carriage wheels faded, Heaven turned to Dr. Logan. "Thank you for giving us at least one night alone."

"They'll be back, you know." He pulled out a chair from the kitchen table and plunked down.

"I hope so." Angel hunkered down by her sister's feet close to the fire while Heaven brushed her hair. "Last time when Ma died, they brought pie. Remember, Heaven?"

"Yes I do. You ate so much pecan pie you got sick." Responsibility burdened her shoulders. Her sister should have pie, meat, and a family. Could she ever hope to fill Angel's needs? Exhaustion filled her body. Her eyelids felt heavy, and the brush she used on Angel's hair weighed more than Mr. Jackson.

"Miss Wharton?"

Startled awake, she straightened in the chair. The brush now rested in Dr. Logan's palm. When had he taken it from her? Anxiety poked its fingernail into her heart. "Angel?"

"She's fine. I finished her hair and sent her to bed. She's waiting for you. I thought I'd carry you there before I head out to the barn."

Carry her? For a moment, she'd forgotten about her ankle. As nice as it would feel to be cradled by someone, she wouldn't allow herself that pleasure. "I can do it."

He sighed. "I thought you'd say that." He reached down and snatched her up before she could breathe in and out.

"Put me down."

"No. You're my patient now. I want you to get better. Tomorrow I'll fashion a crutch for you, and you'll be able to get around without further injury. Tonight I'm taking you to bed."

She watched his face grow red and felt the heat of her own body betraying her.

"Th–thank you." It was only a few steps to the small bedroom, and Heaven couldn't help but wish it were miles away. For one brief second, she allowed herself to feel the safety of those strong arms. Too soon she was in her pa's bed with Angel.

"I'll get the lamps extinguished and the fire banked before I head out to the barn. Is there anything else you might need?"

Her nightclothes, but she wasn't about to ask him to get them. "I can't think of a thing."

The lamplight flickered, giving the room a comforting glow that begged her to rest. Or was it the man in the room that made her feel safer than she had in a long time?

Chapter 9

Travis strolled around inside the barn, stretching his arms over his head trying to loosen the kinks that had settled in overnight. He wouldn't admit it to anyone, but he didn't think he'd ever get used to sleeping on a hard surface. He much preferred a soft bed. He should've known not to spend money on another horse to breed with Pride and Joy. At least not until he'd ridden out and checked the property Caleb had left to him.

This little complication of having to add a wife and her sister to his life didn't sit well with him. He didn't like being a pawn any more than Heaven. But he was stuck. He had to take Heaven with the farm; otherwise, he'd leave them defenseless. His hand brushed his wound. Maybe not defenseless, but not crack shots either.

Caleb's last will and testament would stick in a court of law as far as the farm went, but not the part about Heaven. And it shouldn't. Isn't that what this war had ended up changing? Owning people? Heaven's father didn't own her, and neither did he. Most likely, the old codger just wanted him to leave his daughters cared for. He hadn't mentioned Angel though, and that bothered him until he remembered Caleb's days were filled with thrashing, sweating, and convulsing. Just because he didn't mention his youngest daughter didn't mean he had no love for her. Travis knew he couldn't leave Caleb's daughters to fend for themselves. They could be hurt and forced out of their home. Not to mention the farm was in dire need of repairs. And that is why he had to marry Heaven, like Caleb wanted. Like Caleb ordered in his will. But he didn't want to. He wanted a wife and family after he had his horse farm thriving.

Travis was glad the cabin wasn't all sissified. There wasn't a doily to be seen or a cozy draped over a china teapot. He didn't mind all that stuff as long as it wasn't in his house. A good house needed a chair by the fire, a bed, and a stove big enough to heat the house. Apparently Heaven felt the same way. There might be hope for a compatible match between them. There was a spark; he knew that yesterday when their hands touched on that coffee cup. He felt it and knew she did, too, by the way that cup almost landed on his lap.

A goat bumped against Travis's hip.

Light spilled in as Angel came through the barn door.

"Good morning, Angel."

"Morning."

He scratched the goat's ear. "Friendly goat, aren't you?"

She ran her hand across the goat's back. "Mr. Jackson is my friend. Mrs. Jackson isn't as friendly. You have to be careful around her, because she'll knock you down."

He wondered whose idea it had been to name the goats like married people. He found it odd but funny to be addressing the animals like people.

"You want to meet Mrs. Jackson?"

"I'd like that."

She took his hand, and together they walked to a stall containing an all-white goat. A pregnant goat.

"We don't know why she's so mean. We keep her locked up so she doesn't hurt us."

"Has she always been ill-tempered?"

"No sir. When we got her, they both were nice, but they didn't have names and they were always together, so I named them Mr. and Mrs. Jackson. And she stopped giving milk, too. We haven't had cheese in a long time"

"Might be because she's expecting a little one. They get that way sometimes."

"A baby goat?" Angel squealed and then steepled her hands against her mouth while she bounced on her toes. "When's it going to be here?"

"I'm not sure." It was the wrong time of the year for a birthing. He wondered at God's wisdom of bringing another chance of grief for the small girl bursting with excitement. Then again, God's wisdom in this entire predicament had him wondering.

A black kitten scampered across the floor followed by a gray and white one. At least there won't be a mouse problem. That would have been easier to fix than the one waiting inside the cabin.

"Dr. Logan, I'll tell you what chores are yours. The one thing you must remember is that the chickens are my responsibility."

"Then I suppose it's quite fine with you that I've mucked the stalls and fed the animals in the barn this morning."

She scrunched her face as if she wasn't sure she should believe him. One of her eyebrows dipped. Was she frustrated because she couldn't see if he'd done them? Then she sniffed.

"Yep, it's fine. Doesn't smell as bad in here as when Heaven does it. You can go with me to the chicken coop, but don't forget. . ."

"It's your responsibility."

She turned her face his way, and he saw her toothy grin. "Good. You learn quick."

At the chicken coop, she allowed Travis to open the door that seemed to be hanging from a loose hinge. He would fix that soon. He put one foot inside the door.

"Stop. You can't come in here, remember." She had one hand perched on her hip. "Stand in the doorway and wait for me."

"Yes Little Miss, I'll mind what you say." He watched her work, her lower lip rolled between her teeth as she'd slide her hand under a hen and scoop out the egg. Soon she had a basketful.

"We don't usually get this many. Maybe they knew you'd be here for breakfast." She cocked her head and fell silent for a moment. "I should cook breakfast this morning, because Heaven won't be able to stand without hurting herself."

He could see hope in her face, so he said he'd like that. Now he wondered if she knew how to cook eggs.

As Heaven smoothed the covers on her parents' bed, her sight landed on the small miniature of them. Her heart crumbled. She remembered Ma setting it on the chest of drawers and saying, "This is our home now, Heaven. Always remember, where we are as a family is our home. It's not four walls that make a home. It's family. So no matter where you end up, make those four walls look and feel like your home."

Ma commented on how sad it was Uncle Neal's marriage plans fell through, but if he hadn't made those plans, there probably wouldn't be the nice wood floor and kitchen stove for them to use now.

Heaven had shot back with some stinging retort about the floors not being quality and what good was a stove if there wasn't someone to cook for them? Her head dipped to her chest, and the tears flowed as she remembered how she'd acted. What she'd said to her ma. She covered her lips with her hands, but that couldn't undo words already spoken.

Not long after that, Ma had fallen ill, and she didn't get a chance to make this cabin feel like their home. Before she died, she'd extracted a promise from Heaven to make the cabin into a home for her sister and Pa.

She hadn't kept it. The cabin looked almost the same as when they moved in. Except for the branch Ma had found for them to use to hang their mittens and hats, nothing had been changed. The windows were bare. Great-Uncle Neal's old broken chair still sat in the corner. The few pieces of furniture they'd brought along hugged the walls where Pa had shoved them when they arrived. A happy thought flitted through her sorrow. She could almost hear Pa promising Ma to move them later as soon as she knew where she wanted them and the playful interchange between them.

Now she and Angel were currently without a home of their

own. Unless she could convince Travis to give the farm back to her. Maybe they could come to some sort of arrangement where he could live somewhere else and raise his horses here. She'd be willing to let him do that. She never thought about staying here and making it her home, but now that she was about to lose it, she knew it was too late. The farm had become their home. They had memories here, not all good, but some of them were. She would fulfill her promise, find a way to keep this place, and let it blossom into a proper home.

Proper home? Right now it wouldn't qualify as much more than a shack. She would reread that chapter in Ma's book about what it took to make a proper home. Then she would start doing it right away, because somehow she must convince Dr. Logan to move on and find another farm for his horses.

She'd stuck the book in her sewing basket by the rocker. Eyeing the distance between the bed and the fireplace, it seemed possible to get there without too much trouble. She hopped on one leg and leaned against the wall for support. Winded, she collapsed into the rocker as the door opened.

Angel bustled through and slammed the door behind her. "Got a bunch of eggs this morning for a change. Dr. Logan says if we had more chickens, we could eat some of the hens that aren't laying."

Now why hadn't she thought of that? Ma would kill a chicken and make a nice dinner for them. Heaven hadn't ever even tried to do that. After watching her mother pluck feathers, she had no interest. Chicken with green beans would be a nice change from green beans and biscuits and green beans and potatoes.

"I'm going to make the eggs this morning, Heaven. Dr. Logan says you have to stay off of your ankle." Angel's voice was puffed with importance.

The mouse-ate-the-cat smile on her face took Heaven by surprise. She didn't even know Angel wanted to learn to cook. Maybe she did, know—a little. It was dangerous though, and she hadn't been willing to help her learn. It was much safer to have her roll out the biscuits.

"Think you can manage to roll out the dough while I cook?" Angel's words issued a challenge as she set the egg basket on the table. "I think we'll have to use all of these eggs, because Dr. Logan said he was hungry enough to eat the sides of the barn." She giggled and then slapped her hand over her mouth. "I'm sorry, Heaven, that's probably not a proper thing to say."

Angel held her breath and picked up the still-warm egg. She ran her thumb over a few tiny bumps on the larger end of the oval. She concentrated, not wanting to mess up and have Heaven take over, scolding her and making her feel like she'd never be able to make her own breakfast. She had placed the bowl on the table, and she found it now, tracing the edge closest to her with a finger. Keeping her finger on the bowl, she brought the egg in the other hand to rest next to it. It was time. All she needed to do was smack it against the side and move her hand forward an inch or two. Fast. She let out her breath and took another one.

She smacked it and reached forward. The egg left a satisfying slurp against the bottom of the bowl. She'd done it. Secure in her method, she continued cracking the rest of them in her basket.

"I'm doing it, Heaven. I'm making scrambled eggs. I'm sorry you hurt your ankle, but I'm happy, too, because now I get to make breakfast."

Her sister sat quietly. Then she heard her start patting out the biscuits. "Yes Angel, I do believe you can make your own breakfast. I think I'm going to make a few extra biscuits, just in case there aren't enough eggs to satisfy Dr. Logan."

Angel didn't comment. She was already planning dinner.

Travis's teeth grated against a bit of shell. He looked at Heaven. She seemed to be experiencing the same problem with her breakfast. Their eyes met, and the corners of Heaven's lips began to turn up.

He shook his head, trying to discourage her from smiling. A laugh welled in his stomach, aching for release. He gnawed on his tongue to keep the mirth from bellowing into the room.

"Do you like my yellers?" Angel asked, popping a heaping forkful into her mouth.

Travis waited to see if she would say anything about the shells that had to be in her breakfast.

She chewed and swallowed. "So do you or don't you like them, Dr. Logan?"

He'd try diplomacy. "For your first try, they aren't bad. I could use a bit more salt on them."

"It's hard to hear salt, and I didn't want to put in too much." Angel pushed the saltcellar toward him.

"Thank you." He salted his eggs and began to pick through

them, looking for the offending crunchy pieces. "Heaven, what are you and Angel doing today?"

"I thought you could teach me how to shoot that Spencer so I don't get knocked back into the cabin when I use it." Heaven took a long drink of her coffee.

"Seems to me you didn't have any problems when you aimed at me."

"Heaven can't hit anything with that rifle—except for you. You're the first thing she's shot, and we can't eat you, and even I know that wouldn't be proper." Angel took another bite of eggs. "I think I cooked the eggs too long. They're crunchy."

Heaven set down her cup. "It's the shells, Angel. When you cracked the eggs, a few bits of shell fell in. You'll get the hang of breaking those eggs before long. It took me awhile to learn how to break them cleanly, too."

"I'll try it again tomorrow morning, then." Angel's feet banged against the bottom rung of her chair. "So, are you going to teach her how to shoot or not, Dr. Logan?"

"I'm not sure how I can do that, Angel. You need to stay off of that sprained ankle, Heaven, so it will heal faster." He flicked another piece of shell with his fork to the side of his plate.

"Or you could show me while I'm sitting down. Lots of things we could eat are on the ground anyway, like rabbits."

"It isn't necessary for you to be shooting game." Did she think it possible to sit on the ground and shoot? No wonder she hadn't been able to hit anything.

"Why not? I have to provide for my sister, and I figured while you're here you could teach me some things." Her fork clanked against the plate. Her stare intensified, as if daring him to say that this wasn't where she would be living.

"Because I'm going to do the hunting. You're either going to marry me or move out. Either way, you won't be needing to shoot at anything."

Heaven's chair grated against the wood floor as she pushed back from the table. "I'll not marry you—you arrogant—arrogant doctor!"

"Even though it's what your father wanted?"

She stood, rested her hands on table's edge, and leaned toward him. "He didn't know what he wanted. You said yourself he was delirious with a fever. In fact, I don't think anything written on that paper is real."

"Are you challenging me?" His stomach curdled, and not from the breakfast. What if she was right? Caleb did have a fever, and she might be able to convince the law he didn't have ownership of the farm. Now he was concerned. If he didn't have this place, what would he do with the mare he'd bought to breed?

"I think I'll see about going to the judge with Pa's will and ask him what he thinks."

"I'm pretty sure they'll take one look at you and see you're a woman and not capable of running a farm and tell you the best thing would be to marry me." He stood up and leaned across the table and met her halfway. "I'll be happy to hook Charlie up to the wagon and drive you there."

Heaven's knitting needles flew as she fumed. She wanted to stomp around the back pasture and work off her anger, but instead she was stuck inside with this ankle hampering her every move. Her emotions bubbled. Not the pretty kind of bubbles you got from fancy milled soap—more like the kind you get in your stomach before you lose your lunch. Marry him? Indeed. After the way he spoke to her at breakfast? As if being a woman wasn't worth spit? The most he could do is offer to court her and then ask her to marry him, not assume it would happen because it was written on a piece of paper. Not even if it was signed and legal. She'd take Dr. Logan up on his offer to drive her to the courthouse and fight for this place. Being hitched to him until "death do you part," despite what her father had wanted, wasn't going to happen.

She checked her work and noticed she'd dropped a few stitches. Undoing them, she realized her anger wasn't helping her progress on Angel's Christmas gift.

It was just like Pa to try and fix a mess that never would have happened if he'd been responsible just once. Pa lived by that verse about the birds of the air and fields of flowers never worrying about what to wear. He said God took care of everything, so he didn't need to. Heaven thought that was purely bad Bible reading. It wasn't using your common sense to live like that, if you tried you went hungry and your family had no home to live in.

The rocker under her moved faster. If that verse was true, she wouldn't be sitting here with a sprained ankle, a root cellar full of nothing but green beans, and a man trying to marry her.

It didn't matter how good-looking he was or how nice he was to her and Angel. She didn't love him. But could she? Could she grow to love him? The rocker slowed. Could she marry him? Had God provided for her and Angel? If she wasn't so prideful, she'd march out to the barn where he was probably measuring for expansion and winning over Angel and tell him she would marry him.

But that wasn't right. Ma always said it's best to marry for love. And she didn't love Dr. Travis Logan.

Angel opened the door. Fresh cool air blew through the room, making the flames in the fireplace dance. "Are you still mad? 'Cause if you're not, Dr. Logan wants to know if you still want to learn how to shoot. He said if you're mad though, you shouldn't come out 'cause he doesn't want to hand you a loaded gun in his—his presents."

"Presence."

"That's what I said, but I didn't see any presents."

"Presence means being around somebody, not gifts."

Angel frowned. "That's not interesting. I thought we were going to get presents from him. He oughta give us something since he's getting our farm. Don't you think, Heaven? Why did Pa do that? Give us away like that?"

"I'm not sure." She set her knitting in the basket next to the rocker. "Come sit here with me for a bit."

Angel climbed into her lap and leaned her head against Heaven's shoulder.

Heaven wrapped her sister in a hug and began to rock. "Pa was sick. Remember how Ma was when she had the fever? She would ask us to do strange things like chase fireflies in her room."

"She asked me to bring my pony around so she could feed him a carrot, too. I didn't have a pony."

"That's right, she did. The fever made her see things that weren't real and made her say things she didn't mean."

"Did I do that, too?"

A lump formed in Heaven's throat as she remembered her fight to keep her sister from following her ma to the grave. She didn't want to think about that week.

"Did I?"

"Yes, you asked me to get your pet rabbit and put him in bed with you."

"I didn't have a pet rabbit."

"No, you didn't, but you had a name for him."

"I did?"

"You called him Knocksbury."

Angel giggled. "That's a funny name. Why did I call him that?"

Heaven ached at the memory of the frantic feelings of not being able to bring her sister's fever down and Angel crying out for Knocksbury to help her. "I don't know."

Chapter 10

Travis cracked open the door and peeked inside. "Can I come in? Angel, you didn't come back. Are you both mad at me now?" Travis stepped inside. He'd had a long listen to what God had to say about his behavior. Not that he heard God's voice like Abraham and Moses. If a bush ever started speaking to him, he wouldn't be as brave as Moses. He'd hightail it so fast his feet would melt on the path. He had come to the realization that he had been unkind to Heaven. The verse about taking care of widows and orphans sat heavy on his heart. He was here to eat humble pie and ask for forgiveness.

"Still mad, but not angry enough to shoot you. Angel said you would teach me if I came outside."

"But you're still inside."

"Angel and I had to do some talking."

"About me?" He wouldn't blame them if they'd been tearing him apart, but when he walked up to the door, he'd heard giggles. Maybe they were making fun of him. His heart tore a bit.

"You and Pa." Heaven leveled her gaze at him. "We were wondering exactly what he said to you while he was feverish."

"Did he say funny things like me when I was sick?" Angel smiled in his direction.

"He did say one odd thing over and over. I never could figure out what he was trying to tell me." He pulled a kitchen chair over by them and straddled it.

"Tell us, please."

His eyes followed Heaven's hand as she brushed a piece of that tantalizing blond hair back behind her ear. Why did he want to touch it so much?

He weighed his words before saying them. He imagined they were hoping for words of love about them. He decided to give them the puzzling statements, hoping they wouldn't ask for more, especially Angel.

"Your Pa kept saying something about green beans—to eat enough and I would be sustained."

"Green beans?" Heaven sputtered.

"Those nasty green beans?" Angel laughed.

They broke into gales of laughter. Travis didn't understand the humor, but the sound delighted him.

Once they'd quieted, Travis decided to teach Heaven how to shoot. She was too beautiful and Angel too precious, and he wanted to see to it that Heaven could protect them both if needed. "Get out of the chair. I'll teach you how to shoot."

Angel hopped off her sister's lap, and Heaven rose.

"Angel, get the door please. Heaven, I think if you sit in a chair, we can work out the fundamentals. Stay there, Heaven, and I'll come back for you." He picked up the rocker and held it in front of him. The way her eyes narrowed when he brought the idea up suggested she didn't think it would work. He carried the chair to the yard and turned around to go get Heaven.

She stood on the porch with the front of that ugly black skirt in one hand hoisted just enough to make it easier to walk down the stairs without tripping. The other hand gripped the porch post.

"Heaven, I told you I would carry you out here." The woman was stubborn and independent. Those could be seen as good qualities, but right now he couldn't come up with when that might be.

"I'm able to walk well enough on my own." She took a step, and pain flashed like lightning across her face.

"Stay put, will you?" In a few steps, before she had time to argue, he scooped her up in his arms.

"You didn't give me a choice. Is this how it's going to be? You make all the decisions while you're here?" She squirmed in his arms. "If you'd put me down. . ."

"I will." He dropped her into the rocker.

"This isn't going to work."

"Yes it will. The rocker will give you the feel of needing to keep your balance when you shoot. You can't stand up and shoot, because as your physician I won't allow it."

She sniffed and angled her nose skyward. "I don't remember hiring you for your services."

"Guess they come free with being on my farm."

She scooted against the back of the chair and held out her hands. Her eyes were loaded bullets. "Hand me the gun."

He picked up the rifle from the ground where he'd placed it when he came outside. She still looked put out with him. He hesitated, wondering if handing her a loaded gun was a good idea.

"Are you planning on teaching me today, or do you want me to stare at you like you're one of those marble statues they have in Italy?"

He handed her the rifle. "The first thing you have to do is rest the stock against your shoulder."

She looked at him, questioning him with her eyes.

"This part." He patted the end of the rifle. "If you don't rest it there, it's going to kick back hard and knock you over, not to mention leave some ugly bruising on your shoulder."

Something passed over her face, maybe understanding? He wasn't quite sure. Perhaps she'd already found out the hard way what happens when you don't hold a rifle the right way.

Heaven placed the stock against her right shoulder.

"Now look down the barrel with one eye."

She did as he asked.

"Close the other one." Earlier he'd set up a target. He stood behind the rocker and leaned over, just above her shoulder, and made sure the rifle was snug against her tiny frame. "See that circle I whitewashed on the log?"

She nodded, bumping her head into his chest and causing his breath to flutter.

He needed to concentrate on what that gun barrel was doing, not her pretty head that smelled sweet. He suffocated the attraction. "That's where I want you to aim. Take a deep breath. When you feel you're ready—and only then—pull the trigger." He let go of the gun.

She sat there. A slight breeze lifted her hair and wafted a soft, clean smell his way.

Did she think the target was going to move? No wonder

she couldn't catch any dinner if it took her this long to make up her mind to shoot a log. A rabbit would have hopped away and had a bunch of baby bunnies by now. "Anytime you're ready, just pull the trigger."

As she pulled the trigger, she sneezed. The gun popped off her shoulder.

The rocker flew back, knocking Travis right below his waist. His breath wheezed out, and his eyes burned and watered. He grabbed the back of the chair to keep it from spilling over on its back and him from collapsing onto the ground.

"I think we're done for the day." He squeezed the words out of his lungs. He took the rifle from her. "I'll be heading to the barn to spend time with my horse." And recover. It would be awhile before he'd work on teaching her to shoot again. So far, all that woman managed to do with a rifle was find some way to harm him.

Heaven didn't understand why Dr. Logan had taken off to the barn in such an abrupt manner. He had been so kind before she fired the Spencer. Perhaps the sound brought up memories of her shooting him? He appeared to be limping, and he held his midsection. Maybe he was going to be sick from Angel's shell-filled eggs? Had the hit from the rocker caused him a stomach disturbance? Still, it seemed out of character for him to roughly grab the rifle out of her hands and make off for the barn, leaving her to get back to the house on her own. She wanted to practice more than once.

"Why do you think he quit teaching you so fast?" Angel

helped her sister up the stairs. "I would have thought he would have made you shoot a few more times, especially since you didn't hit the target."

At least her sister had stuck around. Funny how she found herself dependent on her sister after all the times Angel had counted on her for help. She wasn't sure how she felt about that.

"Maybe he thinks I'm hopeless." It was useless. She'd been trying for months to hit something, and so far Dr. Logan was the only living or dead thing she'd successfully struck with a bullet. And shooting people wasn't a useful skill, as she didn't intend to take up a life of robbing and killing folks.

"I don't think you are." Angel opened the door and helped Heaven to a kitchen chair. "You take care of me, and you never give up. Remember how you kept trying until you figured out how to make cheese from Mrs. Jackson's milk?"

She plunked down onto the chair. "I miss that cheese. Dr. Logan says it won't be long though, before the kid is born and we'll have goat's milk again."

Angel looped the handle of her sister's sewing basket across her arm and brought it to the kitchen table. "How long do you think we can stay here if you don't marry him?"

"We're staying on this farm forever. I don't know how yet. I'm wondering if we can buy the farm from him. If we can make cheese and sell it in town. . ."

"Do you think we could make enough money?" Angel's voice rang of hope.

"I don't know. I've heard about making soap, too. Maybe we could learn how to do that." She'd need some kind of fancy mold to form it. They could just cut bars, but she knew from living in Nashville the fancy-shaped stuff sold for more.

"We could make it smell pretty with some lavender. We still have a jar we dried this summer." Angel parked her elbow on the table and rubbed the dimple in her cheek with her finger. "I wish I could still see to draw. I could make the labels."

"You still could. If we used a potato for a stamp with a simple design etched into it and some dye, you could make the labels."

"And you could write our names on them. Heaven and Angel Fanciful Soaps." Angel sighed. "Let's try, Heaven. I don't want to leave our home."

Travis walked slowly around the barn between the stalls until the pain in his groin subsided. That woman was disaster disguised in a pretty package—at least when it came to his body.

He stopped at the pregnant goat's stall and leaned over the half wall. The long-eared white face peered at him from the corner. "How are you feeling, Mrs. Jackson?"

She ambled over and nipped at the cuff of his coat. "I need that sleeve." He pulled his hand out of her reach. "Looks like you're doing fine."

He'd climbed up into the hayloft earlier and tossed down several bales of hay. Separating it with a pitch fork, he'd then strewn it about her pen to help keep her warm. The expecting goat shouldn't be in this condition this late in the year, but it happened sometimes. Heaven was as surprised and excited as Angel had been when he told her Mrs. Jackson was going to have a kid sometime soon. They knew Mrs. Jackson kept gaining weight and accused her of stealing food from the horse and cow. They'd even tried to catch her taking it but weren't successful.

It was conversations like these that made him realize Caleb knew his womenfolk needed a man, and that's why he'd given the farm to Travis. He even saw why Caleb wanted him to have Heaven. Though the man's method was unorthodox, his heart had been in the right place. Heaven's appeal, her kindness and sweet nature along with her resistance to marrying him only made him want her more.

It might be fun to court her—if she weren't so dangerous.

"Dr. Logan!" Angel's holler came from the cabin porch followed by the sound of a bell.

At Angel's call, his heart skipped a beat then calmed as he realized it was time for supper. He went to the barn door to answer her just as she retreated back inside. He wondered if she'd shout again if he didn't come in right away the way his mother did. He didn't think he'd chance it. He was hungry.

Inside he found two women with flushed faces waiting for him. "What's the excitement about?"

"Heaven came up with a plan so we can buy the farm from you." Angel squealed.

"Sit down. Supper is ready," Heaven said.

Travis slid into what he was beginning to think of as his chair. Angel scooted her chair out and sat. "So what is the plan, Heaven?"

"Soap. We're going to get a herd of goats and make fancy soap and sell it at the general store." The spoon she held in her hand kept time with her words. "We need more goats though. I'm not sure how much milk it will take. Angel and I will have to experiment."

"Soap? Fancy goat soap? You think that's going to support you?" Travis knew he'd said the wrong thing as the words were leaving his lips. Too late to call them back and no way to make it appear he hadn't meant it.

The spoon whacked against the inside of the pot as Heaven dished their dinner onto plates.

"Angel and I have a good plan, and while we may not make a lot of money, you should at least consider our offer." *Thwack.* Potato bits sprayed in the air as she emptied the spoon onto a dish. She turned and slapped a plate full of green beans and potatoes on the table in front of him.

How could he fix this? Fancy soaps didn't seem like a moneymaker to him. His mother's words echoed back to him from a time before the war. Her advice on women: "Show some interest in what they are saying." He'd give that a try. "What are you going to name your company?"

Angel slipped out of her chair and made her way to the hutch. "We made some labels. Heaven's real smart, and she figured out a way to use potatoes to stencil them. We were going to write Heaven and Angel Fancy Soaps, but that was too hard to etch. She let me stamp them."

She handed him the label and sat back in her chair. "What do you think? Do you like them? Are they pretty?"

"HA?"

"*H* for Heaven and *A* for Angel." Angel's foot tapped against the chair rung. "Are they pretty?"

He couldn't help it. Having sisters had made it impossible to ignore something so easy to make fun of. "HA. HA. HA. Could I have some of that fancy HA HA soap?" He laughed.

Heaven gasped and whirled around from the stove with Angel's plate of food. "That's mean."

"No, listen. HA—it sounds like a laugh. Get it?"

Angel giggled. "It does, Heaven. Ha-ha-ha."

Heaven slammed Angel's dinner in front of her and then sat across the table from Travis. She narrowed her eyes, and sparks of fire seemed aimed, ready to fire at him. "We are making an effort, and it isn't nice to—to laugh."

She giggled and then broke into a hearty laugh, grabbing her stomach, which surprised him. She was so petite, he'd have thought she'd have a dainty behind-the-hand giggle. At that moment, he knew he had fallen into the depths of Heaven. And just like that, he fell in love with her.

Chapter 11

This morning Dr. Logan had wrapped her ankle tight again after making her soak it. She hated that bucket of cold water first thing in the morning. But once he wrapped the strips around her ankle, it felt better.

She leaned on the branch he had found in the woods to help her take the weight off her hurt ankle. She didn't know what she would have done if he hadn't stuck around to help her and Angel. Getting up and down the front steps took a long time. And in this cold weather, she was outside longer than she wanted to be. Crossing the yard to the chicken coop and barn seemed much farther than it had a few days ago.

Angel had taken to Dr. Logan, following him everywhere and offering such devotion to the man it made Heaven jealous.

She had taken care of her sister for a long time, and Angel had never seemed to admire Heaven the same way.

Angel popped through the door. Heaven noticed she was alone again. "Did Dr. Logan put up a rope for you?"

"No. I showed him I could count my steps and make it to the chicken coop just fine. He said I didn't need a rope, but you might since you had perfectly good eyes and stepped in that hole. Dr. Logan said he was going to teach me how to do a lot of things. He's a nice man, Heaven. I think we ought to keep him."

"He is not an animal, Angel. You don't keep humans. You should have learned that from that stupid war."

"Daddy kept Auntie and Buck." She scurried over to the fireplace and held her hands out to warm them.

"He did not keep them. They worked for us, and Daddy paid them." *Didn't he?* "When he couldn't pay them anymore, they left, remember?" Her stick clunked against the wooden floor as she walked over to her sister.

"Is that why they didn't come here with us?" Angel's bottom lip trembled. "I loved them."

"I did, too, and I would love to have Auntie here right now. I miss her cooking so much."

The door opened, and Dr. Logan came through with an armful of wood and the blustery wind.

"And if Buck were here, we would have lots of wood and fresh meat, don't you think?"

"Fresh meat? I heard that. If it's all right with you two, I might go hunting for some." He set the logs on the side of the hearth. "Think you women could manage to cook a rabbit or two?"

Heaven sputtered. "We could do that."

"What about a deer?" Travis asked as he unbuttoned his coat. He hung it on the branch as if he had every right to do so.

"I've never cooked anything that big." Heaven watched him take a seat in her rocking chair. His dark hair was tousled from the wind, and his cheeks held a red tinge. He was healing well. "I'd like to try. Do you know how?"

"I think I could manage. Might have to throw together a smokehouse pretty quick if I get a deer."

Heaven hoped he would find a deer. That would keep her and Angel in food for a while. Visions of venison stew for Christmas dinner danced in her mind—with green beans, of course.

". . .can get that stove working in the barn so it won't be so chilly."

She shook her head.

"You want me to take you to the Reynolds's so I can sleep inside?"

"No, we're not leaving." She should have been listening. What had he said before mentioning sleeping in the barn? "How long can you stay?"

"Forever. It's my farm."

"Then Angel and I should sleep in the barn and not our home?" She slapped her hand over her lips, too late to capture the words she'd spat out of her mouth.

Angel whirled around and faced her sister. "I don't want to sleep in the barn."

Dr. Logan rose from his chair and towered over Heaven. "That's not what I said. Don't untie my words and restring them so they say something else."

"So you aren't throwing us out of our home?" She wanted him to say it, needed him to reassure her and calm her worry.

"Not today." He strode past her and grabbed his coat. He turned back and cocked his head.

She waited for him to say when. Instead, he shook his head and left the cabin, leaving her stomach scrambling and her mind trying to piece together the meaning of his actions.

The next morning, the kitchen had been straightened and schoolbooks set on the table. Heaven's shoulder still ached from the unpleasant incident with the rifle. She couldn't believe she'd sneezed, once again causing herself pain. She wouldn't let that Spencer win though. After she did school lessons with Angel and implemented a few of her plans for their home, she would go back out there and shoot that log until it grew hands and surrendered.

"I don't know why I have to learn multiplication tables," Angel whined as she slumped in the chair.

"It's part of growing up. There may not be a school here, but you are going to learn whatever I can teach you. Besides, math is important, especially if we're going to be making money. Someone needs to know how to keep track of how much we have."

"I can't see. How am I supposed to do that?" Angel folded her arms in front of her on the table and laid her head on them.

"Sorry, no sympathy from me. You've been following Dr. Logan around, learning all kinds of things. You don't even need me to get in and out of the house now that he's fashioned that stick for you."

"The stick keeps me from walking into things, but I don't see how I can read numbers on paper with it."

"Dr. Logan was telling me about a way you can learn by feeling bumps on paper. I don't know how to make those, and neither does he, but someday you'll learn. And when you have to learn that, you won't have to learn your multiplication tables, because you'll already know them."

"So I can concentrate on learning what they look like on the bumpy paper?" Angel lifted her head. "Where am I going to learn how to do that?"

"Dr. Logan said there are schools that can teach you to read Braille—that's what it's called." This wasn't a conversation she wanted to have. She knew what Angel's next question would be.

"But they aren't around here, are they? Are you sending me away?"

She was right; she knew her sister. "No, not right now. I don't even know where there is a school. Or if they take children your age. But if we have to leave here, I'm going to find one, and that's where we'll move to."

"Maybe we should just go now and forget fighting for the farm." Angel chewed on her thumbnail.

Heaven stilled. Leave the farm? She hadn't considered doing what was best for her sister at all. But once she located a school, what would she do for money? And how would they survive? They had nothing, except what Pa had left on an account at the store. That wasn't enough for transportation anywhere. Where would they live?

"The farm is our home—for now."

"Maybe if you marry Dr. Logan like Pa wanted, he would send me to school."

Her heart couldn't break into more pieces, could it? How did this happen that she would have to give up so much—from her first love to her parents? But how could she refuse her sister's plea? *Please, God, help me. I don't know what to do.*

I know people marry for convenience, but I so wanted to be loved.

"I'll think about it, Angel." And she would, but if she married Dr. Logan, it wouldn't be until she knew his character better. She could grow to love a decent man maybe, but not one who would harm her or her sister. So far Dr. Logan had been a gentleman, but he hadn't been here long enough to know for certain.

Travis rode Pride and Joy across the rough fields and through the tree line looking for good places to hunt. He'd found the creek, but it was too cold to fish.

He ducked as a cedar branch came close to swiping his face, and he held up his hand to push it aside. A light, cold breeze slid under his jacket collar, and he hunched his shoulders. Pride and Joy's gentle walk soothed Travis's jumbled thoughts. Riding a horse with a smooth gait like this one always did that for him.

He needed some time to think and consider the best way to court Heaven. It would take work, because he knew she was against marrying him. She didn't know him yet, and he intended to fix that starting this afternoon.

He liked her spunk. Despite yesterday's mishap with learning to shoot and the head wound—he rubbed the prickly patch on his head where the hair was beginning to grow back— he wanted to spend time with her. He wanted to find out how those lips felt under his and if she fit in his arms just right when he hugged her. The pieces of the puzzle God had placed before him were beginning to come together. God sent him here, not

Caleb. God had chosen Heaven for him. Now he needed a plan to get her to see that, too.

Annabelle had grown weary of the train adventure, as had Mrs. Miles. Jake had remained aloof the entire trip. He'd rented a covered buggy at least for the remainder of the trip. He grumbled about the cost and how he should have seen Heaven by now. It was all Annabelle could do to hold her tongue. The last thing she wanted was to be abandoned by him, and she had no qualms that he would leave her behind.

He was not the Jake that went away. Annabelle didn't think it would be too difficult to convince Heaven to wait a bit before marrying him. She'd need time to reacquaint herself with this new Jake. The outside hadn't changed, but the inside of him seemed gray and disinterested in anything but his cigar.

Mrs. Miles had grown quieter and smiled less often than when they'd left Memphis on the Nashville, Chattanooga & St. Louis Railway.

"Are you warm enough, Mrs. Miles?" Annabelle wished Jake could see how much he was hurting his mother. She missed her own mother dreadfully. That was one of the reasons William's betrayal hurt the way it did. She had looked forward to having a mother, even if it would have been a mother-in-law.

"Yes dear. I'm fine, but looking forward to warming up at Heaven's by this evening. We were rash in this, weren't we? They may not even have room for us to stay."

"We'll make do, and if it isn't possible, I believe there is a hotel in town." Annabelle knew that's where Jake and his mom would most likely stay. Heaven's description of the cabin in the letter she'd written in early spring was that it was quite small. So much so that she and Angel slept upstairs in a loft. She didn't think she should mention the Wharton accommodations now though. They'd see for themselves soon enough, and then a decision could be made. She would stay with Heaven though, even if it meant sleeping in the barn.

Chapter 12

Heaven hadn't counted on rain. A darkening sky replaced the sunlight that warmed the cabin a few minutes ago. She glanced out the front window. They'd had an awful lot of rain this fall. There had been talk of the Mississippi flooding and concerns about how far the water would reach if it did. Dark clouds were bunching up like Baptists at a potluck.

Dr. Logan was out there on his horse somewhere. Right after lunch he'd said he needed to think about some things. What did a man think about? She hoped it was about leaving. No, that wasn't truthful. She wanted her farm, but she'd come to enjoy his company.

Thunder crescendos rocked the air. There wouldn't be any practicing her marksmanship this afternoon. Lightning arched, fracturing the sky. She twisted her apron strings in her hands. How far away had he wandered?

"When's Dr. Logan coming back? If he doesn't hurry, he'll get wet." Angel sat on the tufted, black horsehair, serpentine-back sofa and hugged her doll to her chest while whispering secrets into its ear.

The regal settee against the backdrop of rough wooden

walls was as out of place as she and Angel were in this cabin. So many of the things they'd brought belonged in a fancier home. Still, she was grateful to have these bits and pieces of their old life. They'd arrived at the cabin, expecting it to be furnished. And it was, according to a bachelor's lifestyle, Ma had said. Her brother didn't need much—a table, a chair, and a bed. Heaven thought that's probably why he never found a woman to marry him. He was an odd fellow, Ma had said. As if Heaven couldn't figure that out. All she had to do was look in the root cellar at all those canned green beans.

"I'll check the kitchen window. Maybe he's coming from that direction." She hurried across the puncheon floor, leaned across the sink, and searched through the wavy glass for a glimpse of him or his horse. When had the trees grown so thick? A movement in the grove of cedars caught her eye. Horse and rider burst through the trees. For a moment, his eyes connected with hers, and her heartbeat kicked up its rhythm. Travis was back. "He's coming."

The sky broke apart and released hail. She watched in horror as the ice dropped like eggs from the sky, striking Travis and his horse. The ground in front of them disappeared into a field of white. He angled his head down and seemed to knee the horse to a run toward the barn. Her heart slammed against her chest as she watched him hold his arm across his face in an attempt to protect it from the bruising hail. She wanted to shout at him to use his other arm, protect the wound on his head, but he wouldn't have heard her through the thick log walls. "He's going to the barn."

"That's good." Angel started humming a lullaby to her doll.

Heaven popped on her toes of her good foot to see him better. The hail was slippery, and Pride and Joy could go down. He could roll over and crush Travis. She swallowed even though her mouth was dry. Her mouth formed the words *Be safe*. Be safe, Travis. Travis? When had she decided to call him by his name instead of his title? So informal, and yet his name felt right on her lips. A smidgen of disloyalty to Jake's memory pricked her heart. She'd loved him and promised to forever. But Jake wasn't here to love anymore—the man was dead and not coming back. But Travis was here to love.

Love? She didn't love Travis did she? Impossible. She was just worried about him, that's all. Wasn't it?

He would be wet and cold when he came inside. She reached in the reservoir and dipped out water and filled the coffeepot. She'd make some to warm him.

His footsteps thudded against the wooden porch, and Heaven threw open the door before he reached it. "Come in. You've got to be soaked. Did the hail hurt? How is Pride and Joy?"

Travis's eyes widened as he brushed past her. "He's fine."

She drew back in shock at his brusque reaction. Maybe she was overmothering. And she did not want to be his mother.

Heaven was having difficulty seeing her stitching. She'd have to use precious oil if the storm didn't move on soon. Lightning sparked light through the bare windows and caught her attention. She had planned on making this cabin a home, so why not start now?

Travis sat in her rocker with nothing to occupy him but the drying of his clothes.

Angel busied herself at the table with the abacus they'd brought with them.

Heaven narrowed her eyes and focused on Travis's strong, capable body. She wanted to move the furniture, and with his foot tapping, he became the most likely candidate. But would he willingly move the heavy pieces? Ma had a way to get Pa to do things he didn't want to do. She said all she had to do was be a lady and he'd smile while he did her bidding. Would it work for Heaven?

Angel slid the beads across the wire and softly counted.

Heaven smoothed her long hair behind her ears and remembered what Ma would say about presenting herself as a lady. She straightened her shoulders and wished for a bit of Ma's honeysuckle perfume to dab on her wrists. She could get it from the trunk, but Angel would be sure to notice the scent and ask why she wore it. She'd have to do this with just her charm. Using dainty steps, she walked toward Travis, presenting her best smile.

"Are your clothes getting dry?"

He looked up at her and blinked. "Gettin' there."

"That's good. You wouldn't want to catch your death of cold." She felt silly, like a little girl playing dress-up with her mother's finest hat perched on her head. She let her shoulders fall back to their normal position, but she kept the smile. "You must be wondering why we have our furniture arranged so oddly." She waved her hand around the small room as if it were stuffed with priceless belongings.

She waited for a response, but all she received was a raised eyebrow. "When we moved here, Pa brought our furniture inside and left it. He promised Ma he would put it where she wanted it this winter."

She tried batting her eyes at him, but he furrowed his brow and looked at her oddly.

"Are you all right?"

She covered her face with her hands and rubbed at her eyes with her fingers as if she'd caught an eyelash in one of them. She hoped it covered the heat of the blush that was surely creeping across her cheeks.

"Yes sir. I am, thank you. I'm just feeling a bit sad. It's winter, and now Ma is gone, and so is Pa. And seeing you sit by the fire like he did. . . ." A tear sprang up, surprising her and apparently scaring Travis, for he jumped from the chair as if a cinder had landed on his sock-covered foot.

She thought she'd done all the grieving she could when they buried Ma. How was it possible for a body to hurt this much in one lifetime? Her breath collapsed in her lungs as a sob fought for an exit. Dizziness slammed against her head.

"What can I do to make you feel better?" He leaned toward her with outstretched hands as if he wanted to pull her into a hug, but then he dropped his arms to his sides and backed away. "I know I can't bring them back, and I'm truly sorry about not finding a way to bring your pa here for burial."

"It's distressing not having him lie beside Ma. Not holding a graveside service makes it seem less real. I start thinking, as soon as Pa gets back. . ." She swallowed another piece of her grief. "Then I remember. He isn't coming back. We won't be together again until we're in heaven."

Angel sniffled. The abacus slid across the table.

Heaven turned, and saw her sister's tears dripping down her cheeks. The numbness she'd been feeling since she'd heard about her pa's death finished melting away, leaving behind raw pain. She hastened to Angel's side and pulled her out of her chair into an embrace. They rocked back and forth on their feet together while they expressed their grief through rivers of rain. "It's going to be okay, baby. We still have each other."

Somehow Travis had gone from trying to comfort two distraught females to shoving around furniture. All he'd intended to do was to stop the crying. Watching the two of them mourn and not being able to help them while bearing guilt for not saving their father, he'd blurted out the first thing that came to his mind. He asked Heaven if she wanted him to move the secretary desk, with its bookcase covered with glass doors, closer to the window. The tears had desert-dried in a flash.

"Just a little to the left, I think." She splayed her hands on her hips and tilted her head to the side. Happiness rode across her face. "After this we can move the sofa across from the fireplace and the hutch closer to the kitchen so we don't have to walk so far to put away the dishes. But first it would be best if you would get the carpet from the loft. It will be nice to have that piece of home under our feet again."

Where were those tears? Even Angel strutted around with her hands on her hips giving orders about not scratching the floor. Heaven's smile was as bright as the sun that had gone missing around lunch. He shoved the heavy desk an inch. He hadn't planned on decorating a house, but it was worth it to see her bustling about looking like she'd been given the title to the farm.

She hadn't given up. The little minx was making the cabin into a real home. She probably thought he wouldn't want to take it from them then. She was right, but she was wrong. He had every intention of keeping everything promised to him in Caleb's will. Especially Heaven.

"It looks like you're planning on staying around."

She swung around and faced him, her sapphire eyes sending sparks his way. "Of course we're staying. Why would you ever think we're leaving?"

"Good. That'll make Mrs. Reynolds happy. I'll ride to town tomorrow and talk to the preacher about arranging it."

The smile dimmed and disappeared. Her face hardened. "I never said I would marry you. I said we weren't leaving our home."

Chapter 13

Travis had escaped the cabin right after he set the heavy sofa in place on top of the ugliest rug he'd ever seen. Heaven clapped her hands with joy when he rolled the threadbare thing across the floor. Angel had taken off her shoes and said she needed to feel colors. The design was almost impossible to figure out. Heaven said it had belonged to their family for a long time. He wanted to say he could tell but thought better of it. Heaven's face shone with excitement, and so did Angel's. He didn't want that light to extinguish.

Feeling as if he'd come calling without a chaperone, he left them to putter around. At least in the barn he knew there would be something to do. He spent time with Mrs. Jackson. It seemed she would be dropping her kid any day. For some reason, unlike Heaven and Angel, the goat let him get next to her. As he was in the stall with her, he started thinking about Heaven's idea of making fancy soaps and cheese to sell. She'd need to get more goats to make it profitable. He could get them for her with the little money he had left over from purchasing the breeding mare. That horse would be coming in soon. He'd have to ride to Dryersville to get her.

Travis unfurled his bedroll onto the barn floor. He slipped his suspenders from his shoulders, wincing at the soreness. . . . It was one of many places on him that had taken a beating from the hailstorm. He couldn't remember ever seeing hailstones that big. He unbuttoned his shirt and checked out the purple and green spot. It was warm to his touch; his body already doing its healing work.

It felt warmer in here tonight. He didn't know if it was because the woman had worked him so hard or because the weather was changing. Still, it was December, and that led him to the conclusion it was Heaven's doing that kept him warm.

He settled into his makeshift bed. The night sounds of the barn were comforting. Horse hooves rustled the hay. Pride and Joy might be feeling some soreness from the hail, too. He noticed a lack of livestock, guessing Caleb had planned to send for his daughters the minute he'd found a place to live. There was the one sad-looking cow, the two goats, a horse, some chickens, and no pigs. He was guessing they'd canned a lot of green beans, as it seemed they had them every day. Sometimes twice.

Fresh meat would be good. Maybe tomorrow he'd find a rabbit or two. A stew would go a long way to making those beans tolerable.

He stretched his hands over his head, and something soft swatted his fingers. A barn kitten. He wiggled them again, and a soft, furry ball pounced on his hand. He grasped it and brought it to his chest. A marmalade-orange fluff ball assessed him with wide green eyes.

"You're a young one, aren't you? Quite brave, too, to attack a defenseless man on the floor." He stroked the kitten behind the ears and was rewarded with a noisy purr. It kneaded his chest and then settled for a rest. Travis watched as the kitten's eyes opened and slowly closed a few times before staying shut.

He lay there thinking about what it would take to get Heaven to fall in love with him. If she weren't so stubborn about this being her farm, her home, her whatever she wanted to claim at the moment, she might be able to see him as someone besides the man who wanted to take it all from her.

The kitten's purr quieted. Its little body heated him as well as a woodstove would. He stroked the tiny head, and the low rumble started again. "Shh. Go back to sleep."

Maybe Travis should tell Heaven how nice the cabin looked. That it looked like a home. But he wouldn't. Not yet. He'd wait until she said she would marry him. Besides, the cabin had looked fine before he'd had to shove the sofa, haul furniture, and unfurl a carpet. At least she hadn't hung curtains or spread a cloth across the sawbuck table.

Heaven flung the cotton tablecloth across the kitchen table and then straightened it so the sides were even. She then placed the lit candlestick in the middle. Taking a step back, she surveyed the room, admiring it. "We did it, Angel. It looks like home. I wish you could see it." Heaven grasped Angel's hands, and they twirled in a circle.

"It smells like home." Angel's smile spoke of pleasant memories.

Heaven released one of her sister's hands but held on to the other. She closed her eyes and inhaled the room's scent. She could smell Ma's honeysuckle and an underlying trace of Pa's cherry tobacco. Small moments of time hugged her.

"You're right. It does smell like home and Ma and Pa. I was thinking of using one of Ma's old skirts for curtains. Would you mind?" Heaven knew the perfect one. Ma had a white damask skirt that had a grass stain across the bottom. She could trim that piece off or fold it over, and no one would see it.

"Can I help?"

She squeezed Angel's hand and let go. "Yes you can. We'll work on it tomorrow. Now it's time to blow out the candles and go to bed."

Travis smelled the biscuits burning before he opened the door. He stepped inside the smoke-filled room. "What are you doing?"

Heaven appeared out of the haze. "Leave the door open." She fanned the bottom of her apron, attempting to shoo the smoke from the cabin. "We were making breakfast and talking about the stories Pa used to tell. Then Angel. . ."

"I said we should write them down so we don't forget them." Angel came up behind Heaven with a dish towel flapping in the air.

"Anyway, we found some paper, and while Angel told the stories, I started writing them down." Heaven sighed. "And we forgot about the biscuits."

"Now our home won't smell like Ma and Pa anymore." Angel's lip trembled.

Travis had no idea why she thought it smelled like them in

the first place. He scratched at the wound that was healing on his head. The stitches were probably ready to come out. He'd been looking forward to those biscuits. It was the only thing these two seemed to make with any skill. "Now it will smell like breakfast all the time." He waited for a backlash of angry retorts.

"Burnt up breakfast," Angel said.

"Bad for your belly breakfast," Heaven said.

Angel giggled.

Travis didn't understand. Why weren't they angry—if not about the biscuits—then at him? It seemed that when things like this had happened at home, his father had taken the blame. He never remembered his mother laughing about burned food.

Chapter 14

Heaven took advantage of the unusual day of warmth and opened the window and door to air out the cabin. The oil lamps needed refilling, and she collected them one at a time while balancing on her stick. She set them on the table, removed the glass chimneys, and placed them to the side, thankful they weren't blackened. They would need only a quick swipe of the cloth this morning.

"Angel, the lamps are on the table, so don't bump it."

"Won't it be nice to have something to eat besides a mess of green beans and those walnuts we found, Heaven? I hope Dr. Logan brings back a deer. I've been dreaming about roast." Angel swept the kitchen floor. She wiped her brow.

Heaven trimmed off the ragged burned edges of the wicks until they were straight. Then she filled the lamp bases with oil, stopping about a half inch from the top. "We need to be thankful Great-Uncle Neal liked green beans enough to can a mess of them. Without them we'd be living on others' charity by now."

"We can thank God for sending us Dr. Logan, too. I'm real glad you didn't kill him, Heaven. He's been right handy around here." Angel stopped sweeping and leaned on the broom. "In fact, I think you should marry him. After all, that's what Pa wanted, right? That's what was on that paper."

"Hush! You promised not to tell anyone about that."

"I didn't. You already know about it, and so does Dr. Logan. I didn't mention it to him, but I could if you don't want to. I could be your go-between and fix things between you."

"Angel Claire, you'll do no such thing." Heaven replaced the glass chimneys. Being married to Travis wouldn't be awful. He was a handsome man, and if they had children, they'd be adorable. It wouldn't happen though. Just because her pa wanted it didn't mean Travis did. She wished she still had that paper, because she wanted to see how that part was worded. Did Pa say the farm and Heaven now belonged to Travis, or did it leave any room for her to get out of the contract? Maybe if she didn't marry him, he couldn't have the farm? Where had he put that paper? Back in his saddlebag? She might have to take a walk to the barn later. Guilt of looking at things not belonging to her niggled at her conscience. But what if there was a way she and Angel could stay here and it was on that paper? If there was a chance, she wanted to know. "If we're meant to marry, God and Dr. Logan will see to it."

Angel let go of the broom, and it landed with a dull thud on the wood planked floor. "Sometimes God works a little slow around here. Sometimes I think He's forgotten all about us, what with takin' away most of our family. Sometimes, Heaven, I get real mad at Him."

Angel plunked down in the kitchen chair and lowered her head to the table. "I'm not going to cry. I'm not going to cry. I'm. . ." She sniffled.

Heaven knelt by her sister and stroked her hair, fighting off her own desire to let loose of tears fighting for an exit.

"Angel baby, it's okay to be mad at God. Pa always said God was capable of handling our anger. Everyone gets mad sometimes at people they love, don't they?"

"Uh-huh."

"You don't need to worry about us being a family. We're family, you and me. We're going to be just fine." *An awful small one, God. How are we going to survive if I don't marry Travis? And God, why him? Why, if all if this was going to happen to us, didn't You let Jake live so we could be married?*

Angel raised her head from the table. "How?"

"I'm going to ask Dr. Logan to teach me how to take care of this place as soon as I can walk without this stick. And if he won't teach me, we'll find someone who will."

"But Heaven, this isn't our house anymore." Angel turned and sank into her sister's arms.

"I'm not giving up, Angel. I'm going to find a way to Bells or Dryersville and talk to one of those lawyers. It's not right, Pa giving our home away. And I bet since he had a fever, he wasn't right in the head when he signed that paper."

Angel sat back in the chair, releasing her grasp on Heaven. "Why do you think Pa did that?"

"If he had been thinking straight, I don't think he would have. I wonder if he was worried about us being alone and wanted to fix that before he died." Perhaps that was the answer. It would be like Pa to think about their future. At least he'd cared. What if she'd never heard about his death? What would the awful unknown of being abandoned by her pa have done to her and to Angel? As it was, she'd been limping along thinking they would be leaving any day instead of preparing for the winter. Unless Travis stayed, they'd be eating nothing but green beans and nuts until spring.

"Does that mean he liked Dr. Logan?"

"Maybe he did. I can't see him just being grateful for Dr. Logan's doctoring and then giving away his land and family."

"Well he did, and now we're stuck."

"No we're not. Somehow I'm going to fix this. I promise you, Angel, I will make a home for us, if not here, then in a better place."

"Can I have Ma's lorgnette until that happens? I know I can't use it to look at stuff, but every time I get worried, I can touch it and know you're working on making things better."

Heaven grasped the chain. It brought her a sense of security. When she touched it or noticed its weight around her neck, it was as if Ma were standing with her. Why didn't she think of giving something like this to Angel? Ma didn't have a great deal of jewelry, but there was the brooch that had been passed down several generations. Such a sentimentally valuable piece of jewelry wouldn't be appropriate for a young girl who could lose it, but she had planned on giving it to Angel when she was older.

Angel's sister went silent. No movement came from her—not even the sound of her fingers in her hair. "Heaven? Are you mad 'cause I asked for it?"

"No, I'm just thinking about it."

Quiet surrounded Angel. It was times like this that made her as nervous as a long-tailed cat in a room full of rockers. She couldn't see faces, and that left her without any information about what a person was feeling. Was Heaven angry? Sad? Angel sat still waiting for some indication from her sister.

She heard the lorgnette chain scratch against fabric. Could it be? Then she felt the chain brush her hair as her sister lowered it onto her neck. Angel reached up and touched her chest, but it wasn't there. Sliding her hand down her stomach, she found the beaded chain close to her waistline. Resting it in the palm of her hand, she traced the small metal flower at the end of the slick glass. She brought it up and brushed her lips. "Thank you, Heaven." She wiped a lone tear from her chin. "I'm going to go show Dr. Logan."

Heaven's stick thumped loudly across the floor. Her hand went to the spot on her chest where the lorgnette had rested since her ma died. She swallowed a milk pail full of tears and sunk into the rocker, letting it surround her with its comforting memories.

Chapter 15

The sun had forgotten it was winter. Not even a chill hung on the edges of the morning. Heaven didn't even need a shawl on her shoulders. It was perfect weather to walk off some of the anger she had at her father. Not all of it. She wanted to retain some of it. She'd need it to fight for their home. Her energy fizzled by the time she reached the pond. Slowing, she took in the scenery that graced her home. Friendship wasn't in the mountains, but right now she could almost pretend it was. The land dipped low beyond the pasture just past the straggly line of cedar and poplar trees. That's where she wanted to go. It wouldn't be an easy walk, but it would be an investment in her spirit if she could see beyond her own troubles.

Taking a breath, she hobbled a few steps then a few more. Winded, she stopped and sucked in the fresh air.

Mr. Jackson nudged her hip as if to egg her on. She scratched the white tuft between his large black ears. He wasn't a pet, but he thought he was. She considered how many more goats they'd need to make cheese and soap to sell. And with the extra goats, she wouldn't have to worry about the grass getting too tall where it would hide rattlesnakes.

A few more steps and the pain worsened. She'd have to turn back. She'd come farther than she'd thought, but not far enough to reach her destination. Disappointment took over her mood. She had to make a decision—press on or go back.

She took a step toward the cabin. It wasn't a choice, not when she'd have to cover so much ground to return. "Come on, Mr. Jackson. Let's go home."

"Naaa."

"I'm saying yes, Mr. Jackson. You'd best follow me with that sweet black face of yours. I don't want you taking off on an adventure. You can get lost. You're my hope for the future."

Angel stood in the yard. "Heaven!"

Yelling. She despaired of ever teaching her sister how to act like a lady. "I'm coming."

Angel met her in the yard and held out her hand. "Let's go see Mrs. Jackson. Maybe she'll be nicer to us now that we know she's going to have a baby."

Heaven took her sister's hand, and they walked to the barn. Dr. Logan was inside staring at the hayloft. "What are you looking at?"

"There should be more hay to get these animals through the winter."

"Pa thought we'd be with him by now, so he didn't store much." Heaven defended her father, even though at the time it occurred to her there might not be enough to make it a month if winter came early or the rain quit and the grass dried.

"I wonder who has some extra they would be willing to sell. Any idea?"

"You don't need to worry yourself about that."

He spun around and glared at her. "But I do. My animals need to be taken care of through the winter."

"So do *my* animals." She wasn't going to back down from claiming the animals as hers. And Angel's. They'd been taking care of them, not her pa, and she would fight to keep them, especially Mr. Jackson. "Why do you want to raise horses? It doesn't make sense to give up being a doctor. Can't you do both?"

"I could, but I'm not going to." He hung the milking pail on a nail outside the cow's stall.

"Why not?" Angel stroked Pride and Joy's nose. "It's not like you're going to make lots of money with horses or fixing people."

"Angel!" Heaven racked her brain. What did Ma's book say about tactless thoughts expressed? "That's not nice. It's not proper to talk about money, not even to your husband."

Travis's eyebrows slanted down. "Where did you learn that, Heaven?"

"Ma taught me that. It's the husband's job to take care of the family and the money. Wives don't need to be concerned about such things." She wished she believed it with the conviction her words carried. It seemed to her that Ma was much smarter when it came to taking care of things. Pa seemed to be selling things almost as soon as they got them. One of them had been that sweet little pony he'd bought her for her eighth birthday.

"Guess some families are different than others. My mother was adamant about her daughters learning how to take care of themselves in case they ended up with a good-looking man worth his weight in dirty dishwater."

He had sisters? Heaven pondered that for a moment. What would it be like to be able to take care of herself and Angel and not be dependent on anyone? She'd have a bigger family. Could she do that? With Pa dead, she didn't have a choice unless she married Travis. If he would marry her. If he did, would he let her tell him how to spend his money?

"How many sisters you have?" Angel tugged on Travis's coat sleeve.

Heaven winced. She'd been trying for months to get Angel's speech correct. "How many sisters *do* you have?"

"*Do* you have, sir? Is one of them Mary?"

How had Heaven forgotten about the woman he'd called for when he was feverish? She watched Travis walk to the shelf where they kept the grooming supplies. Why didn't he say something? Was Mary someone he loved, and then Pa threw Heaven in with the farm? And now that he knew Heaven was a person, he didn't know what to do about Mary?

Travis picked up the currycomb and brush. "No, Mary— well, she was someone who promised to wait for me until the war was over, but she didn't. Married my best friend." He opened Pride and Joy's stall door and slipped in next to the horse. He scratched the horse's neck.

Happiness fluttered in Heaven's stomach. Mary didn't matter. Or did Travis still love her?

"I have three sisters, and all of 'em older." He tousled Angel's hair. "They were always picking on me or making me play house with them."

"I bet they miss you," Angel said. "Why don't you go home and be with them?"

Heaven grinned. She wanted him gone, too.

"They're all married and have their own kids now. It felt right to start off in a new place."

"I'm sure they miss you. Where are you from?" Heaven wanted him gone, but if he did go, what would happen to her and Angel?"

"A ways past Knocksville." He stroked his chin. "They might miss me, but not likely. I haven't been around much, what with the war and all."

"Did you go home when it ended?" Heaven leaned against the barn wall. The wind blew between the boards, and she tugged her coat closer.

"Yes ma'am. I went to see my parents and stayed for a bit. I ate a lot of good dinners, and one day my father asked if I would be starting a practice in town. That started me thinking about taking care of people. I didn't want to do that anymore."

Chapter 16

Travis led his horse, Pride and Joy, out of the barn. Every day he stayed here he grew uneasier about Caleb's will. He'd been right about one thing—there was plenty of room to raise horses here. Caleb's property could be fenced in the back and would be a nice place to train horses. The barn was a bit small, but that could be fixed easily enough. It just didn't feel right to take it from Caleb's family and to take Heaven as a bride if he couldn't love her the way Christ loved him. Then again, she was a cute thing and not dull to be around.

If Heaven was capable of taking care of the place, he might consider leaving. He felt sure Caleb had sent him here for more than the land though. Two women alone were an easy mark. Was that enough reason to marry her? If he did, he could be sure she couldn't betray him like Mary. You can't betray someone you don't love.

He whispered in the horse's ear. The horse nickered back.

"Do you and your horse talk to each other often?"

Travis looked up to see Heaven grinning while holding on to the porch railing.

"Thought I'd give him a good grooming since my head is feeling better."

"I'm glad it's healing. It's awfully warm today isn't it?"

Travis tied the horse to the porch railing. "A bit unusual. Might try and catch a few fish down at the creek today since it feels like fishin' weather."

"Fish would taste good for dinner since you didn't find anything yesterday." Heaven winced.

"Ankle hurting you?"

"A bit, though it's getting better. Could you bring out my rocker? It's such a nice day, I'd like to enjoy it before it turns cold again."

He pointed at the ball of yarn in her hand. "Going to do some knitting? That's a pretty blue. Are you making it for Angel?"

"Shh, I am working on something for her for Christmas. She can hear my needles, but as long as I keep it away from her, she doesn't know what I'm doing."

Travis smiled. "I can do that." He climbed the steps and stopped next to her. "You have some flour on your cheek."

"It's from making the biscuits this morning. Sorry there isn't a cake baking." She raised her hand to wipe it off.

He stopped her with his.

"Let me. I can see where to wipe." He used the edge of his hand and gently brushed away the white dust. Her skin was as smooth as his mother's prized china but as warm as a kitten. He leaned in closer. "I do believe"—he looked into her eyes and almost drowned in the shimmering blue—"you have a speck on your eyebrow." He moved his thumb from her cheek and slowly slid it across her brow.

Her breath came a little quicker, but she didn't back away from him. "Dr. Logan? Did you get it all?" Her soft words fell from her lips.

Lips full like ripe peaches ready to be picked and handled with great care so as not to bruise them. He might have lost his mind, but all he could think of was that Caleb might have been right. He may have found a piece of heaven on this side of the curtain. He lowered his head and brushed his lips against hers.

She gasped but did not move, so he kissed her again, brushing the back of her hair with his hand. Her lips melted into his.

"Heaven," he said, his own breath coming a bit hard. "I do believe your father was right to name you that."

"What are you all doing out here?" Angel stuck her head out the door. She appeared to be staring right at them.

At that moment, Travis was thankful the little girl couldn't see. He had surely broken every rule there was by kissing her sister.

Heaven kept her eyes connected to his as she stepped back from him. "I am waiting for Travis to bring out the rocker. It's such a beautiful day. I thought I could keep my weight off of my ankle and still be outside."

"Well, standing there looking at each other is not going to bring the rocker outside," Angel said.

Travis broke away from Heaven's magnetic eyes.

They both stared at Angel.

"How do you know we are looking at each other?" Heaven's hand went to her cheek.

"I can't see you if that is what you all are thinking." Angel grinned. "But I listened to your footsteps, and I can tell where you are, and *Travis* stopped right by yours, so I guessed you were looking at each other. Was I right?"

Heaven's face was beet red.

Her sister had caught the informal use of his name. Travis rubbed his hand over the back of his neck. "Yes Little Miss, you're right."

"But what I don't understand is why you stopped moving and then didn't say anything. Are you mad at each other?" Angel stepped out on the porch close to her sister as if she could protect her from Travis. And Travis thought she probably just did protect her sister from a few more kisses.

"No, we aren't mad." Heaven finally spoke. "Why don't you get the Bible, and I'll read to you. Travis is going to groom his horse, so he can listen, too."

"I'll get it. Can we read about Jesus being tempted by Satan? I like that story, because I always get tempted by stuff, but Jesus always wins." Angel went back into the cabin.

Travis let out his breath. "Do you think she knows?"

"I don't know. It's one of her favorite stories, but it does seem fortuitous that she picked it for today. Maybe it would be a good one for us to pay heed." Heaven touched his arm gently.

Travis nodded and stepped away to get the chair.

"Travis?"

He turned to face her. "Thank you. It has been a long time since I was kissed. I had forgotten how wonderful it feels, but I think it best that it not happen again."

"You're welcome." Who had kissed her before? And why

didn't his kisses feel better than those of whoever had kissed her before? Travis didn't care for that thought at all.

Glory be. Heaven wanted another one of those kisses. She was sure when Travis's—she could call him that now that he'd slid his lips across hers and she'd let him—lips touched hers, the whispers from the cedar trees stopped, the chickens quit cackling, and her world grew a lot warmer.

And then Angel had bounded out the door. Good thing, too, because Heaven would have gone back for more of those block-out-the-world, good-feeling kisses from that man.

Chapter 17

Annabelle hadn't been this hot since last August. She fanned her face with her hand, wishing for a real fan. Mrs. Miles's face was gleaming, and she kept dabbing it with her handkerchief. Both of them had dressed for the winter temperatures. It surprised her that the climate was so different from back home.

"Why don't you take off your coat, dear?" Mrs. Miles asked while peeling off hers. "It's so hot."

Take it off? She couldn't, not until she had a safe place to put it. "I'm fine, really. This way I can keep my traveling clothes a bit cleaner." And she wouldn't have to worry about misplacing her future.

The carriage wobbled and bobbed for hours it seemed. Jake had been silent for this part of the trip, as had his mother. Annabelle brushed her forehead with her hand. A headache edged sideways and slipped into her body the minute she climbed in the carriage, and it proceeded to swell with each mile that passed.

"Do you know how much longer, Jake? I think we could all use a break. It would be nice to get out of the carriage and walk a bit." She smiled her best save-the-next-dance-for-me smile.

He scowled at her.

Was this what it would have been like to have a brother? If so, she was glad to be an only child. When they were younger, she'd wanted Jake for a brother because he was fun and even his teasing made her feel special.

"We should be coming to the town soon." He squared his shoulders and looked straight ahead as if making sure she wouldn't continue making conversation with him.

"Are you feeling okay, Mrs. Miles?" Annabelle patted the woman's hand.

" 'Tis hot today, isn't it? So odd for this time of year." Mrs. Miles waved her hand in front of her face to stir the air.

"Do you think it's like this all the time? We are far west of Nashville." Annabelle tugged at her collar, hoping to allow a small breeze to flow into the neckline. Nothing but humidity entered. They rolled past another long line of cedar trees.

"I really don't know, dear."

Annabelle was tired of seeing cedar trees and poplar trees and cypress trees. At first she thought the cypress were interesting, with their multifingered roots rising out of the low-standing water. Now they held no interest. She wanted to see Heaven and was quite ready to get away from grumpy Jake.

"Friendship's up ahead," Jake said. "We'll need to water these horses before going much further."

"Heaven doesn't live far from here then. Her letter said she was on the west side of town." Joy fluttered through her. She needed to hug her friend, someone who understood what it was like not to have a husband and a baby on her hip.

"We'll stop in town and ask someone. You and Mother can get out for a bit."

"It would be nice to get some refreshments before we rush to the Wharton's. We don't want to embarrass her by dropping in unexpectedly and catching her unprepared for visitors." Mrs. Miles brushed her graying strands of hair with her hands. "Do I look presentable, Annabelle?"

"Yes ma'am, you do." She patted her own coif to make sure all the strands were neatly tucked inside the net. Her excitement grew as the carriage climbed the small hill. Soon her life would change for the better. She closed her eyes and envisioned her shop, but beyond a building painted yellow, she couldn't see the store's sign. She needed a name for her business. Once she had that, she was sure the vision in her mind would be complete. Heaven would help her think of a good one. She had a knack for that sort of thinking. The carriage wheels slowed, and she opened her eyes. They had arrived.

Jake stopped the carriage in the middle of the street next to the public well. "I'll water the horses. Why don't you two go inside the general store we passed on the corner and see if you can get directions to the Whartons."

The carriage swayed as Mrs. Miles stood. "I do hope they have something cool to drink."

Jake climbed down and raised his arms to help his mother to the ground. "We might need to find a café if you are wanting a snack. You can ask about that as well."

Annabelle waited for him to turn and help her disembark. When her feet hit the ground, she gave him a half smile. "Thank you, Jake, for being so considerate of us on this trip."

She linked arms with Mrs. Miles, and they crossed the street to the boardwalk that ran along the buildings.

The store held a slight touch of coolness between its wood walls. Not enough to cool off a man who'd been driving in the hot sun, but enough to appreciate. Jake blinked a few times to adjust his eyes. After the bright sunlight, it took a bit to adjust to the store light.

It was bigger than he'd thought from the outside. A few women stood close to the counter. They had several bolts of fabric in front of them. He didn't see Annabelle and his mother.

He glanced around at the various items offered for sale, including a selection of Christmas gifts. He supposed he should get something for his mother before he left for the West. He'd come back into town later and pick it up. Annabelle could give it to his mother for him.

He found the women at the front of the store standing in front of a china display. He almost smiled at the coat draped over Annabelle's arm. She'd finally admitted to being hot and taken it off. "Annabelle, did you ask for directions?"

"Um, not yet. We saw this pretty dish"—she held up a small china dish covered in roses—"and we were trying to decide if we should get it for Heaven."

"Doesn't look all that useful to me. Guess I'll get the directions while you two shop." To get to the counter, he scooted past the two chatting women with the fabric. He noticed they'd added lace to their selection. Jake excused himself and scooted around them so he could talk to the clerk who waited behind the counter.

"I'm looking for the Wharton place." Jake's nose twitched at the brine odor rising from the barrel of pickles next to the counter.

The clerk's eyebrows edged up, "You are? That other fellow that went that way awhile back never came back."

One of the women at the end of the counter gasped, distracting Jake.

"Mrs. Reynolds, you didn't just leave her there?"

"She wouldn't leave. Besides, he is a doctor, and she's hurt."

Jake brought himself out of the women's gossip and back to the conversation he'd started. "Another man?"

"Yep, he was looking for Caleb's place. Told him he'd better have a gun with him."

Another gasp behind him. Really, women were so emotional, full of gossip.

"She really shot him?"

That got Jake's attention. He whipped his head toward the gossipers.

"So, son, what do you want with Caleb's place?"

Jake turned back.

"I was asking why you needed to get to Caleb's?" The clerk leaned forward on the counter, searching Jake's face for something.

"His daughter is my—my friend. I've brought her best friend and my mother along as well. For a visit."

"I'm sure she'll be glad to see her friends."

"She said she was aiming over his head and missed." The other voice piped up. Mrs. Reynolds, he guessed. She must be the town gossip.

"God was watching out for him."

"Heaven, too, and Angel. Where would that girl go if her sister went to jail?"

Jake stilled. Were they talking about his Heaven? Had she found someone else then? She'd shot him? And he was living with her? Without marrying her?

A crack of thunder rolled through the building, shaking the glass windowpanes. Jake whirled around. The widows no longer let in the hot sunlight. The sky had taken on a bruised appearance.

A man burst through the door. The wind came from behind him, banging the door against the wall, shattering the glass. "Tornado's a comin'! Everyone in the cellar!"

Chapter 18

Travis stared up at the bunching clouds. The sky had turned dark gray green. The wind whipped away the heat. A branch snapped and splashed into the creek. He didn't like the dropping temperature. He pulled the fishing line back to the shore and collected the bucket of caught fish. He'd clean them back at the cabin. He wanted to get there, just in case the weather took a turn for the worse.

He did. He wanted to be with Heaven. One kiss and she'd filled the giant hole left in him from Mary's devious behavior. *Thank You, God.* Caleb was right, heaven did wait for him here in Friendship. Now he needed to convince Heaven that being married was the best thing to do. He had a feeling she was going to fight him on this. She kept asking him questions about how to do things so she could do them when he moved on, even though he told her repeatedly he wasn't budging from this land.

The air felt heavy and thick on his face.

Lightning filled the sky, followed by a volley of thunder close enough to make a hardened soldier jump. The wind rushed around him, pushing him forward, urging him to take bigger strides. The clouds ripped open and sent driving rain so solid it felt like nails piercing his face. He dropped the fish and the pole. Thunder sounded overhead, his ears popped once, then twice, and the sky turned pea green. A loud rushing of wind buffeted his face, making it sting. It grew darker, and it seemed time had skipped ahead to midnight. Then he heard it. Wind that strong had to mean—a tornado!

He ran but gave up and dove for a gulley when the dark gray cloud spiraled just north of him. His breath caught. He wasn't in danger, but Heaven and Angel were. He struggled against the wind. He had to get to them. The wind knocked him to the ground, and in desperation he crawled toward the cabin and prayed as he'd never prayed before.

The sky had grown darker. Rain again. Heaven was sick of it. She collected her knitting and went inside. "Angel, another storm is coming. Do you think you can get the rocker back inside? It's heavy, and I don't think I can help because of my ankle."

Angel set the doll she'd been playing with on the settee. "I can try."

Heaven followed her to the porch.

Angel tried pulling, but the rocker barely moved. "It's too heavy."

"That all right. Maybe Travis will come back before it rains. I'm sure he'll notice the clouds piling up. Then he can bring it inside."

"It won't hurt it to get a little wet, since it's just wood."

Angel pushed past her and went back inside and curled up on the couch with her doll.

Heaven shrugged. "I guess it would eventually dry out." She dropped her knitting basket onto the kitchen table. She touched the coffeepot on the stove to see if it was still warm. It wasn't hot but warm enough. She flipped over a china cup she left out to dry and filled it halfway. She didn't want to risk spilling a full cup while she hobbled back to sit by Angel.

She sat next to her sister and set the cup on the small table next to the settee. "Would you like me to read to you while you play?"

"Can you read the story about David killing the giant?" Angel kissed her doll's cheek. "I like that one."

"Me, too." Heaven picked up the heavy Bible from the side table and flipped it open to 1 Samuel and turned the pages until she reached chapter seventeen. "Here it is." She began reading the story and had just reached the part where David asked what the reward would be for killing Goliath when Angel grabbed her arm. "What?"

"My ears are popping. Something's wrong." Angel cocked her head.

"What do you mean?"

"I hear something different. Like the wind is going faster than I've ever heard it go before. It's noisy." Angel paced the floor, fiddling with her ears.

"It's just the storm." Heaven placed the ribbon bookmark inside the Bible and closed it. "I'm sure it is." But Angel might be right. She'd never seen the sky turn so dark in the middle of the day.

"No Heaven. Listen. It's not just raining. The wind— it doesn't sound right. We have to get in the cellar." Angel grabbed Heaven's hand and pulled. "Please believe me. We have to go now!"

Heaven sprung to her feet and followed her sister. She pulled open the trap door to expose the wooden ladder. "Angel, you go first." Heaven feared it would take her too long and Angel wouldn't have time to get down the ladder. At least Angel would be safe in the cellar.

Heaven left the trap door open. She couldn't close it, because she would have to put more weight on her sore ankle. Just as she made it to the bottom rung, something blew through the window, and shards of glass sailed down the steps.

Heaven screamed. She grabbed Angel around the waist, and the two of them squatted against the back row of shelves holding the canned green beans. Thunder shook the shelves.

A roar rushed over the house. A high pitched screeching made them cover their ears. Then it grew quiet.

"The animals!" Angel grabbed Heaven's arm and pulled her toward the stairs. "Mr. Jackson was outside!"

"So is Travis, but we can't go yet. It might not be over." Heaven yanked Angel back from the bottom stair. They toppled to the dirt floor.

A rush of wind once again roared over their head. And then there was only the patter of rain.

"How did you know we should come down here, Angel?"

"On a walk last spring, Pa and I saw a tree pulled up by its roots. Pa said sometimes wind out here blows hard enough to do that, and if it happened, I should get in the cellar."

"I'm glad Pa told you, because I didn't know that." Heaven couldn't wait any longer. "I have to see if Travis made it back."

"I'm coming with you." Angel hopped off the floor and followed her sister upstairs.

In the kitchen, Heaven grasped Angel's arm before she went past her. "The glass windows are all broken, and. . .and nothing is in the right place."

"But we just made it a home." Angel's voice wavered.

Heaven wanted to cry, too. "The front door is gone, and the table is upside down." A chair leg impaled the glass book case and hung like an oddly shaped coatrack. Then she noticed the cold wind coming from the side where the bedroom was. Only it wasn't there anymore. The doorway led to the outside.

"Angel, this is bad. Ma and Pa's room is gone. Just gone. Hold on to my hand, and I'll tell you what's happened. I want to go outside and see if any of our things are there."

"Is Pa and Ma's picture gone?"

"Probably." And a lot more. She had left the Bible with their family records on the settee, and it was on its side. The rug under it hadn't moved, and. . . She stopped, and Angel bumped into her. "Angel, that is the oddest thing."

"What?"

"The cup of coffee I was drinking is still sitting undisturbed on the little table. If you only looked at the table and cup, you wouldn't know anything happened in here."

She stepped through the doorless opening onto the porch. "The rocker is gone, too." She'd never be able to get another rocker that brought so much comfort through memories. The sun was now shining as if there had never been a storm. Heaven gazed upon the pieces of the bedroom walls scattered across the yard. There was no sign of the bed or the quilt that had covered it. Something glimmered, and her heart raced. Could it be the photo of her ma and pa? "Wait here, Angel. I think I see something."

She hobbled down the stairs, ignoring the twinge of pain, stopping where she'd seen the sparkle of glass. She bent down. Her spirit crashed.

"What did you find?" Angel hollered.

"Nothing, just a piece of glass."

Rain hammered the store windows. Thunder crashed overhead, startling Annabelle with its intensity.

Mrs. Miles grabbed Annabelle's arm. "Hurry!"

Annabelle slid the pretty dish back on the shelf, giving it an extra push so it wouldn't sit on the edge. She looked in the direction of where she'd last seen Jake. He wasn't there. Had he left without them? She turned back as Mrs. Miles again tugged at her arm. "Where's Jake? Shouldn't we wait for him?"

Mrs. Miles shook her head and pushed Annabelle toward the front of the store. "He was at the counter conversing with the clerk."

Jake appeared at her side. "Mother, Annabelle, come on."

Mrs. Miles pulled at Annabelle's arm, dragging her forward. "We have to go."

Annabelle's mind connected with the warning in Mrs. Miles's voice. As she rushed for the stairs to the cellar, her coat slipped off her arm. She stopped and turned to go back.

"Leave it!" Jake grabbed her arm and yanked her along with him.

She stumbled forward, looking back at her future disappearing under feet.

After first herding the women into a corner of the store's cellar, Jake moved closer to the entrance and away from them. Annabelle huddled in the corner next to Mrs. Miles, who clung to her like a wet cloth while her son ignored them both. She couldn't understand his need to be alone. Except down in this hole in the earth, he couldn't really distance himself from them. Still, he had managed to remove himself as far as he could.

She must get upstairs as soon as it was safe and get her coat. She hoped everyone thought her breathlessness came from the fear of the storm and nothing else. If they knew or suspected it was more than a coat, it would disappear. The store above them creaked and groaned as the wind pushed and shoved against its wooden sides. Something fell on the floor upstairs. Annabelle jumped.

The coat had to be there. It couldn't have been caught up in the twisting winds. If it had, she would be forced to go home. Shards of fear hammered against her nerves. Why had she sewn all of her money in the hem? Her desire to get away from her ex-fiancé's new wife and lead an independent life had led her to act with foolishness.

The tight quarters and smell of fear rode Jake's bones. He hung his head and studied the dirt floor. He should help calm Annabelle and his mother, but he couldn't. His only desire was to get out of this town and move on to where no one might find out what had happened on that battlefield. He tapped his foot, eager to get above ground and complete the task he'd come this far to do. With all the prattling from his mother and Annabelle about Heaven on this trip, he'd begun to think he was making a mistake by not marrying her.

He remembered how soft and small her hands were in his and the way she laughed at his silly pranks rather than crying like the other girls. Heaven always looked at him as if he were responsible for all the good in her life. A man could get caught up in feeling like a woman's hero in moments like that. Those memories had been circulating in his mind for most of the trip.

Then the storm came. He was glad. It reminded him that his reasoning was correct. Heaven shouldn't be tied to a man like him. He couldn't even comfort his own mother in a storm. He wasn't worthy of any woman, much less Heaven. On the inside, he still wore the colors of a coward.

Chapter 19

Heart thumping, Travis slipped and slid as he ran across the wet pasture. He brushed the rain from his forehead as it dripped into his eyes. Trees were snapped and lying on their sides. A tree stuck in the ground, trunk side up, next to a section of splintered logs in the pasture. He moved faster. The tornado had touched down here, but what about the cabin? Were Heaven and Angel safe? He had no idea if they would know to go to the cellar in a storm like this.

He slipped on the wet grass and fell on the ground. Breathing hard, he stood up and bent over with his hands on his knees and sucked in a breath. His head throbbed where he'd been shot. He touched it. The stitches held, and his hand came back clean. With his breath more even, he ran for the cabin. *Please, God, let them be all right. I don't care about the cabin and barn. They can be rebuilt, but Heaven and Angel can't.* He pushed through a stand of cedar trees and saw it. The cabin stood, but the added-on bedroom was missing. The barn stood, and on the front porch, the woman he cared about waited.

"Heaven, are you and Angel all right?" He ran like a little

child runs to his mother after he's had a nightmare. He stopped at the bottom step and grabbed the railing.

"I came—as—fast—as I could run."

"We're okay." Heaven rushed down the steps and hugged him. "Angel heard the wind coming and made me go to the root cellar."

"I told her so, and for once she listened to me," Angel said. "Are the animals okay, Dr. Logan?"

"The barn is intact, so I think they are. I'll check on them in a minute."

"But Mr. Jackson wasn't in the barn." Angel's voice wobbled. "Mr. Jackson! Mr. Jackson, where are you?"

Travis's heart split as he looked around and didn't see the troublesome goat anywhere.

"Can you see him, Heaven?" She trotted down the steps. "Mr. Jackson!" She turned back toward the cabin. "I don't even hear him. We have to find him. He might be hurt."

Heaven went to her sister and hugged her. "We'll find him." She turned to Travis. "Won't we, Travis?"

"If you're okay, I'll start searching right away." He brushed a hand over Angel's hair. "I'll do my best to bring him back to you, Little Miss. For now, why don't you and your sister see if the other animals are okay? Can you do that? Check on Pride and Joy for me and tell him I'll be back soon with his new pal Mr. Jackson."

"I'll pet him on the nose and scratch his ears, too, Dr. Logan. Please find Mr. Jackson. He's my favorite animal in the whole world."

Travis's eyes met Heaven's troubled eyes. What if he

couldn't find the goat? Would it be too much for Angel? She'd lost so much in one year. Humans couldn't take that much pain, could they?

"When I get back, I want to ask you something, Heaven. But first I need to find a goat."

A horse thundered down the lane.

Heaven twirled around as if to run to the house. Travis grabbed her by the arm. "No need for that rifle. I'm here."

The rider was at the house in mere seconds. He didn't even dismount. Rather, he rode up next to them. "Doc, you have to come to town. Preacher sent me. There's people hurt."

His medical instinct kicked in, but he fought it. He'd given up this emergency way of living. He felt the tension of his decision rumbling through his veins. He could stay and search for a little girl's lost goat or help save lives. When he looked at it that way, there wasn't a choice.

"Heaven, Angel. . ."

"You have to go. Angel and I will look for Mr. Jackson." Heaven touched his arm. "We'll find him."

"Preacher told me to fetch you and Angel, too. He said Mrs. Reynolds was needing help at the church. She's organizing something so people will have a place to sleep and eat."

"But Mr. Jackson!" Angel's lower lip trembled.

"I think he'll find his way home, Little Miss." Travis took her hand. "He'll get hungry for your petting, and he'll find his way back. As soon as I can, I'll come home and see if he's here. If not, I'll start searching."

"You promise?"

"Promise." He hoped the goat would come home, healthy.

He didn't want the responsibility of a dead goat heaped on top of all his other failures.

Heaven's mind buzzed like a hive of bees. What did Dr. Logan want to ask her? Had he changed his mind about taking the farm? Maybe he wanted to know if he could buy it from her. The more she thought about him and the kiss, the lighter her step. At least thinking about it and Travis was taking her mind off the cruel reality that half of her home was possibly in some other county. She wanted to change before going into town. She opened her mother' trunk. Her perfume sat on top. She pulled out the stopper and dabbed the honeysuckle scent behind her ears and then set it aside. She'd wear one of Ma's skirts, maybe that pretty gray blouse with the black trim and ruffles on the cuff as well.

"What are you singing about—Travis?" Angel said. "Are you in love with him?"

"Certainly not, and why are you calling him Travis? And I wasn't singing."

"If you aren't in love, why did you put on some of Ma's honeysuckle perfume?"

"I was missing her, that's all."

"Well, I miss her, too. How come I don't get to wear any?"

"You aren't old enough." Angel should change, too. After landing on the dirt floor, the back of her dress was filthy.

"You need to wait here while I run down to the cellar. Don't move around in here, or you might get hurt."

"I'll just stand here and make up songs about Travis for

you." Angel leaned against the doorway where the door used to be hinged.

"I wasn't singing about him," Heaven said under her breath. She picked up the small vial of perfume and walked over to her sister. "Angel, you're right. Hold still, and I'll put a little bit of Ma's scent on your neck."

Angel took a deep breath. "It smells just like her."

"Yes it does." Heaven replaced the bottle's stopper. "Now stay here while I run and get the green beans."

Down in the earthen cellar, Heaven gathered several jars of green beans in a basket to take to the church, glad the exchange with Angel had stopped for now.

"It's time to go. Travis will have Charlie at the door in a minute." She nudged Angel out the door and then set the basket on the porch. The temperature had plummeted. It was hard to remember the brilliant sunshine and warmth of the morning. She slipped her coat over her shoulders.

"I don't understand why I can't stay here," Angel whined. "Please let me stay on the porch and call Mr. Jackson. He might hear me and find his way home."

Heaven tried to focus on the fact that Angel was younger and had lost so much, but then so had she, and her sister was wearing her thin. "I'm not leaving you here alone. Button your coat. It's getting colder."

"Is it because I'm blind? Is that why you won't let me stay here? 'Cause I can see, you know."

Heaven spun around, wincing at the pain in her still tender ankle. She grabbed her sister by the shoulders and pulled her close.

"What do you see, Angel? Can you tell me what color Dr. Logan's eyes are? Or show me where the stain is on my skirt? Can you see if someone with a gun is standing in front of you threatening to take our home? No you can't. You're coming with me, and not because you're blind but because you're eleven and you're all I have left."

"Mr. Jackson is all I have." Angel shoved Heaven's hands away from her and stomped to the porch railing. She hung over it and bellowed. "Mr. Jackson! Mr. Jackson, please come home!"

That stung. The goat was the only thing her sister had? She took a breath, ready to respond with her own hurtful words, when Charlie's nose edged out of the barn door followed by the wagon. Travis stopped the horse at the porch steps and hopped to the ground. "You ladies ready?"

Angel stormed down the porch steps. "If I have to be. It's not like anyone is going to let me help. I'd be more useful here calling for Mr. Jackson."

Heaven snatched up the basket of canned green beans from the porch floor. "Thank you, for taking us to town with you. I'm sure you wanted to ride off immediately to see to the people in town."

"I couldn't leave you here. You're my first responsibility. How would you get on Charlie to ride to town when your ankle isn't quite healed?" He bent down and scooped her off the porch and carried her to the wagon.

Yes, indeed, how could she? She'd have managed, but she doubted anyone from town would have ridden out to tell her they needed help if she didn't have a doctor sleeping in her barn. She settled on the bench next to Angel, who hugged the outer edge. That meant Heaven would have to ride shoulder to shoulder with Travis. She smiled.

Travis climbed into the wagon and signaled Charlie to get moving with a jiggle of the reins.

Angel leaned into her sister and pulled Heaven's head close to her ear and whispered, "His eyes are brown. You don't have a stain on your skirt, because you changed into one of Ma's skirts right after the tornado. And if the sun hits a man's gun just right, I can see a light. So I can do all those things you think I can't." Angel turned her body away from her sister, scooting as far away as she could.

Shock waves ricocheted through Heaven. Was it possible? She wrapped her arm around her sister and pulled her tight and leaned close to her ear. "How do you know his eyes are brown, Angel? Can you really see them?" Heaven hoped it was true. Could her sister's sight be returning? *Please, God.*

"I know, because I heard you singing to yourself about his lovely puppy-brown eyes."

Travis couldn't help the grin on his face. She'd been making up songs about his eyes? Sure, it had only been a week, but he could see why her father thought she was Heaven. Except when she didn't get what she wanted. Then she was like an old rooster that ought to be put in a pot and boiled. If she had her way, he'd have taught her everything he knew about guns, horses, and doctoring in one day so she could send him packing. He hoped that kiss changed some of her mind about that. It changed his.

But he had no plan to marry the woman if there wasn't love between them. He'd watched his parents' marriage, and that's the kind he wanted. A partnership so full of love that he and his sisters were always complaining about the quick kisses by the stove if they happened to walk in while his parents were so engaged. Kissing Heaven by the stove sounded good to him. He snuck a glance at her. She did have on a nice skirt, still black but a softer material. He knew from picking her up that it wasn't a work-on-the-farm skirt, more like what his sister would wear to church. Even her blouse had lace on it—black, but it was lace.

Angel hadn't changed though. He'd heard the arguing all the way in the barn. From what he'd learned about Heaven this week, she'd be upset about Angel choosing to keep on her old clothes. He'd keep that to himself, but it was nice to know she wasn't all prim, proper, and perfect.

"How long do you think we'll need to stay in town?" Heaven caught him staring at her, and her cheeks turned a pretty pink.

Charlie splashed through a puddle, sending dirty water up his leg. He'd need a good brushing tonight. The wagon creaked though the same hole in the lane, tilting enough that Heaven leaned against him.

She put distance between them fast.

He bit his lip to keep from smiling. He'd kissed her, but leaning against him in a tipping wagon must be against some rule.

"Not sure. It depends on what kind of injuries. If no one is seriously hurt, it won't take long; otherwise I might need to stay overnight."

"Overnight?" Her eyes widened. "I planned to be back before dark. I have animals to take care of, including your horse."

"Don't fret. I can always take you home, or someone else can drive you and then ride Pride and Joy back to town for me if I can't take you."

"That's good. I don't want to stay in town. Like I said, I have a farm and. . ."

"And we have to find Mr. Jackson. Don't forget. You said, Heaven, that we would leave as soon as we helped get the dinner served." Angel's voice rose on each word. "You promised!"

"I did, but I didn't think about Travis not being able to return right away." She sighed. "We're going to find Mr. Jackson perched on the porch when we get home. He's making you worry for nothing."

"You know how to drive the wagon. You can take us home."

Travis scratched the side of his head. They sounded like his sisters getting ready to go into battle. "Angel, your sister is capable of driving the wagon home. She cannot jump out of it though, because her ankle could be reinjured. Unless you'd like to continue doing her chores?"

"I could, you know. I'm capable, too." Angel slapped her arms around her middle and tucked her hands under her arms. "But you probably don't want to keep eating my cooking. Heaven says I have a lot to learn."

She was right about that, but he had learned from his experience with his sisters about speaking the real truth. "I think you scramble eggs better than anyone." He just didn't have a desire to eat them again for every meal next week.

Heaven rotated the basket of green beans on her lap. She tapped her fingers on the lid of one of them. "I hope they weren't expecting something baked."

"I'm sure the beans will be appreciated. Mrs. Reynolds has probably mentioned your ankle being sprained to a few people, so they wouldn't expect you to be baking pies and bread this week."

He couldn't read the expression on her face, but he thought it might be relief. Maybe she couldn't bake any better than Angel scrambled eggs.

"I'm sure you're right, since they knew to ride out to my farm and ask you for help."

Chapter 20

Heaven concentrated on the bobbing jar lids riding in the basket on her lap. They were screwed on tight, holding in those green beans, just like she was trying to keep her fears from getting loose and making a mess. When she went back into the cellar, the first few jars she'd picked up where heavy, and she worried that their one never-ending supply of food was going bad. What would Travis do once he figured out there wasn't much else to eat?

She should have stayed home with Angel. They could have searched for more of their belongings, maybe found a way to block off the open doorway and the windows. In town she would be subjected to questions about her father and the man that brought the news. Questions she didn't have answers to give that she liked. If they knew Pa had given Travis the farm, she wouldn't stand a chance at getting it back. They thought women shouldn't be in charge of their own lives, even though they'd proved themselves as a whole for generations and through this last mess when their men took off to fight. She'd watched as some of them returned and shooed their wives back into the parlors, as if they didn't have an ounce of wisdom about what to do without their husbands telling them what to do.

She did not want to be one of those women—ever.

The cedar trees thinned as they reached town. From the distress in the messenger's verbal demands about getting the doctor to town quickly, she'd expected to find everything flattened. Instead, she could see a path were the tornado had touched down. The tops of some of the trees were snapped in half, while those around them bent as if trying to bow to those untouched by the wind.

"What's it look like? Is the store still there? The post office?" Angel bounced on the seat next to her as the wagon dipped in and out of the low spots on the road.

"We aren't quite there yet," Travis said. "I can see rooftops though."

Heaven straightened her back and lifted her head, trying to see what he could see, but couldn't. He was much taller. "I hope it skipped most of the town—all of the town would be even better."

"It might have; tornados are odd like that. Taking a house and leaving the barn or. . ."

"Do you think it took Mr. Jackson?" Angel's voice, no longer demanding, had faded to one without hope.

Heaven squeezed her sister's hand. "I'm praying that didn't happen."

"Me, too," Travis said as he reached over Heaven's lap and covered their hands with his.

Heaven didn't know what surprised her most—that he was praying to find Mr. Jackson or the warmth and security flowing through his touch. That he cared about her sister woke something in her heart she'd thought long gone.

As the wagon reached the crest of the hill, Heaven gasped as a man darted across the street and climbed into a buggy.

"What? Tell me, is it all gone?" Angel squeezed her sister's arm with both hands.

She watched the buggy pull away from the hitching rail and head out of town.

"Why'd your arm go all stiff? What aren't you telling me? Are there dead bodies on the street?" Angel tugged hard on Heaven's sleeve. "Were you two doing something naughty 'cuz you think I can't see? Did he sneak a kiss?"

"Hush, Angel. There aren't any dead bodies, and no kisses have been exchanged. Please be still. All that bouncing around you're doing hurts my ankle when you bump it, that's all."

Could there still be some of that laudanum in her brain causing her to see things? Maybe she was tired. Sleep hadn't come easily this week. Jake was dead, right? Or had his death been a mistake? She'd heard of that happening, but the war had ended last year. If he was alive, he would have come to her by now. Wouldn't he? And if it was Jake, why wasn't her heart singing love songs?

Annabelle snuggled in her coat, secure in the knowledge she still had her money and her plan was intact. She had left Mrs. Miles behind as she raced upstairs. The coat wasn't where it had fallen from her arms, and prickles of fear had raced through her. Then she noticed it draped across the store counter. Some kind soul had placed it there, and he or she hadn't discovered the secret in the hem. She wouldn't take it off again until they reached the farm. She was glad it was cold again. Now there would be no need to pretend it necessary to wear it.

"We'll be there soon." Jake put the horses in motion. "When I exchanged the carriage for the buggy, I asked the livery man where the Wharton's farm was located. He said it's about a mile out of town."

Annabelle tapped Jake's arm. "Did he think the tornado hit their farm?"

"I asked, but he didn't know. He said a few homes on the west side of the town got hit hard. He hadn't heard about the outlying farms."

"Jake, maybe we should stay and help these people." Mrs. Miles twisted her gloved hands in her lap.

"No, we need to get to the Wharton's farm. If they're fine, I'll leave you as soon as I speak to Heaven and then come back to help."

Annabelle wondered if he would come back to the Wharton's if he went into town. She needed to talk to him. It was time to tell him she wouldn't be returning to Nashville either.

Heaven waited for Travis to help her down from the wagon in front of the church. His strong hands surrounded her in security. Except there was no secure place or person. She knew that now. The cabin hadn't been flattened by the tornado but might as well have been. With the back room ripped off and an open wall exposing them to the elements, she knew there wasn't a way she could repair it. She didn't have the funds or the skills. Her father was right to leave the farm to Travis. But to leave her and Angel without means was unthinkable.

Travis carried her over the small muddy stream that had formed in front of the church and placed her on the wooden porch. He waited until she was steady on her feet. "I'll get Angel."

Her heart was turning to Travis, but she was afraid. Did she want to love him because he could save her and Angel? Or was she truly falling in love with him as Angel had suggested on the drive into town? She watched him carry her sister to her as gently as he'd carried her. She touched her lips and remembered this morning's kiss. It had been more than pleasant. It had warmed her in places that never before felt heated. Not even with Jake.

Dear Jake. She did miss him, and when she thought she'd seen him, she'd been glad. But not in a way that shouted love. It didn't matter anyway; the only man she had to choose was Travis. Things had changed much since she'd had her coming out party in Nashville.

"Thank you, Dr. Logan." Angel slid from his arms and stood next to her sister. "Don't forget we have to go back soon to find Mr. Jackson. You promised."

"I'll not forget, Little Miss." He tipped his hat to them and climbed back on the wagon. "I'll tie Charlie up by the post office, since that looks like the only place where the wagon won't sink in the mud. I'll come back here to find out where they need me."

Heaven stiffened. She didn't consider answering all the questions alone, without Travis. "We can wait for you." She shifted the basket to her other arm.

He cocked his head and grinned. "I'd like that, Miss Wharton, but don't you think that would fuel the gossip about us?"

She bit her bottom lip. He was right. It wouldn't help matters if she walked into the church holding onto his arm. She nodded and touched her sister's shoulder and turned away from him. "Are you ready, Angel?"

"Of course. Why, shouldn't I be?" Angel held her hand up for her sister to grasp. "I like being at church. You're the one who gets upset."

"You didn't like it when the Rush boys were pulling your pigtails and making fun of you not being able to see." She held tightly to her sister's hand, directing her to the door.

"They're stupid boys. Dr. Logan says when boys make fun of you, that means they like you."

Heaven looked at her sister's smiling face and wanted to hug Travis. She wished she had remembered that from her youth. "When did he tell you that?"

"The other night when we were checking on Mrs. Jackson."

Heaven pushed open the heavy door. The enchanting smell of fried chicken made her mouth water. How long had it been since she'd had some? She could taste the crunchy skin mixed with the salt and pepper. Her stomach begged for a piece.

"Do you smell that, Heaven?" Angel inhaled. "It smells like the best part of church."

"I think God is the best part, Angel."

"I know. But doesn't it smell like church—the dinners on Sundays and all the starched, clean clothes?"

She took a deep breath. "Yes, you're right, it does." The

sanctuary was full of apron-wearing women. The high-pitched voices seemed overwhelming after the quiet of her home. She glanced about the room for someone she might know.

Mrs. Reynolds caught her eye. With a load-bearing smile, she squeezed through a group of women to get to them.

"You came! I'm so glad you did." Mrs. Reynolds cut off any more discussion Heaven might have had with her sister.

Heaven thrust out her basket of green beans. "I hope this is okay. We didn't have anything baked, and then the tornado took off part of the cabin."

"It did? And you came to help anyway? Thank you." Mrs. Reynolds gathered Heaven in a hug. "You two have been through so much this year. You're such very strong—yes, strong—women."

Heaven felt the moisture in her eyes gathering reinforcements. "Ma used to say that to us."

"I hope it didn't make you sadder to hear it from me then." Mrs. Reynolds stepped back. Concern crinkled around her eyes.

"No, it's a nice memory. Thank you."

"Is your ankle better?"

Angel piped up. "Heaven's better, but she's going to get tired fast. We'll have to go back to our farm soon because Mr. Jackson is lost."

"Mr. Jackson? You have another man at the farm?" Worry worked the preacher's wife's brow.

"He's my best friend, and he's going to be a daddy soon, so he needs to get on home," Angel continued.

Mrs. Reynolds's lips pursed, and her glance shot from Angel to Heaven.

"Mr. Jackson is our goat." Heaven stifled a laugh. Had the woman really thought they had another man hanging around the place?

"My goodness, Angel! Bless your heart. You had me worried that there was a missing man out there at your farm."

Angel giggled. "I'm sorry."

"If you two will help me and the others, we can get this noon meal together. I have some of the older boys assigned to set up some chairs along the walkways. It's a bit too wet to have people sitting on the ground. As you can see, they've already moved the pews around. My husband won't like that, though I suspect God wouldn't mind."

"There isn't much choice is there, since there isn't a school building?" Heaven said as she followed Mrs. Reynolds.

"Not yet, but there has been plenty of talk about getting one started."

"Angel!" A bouncing blond girl about Angel's age wove through the women. "Remember me? I'm Cassie."

Angel straightened. "I do."

"Come help me cover the tables. It'll be fun." Cassie grasped Angel by the hand. "Say you will. Please."

"Heaven?" Angel tipped her head, waiting for her sister's answer.

"Yes, of course." She listened to the girls' lively chatter as they moved away. Guilt slammed her. They should have been coming to church. Angel had friends here, and maybe Heaven did, too.

Mrs. Reynolds held out her hands. "Let's get those green beans heated up. I bet you are getting tired of eating these."

"Great-Uncle Neal seemed to enjoy them more than we do. I am grateful to have them, especially now that we won't be leaving Friendship."

"Neal was a bit odd, but our church family loved him and still misses him. Do you know why there are so many green beans?"

"No, do you? Angel and I have been wondering why he didn't can anything else." Heaven picked up her steps to match Mrs. Reynolds's quick ones.

"He was a funny man. He loved those green beans, and one day he announced that's all he was planting since he couldn't find a wife to make him anything else. He said they were a life-sustaining vegetable. We never could figure that out. They must not have been, since he died not long after canning his crop."

"Maybe not for him, but they've been keeping Angel and me alive. Pa, in his grief, didn't plant a good garden last spring, and what he did plant, I didn't know how to can." Heaven wanted to slap a hand over her mouth. Why was she telling this woman about their lack of food? Maybe it was the motherly way Mrs. Reynolds had about her.

"Goodness, child! We'll have to see what we can do for you. Might be some people willing to trade green beans for peaches and such."

"That would be lovely. Thank you so much for thinking of that. Angel and I don't want to take help from others, but trading would work out right nice." Her gaze landed on a basket of fried chicken. She wanted some of that, and Angel needed to get her hands on a leg or two as well. Her stomach growled.

Mrs. Robinson stopped. "Dear, why don't you find your sister and get something to eat and then come help us? I imagine what with the tornado hitting your place, you didn't have time for eatin' before you came here to help."

Heaven hoped the relief didn't shine like a full moon on her face.

A tiny hand escaped the tightly wrapped bundle and brushed Travis's cheek as he handed it over to Mrs. Shaw. "She's a pretty one, and looks healthy, too." This was the best part of being a doctor. A healthy newborn baby fresh from God always made him happy. That perfection could be formed unseen in the womb was something only the great Creator could do.

Mrs. Shaw rubbed a thumb across the baby girl's cheek. "I'm so glad you came, Dr. Logan. She wasn't supposed to be here for two more weeks. I don't know what we would have done." She looked at him for a second, then her attention fixated on her daughter.

"I'm sure Mr. Shaw would have figured out how to get you some help. Babies seem to pick to be born during the oddest times." Travis stood back. "You take care now. Let the others do the work around here while you get your strength back. I'll ride over later and check on you unless you'd rather your doctor come."

Mr. Shaw patted his wife's hand. "We don't have a doctor in town. There's a midwife that helps with birthing and minor cuts. The town's been trying to get a doctor to hang his shingle. Trying to get a school started for all these little ones we have running around town, too. It's time to get on with living now that the war is over."

Travis slipped his coat over his shoulders. "A school's a sure sign of a prospering town." He slid his arms in and buttoned two buttons. "I need to head back to the church and see if there's anyone else needing help."

"I'll walk you out." Mr. Shaw gently touched his wife's hand. "Be right back."

Travis took note of the sparsely furnished cabin. It didn't hold near what Heaven's cabin did, but he could see touches of love sprinkled in the room. A hand-carved cradle waited next to the hearth, and a quilt of blue and yellow squares rested in the rocker. That's what Heaven and Angel had been missing. He understood their need for moving that furniture around and saving their father's stories. Even that ugly threadbare rug made sense to him. And now their home was ravaged by the storm. He'd see to fixing that right away. For tonight he wasn't sure they should sleep there, but he had a feeling he wouldn't be able to keep Heaven in town. Or Angel, at least not until that rascal Mr. Jackson was found.

Mr. Shaw held out his hand.

Travis took it in his and shook it.

"Thank you again for coming for my Etta. We were both unnerved when she started having those pains. And this being the first one. . .well. . ." Mr. Shaw's Adam's apple bobbed. "Helping your wife is not the same as helping a cow along. You wouldn't be thinking of settling down here, would you? You'd have plenty of patients."

"We'll see, although my heart is leaning toward raising

horses rather than doctoring."

"Me and the missus are going to be praying that you'll stay and take care of our little girl as she grows up."

Travis hopped on Charlie, glad he'd left the wagon in town. He'd be able to get back to the church faster. His work for the town folk was done, and the sun was still shining. He'd pick up Heaven and her sister and begin the process of finding pieces of their home.

Angel hadn't been this excited in quite a while. Cassie introduced her to Debbie and Luanne. They didn't treat her like she couldn't see, and they made sure to tell her where to be careful. Not that there had been a lot of opportunities for making friends with Heaven hovering close by.

"I'm sure you could still be in the play. We have to ask Mrs. Reynolds. You could be the angel that doesn't speak," Debbie said. "That's what I'm doing. I get to wear wings, and I don't have to say any lines. Mrs. Reynolds said my role is to look angelic and smile."

A tablecloth flapped, and Angel heard it swoosh across the smooth tabletop.

"Robert Rush is going to be Joseph. Can you imagine?" Luanne giggled. "He's been swaggering around town like he has the most important role in the play."

Angel took in all of the back-and-forth conversation, cherishing the closeness of her new friends.

"So do you want to be an angel?" Debbie touched her arm. "It would be fun."

"I'll have to ask my sister."

"Go with me, Debbie, to get the rest of the cloths," Luanne said. "Angel, if Mrs. Reynolds isn't busy, we'll ask her if you can still be in the play. We'll be right back."

Angel listened to their footsteps and giggles fade.

"I think Robert's brother is cute," Cassie whispered to Angel. "But they say he's even meaner than Robert."

"Thomas was mean to me. He didn't even know my name, and he pulled my hair. Then he called me a dumb blind girl."

"Then I'm not going to like him."

Angel covered her lips with her hand and leaned close to where Cassie was sitting. "It's okay. It means he likes you if he's mean."

"Then you can have him, since he's been nice to me. I guess he doesn't care for me."

Angel didn't know what to say to her new friend. Dr. Logan didn't say anything about what to do if a boy likes you. "Maybe when a boy really likes you, he starts being sweet to you."

"Do you think so?" Cassie's voice trilled with hope.

"Guess we'll have to wait and see." Angel didn't have any answers about boys except what Travis had told her, and she had never cared before, but now she had a flaming interest in finding out about these brothers and how she could get them to like her.

And she knew just who she would ask. Dr. Logan would give her answers her sister wouldn't.

Chapter 21

Angel squished in between Heaven and Travis. Heaven tried to conceal her disappointment, but the upturned corners on Travis's face led her to believe she'd failed miserably.

Angel tugged on Travis's coat sleeve. "What kind of baby did you get?"

"A human one."

"I mean, boy or girl?"

"A tiny perfect little rosebud of a girl. Looks like her mother."

Travis looked at Heaven and winked. Her stomach flipped. Was he thinking of having babies with her? She ran down that path with him, picturing not one but three little ones.

"Did they name her yet?" Heaven tried to focus on the scar on Travis's cheek, because if she looked him in the eye, she was afraid he would read her thoughts and see those three little ones.

"No, not yet. When I go back next week, I'll find out."

The wagon didn't sway as much as it did on the trip into town. Heaven noticed a roll of canvas in the back and some—could it be; had he bought flour and sugar? Her spirits lifted. "What's the stuff in the back for?"

"Thought we'd close up that hole in the cabin so you won't be so cold tonight. I was hoping if I bought some flour and sugar you might be convinced to make me a cake. It's been a long time, and I'm hankerin' for something sweet."

"I'll make it for you. I can cook now." Angel nudged him with an elbow.

Travis coughed. Panic widened his eyes. "I'm sure you can, Little Miss, but I was thinkin' it was time for your sister to start doing some of the kitchen work again. Her ankle is much better."

"Maybe I can help?" Eagerness trickled through her words.

"You can lick the spoon. I won't fight you for it—this time." Travis ruffled Angel's hair. "Next time though, look out. I'll be first in line for that spoon licking."

Next time? Heaven added that to her tangled thoughts. She draped an arm around her sister. "I'd appreciate your help. We'll make it tomorrow. We'll have a treat after we clean up from the storm. Thank you, Travis. We'd both be happy to make your cake for you."

"Heaven, do you know how to mix a cake?" Angel whispered.

"I have Ma's recipe box. There has to be a recipe in there that's good. I'm sure it will turn out fine." Just like going to the church had turned out better than she'd expected. Angel had been accepted by a group of girls her age and managed to convince Heaven that her sister had to be in the play. To her surprise, she'd agreed.

And she'd learned some things about her uncle.

"Do you think Mr. Jackson came back home?" Angel twisted her hands together, let them go, and then did it again.

"If he's as smart as you say he is, then I think he'll be waiting." Travis pulled up on the reins. "No need to run home, Charlie. We'll get there soon."

"He always does that—tries to run home. It ain't even time for him to eat," Angel said. "I made a lot of new friends today. They didn't even care that I couldn't see them, Dr. Logan."

"A true friend won't care if you see the same way they do. There's more to a person than sight."

Heaven glanced up and got hooked by Travis's eyes. So full of compassion for her sister. And she wanted him to kiss her again. And the way he was looking back made her think he wanted the same. She had never felt this way about Jake. Maybe this was what love was like. It stole your heart when you weren't willing to let it go, and gave it away.

The sun poked through the clouds but didn't give up any of its warmth. Heaven shivered. The night would be cold even with the exposed places covered. She and Angel would have to sleep on the floor in front of the fire.

Charlie turned down the cedar-lined drive.

Angel scooted to the edge of the bench seat. "Can you see Mr. Jackson yet?"

"We can tell in just a minute. Be patient." The right side of the wagon dipped into a gulley, jarring Heaven. She grabbed the side of the wagon to steady herself.

"I see him. On top of the wood pile." Travis laughed. "Looks like he didn't wait on us for dinner. He's chewing on something. Looks like paper."

Heaven abruptly lifted her head. A piece of paper fluttered from Mr. Jackson's mouth to the middle of the logs. "It's a book.

Hurry Travis, hurry. That might be our family Bible."

Travis clicked his tongue.

Charlie needed little urging, and he lunged ahead.

Heaven chewed her lip. *Please don't let it be the Bible unless it's the only way we're going to find it. And if it is the Bible, please don't let him be eating the page with our family history.*

Travis stopped the horse close to the wood pile and jumped from the wagon. "I'll get it."

"I'm coming, too." Angel climbed to the ground and stood. "Which way do I go, Heaven?"

"Got it." Travis called. "It's not the Bible." He walked over to the wagon. "I'm sorry Angel. I didn't mean to leave you here. I wanted to rescue the book before any more damage was done to it."

Heaven scooted across the bench and waited for Travis to help her down. "What is it?"

Travis smoothed out the paper and held it up, "I'm not sure."

Heaven recognized the illustration on the back side. Her heartbeat picked up.

He flipped over the paper and chuckled. "Seems to be from a book or magazine—*A Guide to Raising Proper Ladies.*"

Mortification numbed Heaven. She wanted to reach out and grab it from him, but Angel stood between them.

" 'Important rules to always remember. A proper lady never speaks with—' " he read.

" 'Her mouth full of food, lest she resemble a pig at the table.' " Angel finished the rule. "That's Ma's book. Heaven's been teaching me from it. I know lots of rules, but they're hard to follow. There's one about not asking to go to the outhouse."

"Angel Claire Wharton!" Heaven wished the tornado had swallowed her sister instead of her Bible. She pushed Angel aside and tore the book, or what was left of it, out of Travis's hand. "Give it to me."

He held on to it for a second.

She tugged again.

He released it. "Heaven, I'm sorry."

She limped off to pick up the other pages that were scattered across the yard, not wanting to hear an apology from him.

"Heaven, my mother has the same book," Travis yelled. "She's used it to teach my sisters. Why, I bet I could quote a few of those rules myself."

She wouldn't answer him. How dare he laugh. Ma had only tried to make her a desirable bride for Jake. And she would have been a proper wife for him, too, knowing all that she did, unlike what you needed to know to be a farmer's wife. She knew what fork to use but not how to clean a chicken. Ma's little book would have worked for her if Jake hadn't died. Jake was somebody. The only son, destined to take over his father's business. She'd have been hosting afternoon teas and soirées instead of feeding farm animals and mucking stalls.

"I'm going to put Charlie back in the barn and unload the wagon since you're not ready to speak to me. Just don't forget you promised to make me a cake."

"I'm going with him," Angel yelled.

Traitor. Even Angel didn't understand the injustice of Heaven's life. She continued to ignore the two of them, even though they were laughing and seemed to be having a good time. Once she heard the wagon roll inside the barn, she stopped and sat on a log. She pulled her knees under her chin and encircled her legs with her arms as she'd done when she was small. A tear trickled down her face, and she let it slide to her skirt. She didn't care, not anymore. God had abandoned her and her sister, left her to some man who thought her previous life was amusing. How brazen of him to think that.

She scooted off the log, landing on her bad leg first. Her ankle screamed, but she didn't. There was no need to bring that man out of the barn to help or lecture her. She was not in the mood to be appeased.

Annabelle's patience had been stretched slingshot tight, and she was about to fire. "I do hope this time you got the right directions, Jake Miles." She held out her arm and let him help her into the rented coal-box buggy.

"Everything has turned out fine. Mother was able to freshen up at the hotel, and we unloaded the luggage she brought."

He didn't mention they'd toured the countryside going east instead of west, which is why his mother needed time to freshen up. "Jake, I'm not returning to Nashville."

"You have to go back. I'm not going, and Mother needs a chaperone to get home." Jake scowled at her.

"Here I am," Mrs. Miles called from the steps. "It takes me a little longer than you young people to navigate those steep stairs."

Jake rushed forward to take his mother's arm. "That's fine. Annabelle and I were conversing about travel arrangements."

"I don't want to talk about traveling anywhere for a while. I need to rest before I take that journey back home." The buggy sagged as Mrs. Miles stepped into it. She slid across the leather bench next to Annabelle.

Jake climbed in after her and took the driver's seat without a word. His sullen slouch let Annabelle know this discussion hadn't ended.

She wouldn't let him convince her to return. Not when she'd made it this far. And besides, she'd left her father that good-bye note. If she returned now, she'd never be able to leave. Her father would make sure she never got the chance. All of her freedom would disappear faster than Cook's special tea cakes on a Sunday afternoon.

"It's quite pretty out here, isn't it?" Mrs. Miles peered out the buggy.

Annabelle watched the cedars—some standing tall and others bent in half—and wondered what Jake's mother found so pretty. The cedars weren't even a pretty green this time of year. More of a green mixed with mud.

"It's nice, Mother, but it's not Nashville. I'm sure you would be fighting boredom without your ladies' societies."

"You would be surprised, Jake. Since we lost you"—she leaned forward and grasped her son's shoulder as if to remind herself he was still there—"or thought you were. . .gone, your father and I didn't see a need to keep socializing with people. We told you that at dinner, remember?"

"You mentioned it."

"It didn't seem right to try and advance ourselves in the social circle without a son to carry on the business or the family name." She squeezed her son's shoulder and let go.

Annabelle ached at the motherliness of that touch. Her eyes burned with tears for what she didn't have.

"There, that's the broken wheel up ahead. The one the clerk at the store mentioned." Jake pointed.

"And the split rail fence!" Annabelle wanted to stand up and shout, but instead, she tightly folded her hands and settled them on her lap. "Hurry, Jake. It's been so long since I've seen my friend."

"Or my son's fiancée." Mrs. Miles leaned back and smiled. "I cannot wait until you have children, Jake. Imagine! I had lost hope, and now it seems God has blessed me with a future."

Annabelle cringed. Jake's mother was going to be powerfully disappointed when her son told his fiancée he no longer wanted to marry her.

Travis hopped back onto the wagon, disengaged the brake, flipped the reins, and directed Charlie back into the barn.

Angel was waiting for him. "Now Mrs. Jackson is missing."

Travis jumped off the wagon and tied Charlie to a post. "Wonder how she got out." He strode over to the goat's empty pen. The hay was pushed about in small piles, some of them flatter than others, as if the top layers were tastier to the pregnant goat. "Looks like she managed to work open the latch, or maybe the wind jiggled it loose."

"I have to unhitch Charlie, and I'd like to get some of this sweat off of him before I head out and look for her."

"I hope she's okay. Mr. Jackson would be sad if she isn't."

Angel rubbed Pride and Joy's nose.

"She's probably out looking for a snack. There's a lot of tempting goat treats out in the woods." Like Heaven's Bible and an apron or two, he suspected. "I don't think she'll wander far. She'll tire out quickly."

"Do you think she'll have the kid before we find her?"

"I'm not sure. I don't know when it's due. It will come when it's time. Could you get me the brush and currycomb, Little Miss?" Travis tied Charlie to the barn post.

Angel showed a tooth-filled smile. "I sure will, Dr. Logan."

"I bet you wish you didn't laugh at my sister." Angel headed for the corner where the tack was stored.

"She doesn't scare me." Her eagerness to please and do something on her own warmed his heart. She had that same no-nonsense face her sister seemed to wear often. He wondered if their children would acquire that look from Heaven. *Humph. Children.* First, he had to get the woman in front of a preacher.

"Why not? She makes me want to hide in the chicken coop sometimes."

"Is that why you came in here with me?" The little orange cat scampered across the floor and rubbed her body against Travis's leg. He bent down, picked her up, and cradled her to his chest. Her purr rumbled bigger than her body.

"Yes. Sometimes she needs to work things out all by herself without anyone to boss while she does it." Angel spun around and headed for the tools he'd asked for.

"Why don't you just call me Travis?"

"Wouldn't be proper. Heaven calls you Travis though, so maybe she won't be mad if I do, too." Her answer fluttered back to him as she scooted things around on the shelf.

Of course not. Wasn't that the reason he was in here hiding from Heaven? The usage of proper manners and behavior? He should have paid more attention to what his mother was teaching his sisters.

"Here." Angel thrust the tools out in front of her.

He grabbed them with one hand. "Little Miss, I've got something for you." Travis handed her the kitten.

"Oooh."

"She needs a name, since she's decided to sleep on my chest at night."

"She's so soft." She put the kitty next to her nose. "Hi there."

The kitten responded with a soft meow and more purring.

"What color is she?" She stroked the kitten's back.

"Reddish orange, with a few stripes of cream licking her face. More like a fresh-picked persimmon now that I look at her. Do you remember what they look like?" Travis whipped the currycomb and brush in an easy rhythm across Charlie's withers.

"Um-hum, they taste good in cookies. I think I'll call her Miss Simmons, because she's too little to get a husband. Not like my sister."

Travis's hand stilled. "Do you want your sister to get married, Angel?"

"I wouldn't be opposed to her marrying you. You're nice. Jake was always mean to me. I was sorry he got killed, and that made Heaven cry a lot, but I wasn't sad that they weren't getting married."

Travis decided he didn't much care for Jake—even if the

man was dead, God rest his soul. Angel was too precious not to show kindness to.

"Do you hear that? I hear a buggy coming down the drive."

"We'd better get out there, or Heaven will be going for the shotgun."

"If she can find it in all that mess." The kitten in Angel's hand wiggled, its thin, sharp claws connected to her sleeve. "Time for you to get down and explore, Miss Simmons. Come on, Travis, we'd better hurry just in case." She took three confident steps and then stopped. "Don't tell Heaven I called you by your given name, please."

"I won't. We'll keep that between ourselves." He smacked the horse on the rump, and into the stall he went. "I'll toss him a bit of hay and be right there. And don't worry, she can't shoot anyone, because I took the gun."

Chapter 22

Heaven heard wheels rumbling down the road. Where was that rifle? Did she have time to run inside for it? She gave a frantic look at the barn. Where was Travis? Why didn't he rush out here and make sure the company a-comin' wasn't coming to harm them?

Through the cedar trees, she caught flashes of the black buggy. Then it came into view. Intrigued, she stopped in her tracks. She'd seen this one for rent at the livery. Who would have rented a buggy to come see her? Not someone who wanted to trade peaches for green beans.

The driver wore his hat low over his eyes, but that wasn't unusual for a hired driver. She waited for him to stop the horses. Then he climbed down and helped a familiar-looking woman step down.

Could it be? Was it? The red hair, the way the woman stood. Unfamiliar feelings sprung up, and then she recognized them as joy. The woman turned, and Heaven felt her anger at Travis fly away, and the corners of her mouth lifted as if strung by string. She didn't care about manners or being a proper lady. This was her friend. Her best friend.

"Annabelle!" She tried to hurry, but her ankle kept her at a slow walk. "Is it really you?"

"It is!" Annabelle's feet made quick time across the trampled grass drive and gathered her friend into a hug. "Heaven! What happened to you? You're limping."

"I fell in a hole. I'm much better."

"Annabelle!" Angel hollered from the barn door. "Is that Annabelle? Did you bring any jam?"

Heaven felt her face flush. "I'm sorry. I've been trying to teach her better manners. She just doesn't want to learn."

"Neither did we, if I remember correctly." Annabelle's laugh fit her name with its gentle, rolling peals.

"We don't need to inform her of that though, do we?" Heaven couldn't stop looking at her friend. God had provided her with the best gifts today, even if He didn't stop the destruction of her home. "Annabelle, did you get caught in the tornado?"

"We were in town at the store. They had us all go down into the root cellar." She waved her hand at the front of Heaven's home. "It looks like it hit you."

"It did, but we're okay, and we'll get it back together. Although I don't know that you'll want to stay with us. There's not much to eat unless you like green beans. We do have plenty of those. And sleeping conditions might be a bit cold tonight, what with the windows, door, and part of the house out in the yard."

Angel charged forward with her hands out. She reached Annabelle and touched her skirt. "It is you!" She threw her arms around Annabelle.

Heaven understood that need. Annabelle represented home and all of its memories. Her eyes burned from salty tears, and she wiped them away with the back of her hand.

"Angel, I know how much you like Cook's jam, so I brought you some. I'm glad you didn't change your mind about liking it."

Angel let go. "Never. It's the best, and all we've been eatin' is green beans."

Annabelle grinned, but her eyebrows twisted in confusion.

"Angel!" Heaven wanted to yank those words out of the air before Annabelle understood the truth behind them.

"Did you come alone? Without your husband?"

Annabelle's toothy grin slid to the ground. "No, I'll explain later. But I did bring you a surprise."

"You shouldn't have. Having you here for a visit is surprise enough."

"I think you'll love this one, better than seeing me." Annabelle pointed at the driver.

Heaven looked away from Annabelle's smiling face. "A surprise?" She went cold all over. Her eyes were deceiving her, not once but twice today. *Jake is dead. He's not coming back. That is not him.* "The driver looks like Jake, but that can't be."

The man walked closer. "It is me, Heaven."

Heaven's good leg gave away. Her eyes strained, almost popping out of her head. She swayed. Annabelle steadied her.

"It's a shock, I know. That is why I made him bring me along. When he showed up in Nashville looking for you, I didn't believe it either."

Jake and his mother stood in front of her. "I am so sorry, Heaven. I know they told you I was dead. I was captured and put in prison up North. I was so sick I did not even know who I was. I guess someone saw me go down and wrote home to tell everyone I was dead."

Heaven reached with her fingertips and stroked his cheek. "Jake."

He reached his arms out and pulled her into them. "Heaven, I have missed you so much. Thinking about you got me through the terrible times. I could not wait to get home to you."

"Hi, Jake. 'Member me?" Angel tugged on his sleeve.

He let go of Heaven and turned to her sister. "This can't be little Angel. You're all growed up. I bet you got beaus lining up at the socials out here."

"No, Heaven says I'm too young." Angel spoke as if he were standing a further distance from Heaven instead of right next to her.

Jake quirked an eyebrow. "Something wrong with her?"

"Jake!" his mother warned.

"I'm right here. I can hear you; I just can't see you." Angel stomped her foot. "Why do people think that?" She went back toward the barn.

"Sorry, Heaven, I didn't know she was so sensitive."

"Annabelle, why didn't you write me and tell me Jake was alive and you were coming to see me?"

"Heaven, I've been wanting to come since your letter came saying your papa had left for Chicago. Then Jake turned up in town, and I couldn't' wait for letters to be written and sent. Jake wanted to come out right away." Annabelle smiled at Jake. "He's a hero. Did you know that?" Her face glowed.

"A hero?" The pain on Jake's face hurt Heaven. All this time, she'd thought he was dead. Thought about marrying another man, even kissed one. That wasn't her fault though, not when she thought he was dead. But why didn't he write her himself?

"I am not a hero. Far from it." Jake dropped his gaze to the ground. "Sometimes you just do things without thinking, and the ending turns out for the good. I don't like to talk about it, but since you want to know, I was supposed to be on guard duty, but I had a cramp in my leg and was moving slow. If I hadn't been, I wouldn't have seen the band of blue coats. I sounded the alarm, and there was a lot of shooting, but most of my unit survived. Then later that day, we ran into another band. When I woke up, I was in a transport to a Yankee hospital. I didn't know my name, only that I was a rebel, because I had on a gray uniform."

Annabelle reached over and patted his arm. "It's okay, Jake."

"How about a kiss for a returning soldier?" Mrs. Miles tweaked Heaven's cheek. "I've been waiting to watch this reunion."

This was too much for Heaven. Jake was alive, a hero, and now his mother was demanding kisses for him just when she was thinking about Travis and how she wanted him to kiss her.

"Mother, it might be too soon." Jake raked his eyes over Heaven. "Then again, it's been a long time since I've had a kiss from this pretty woman."

Before she could stop him, he pulled her into his arms and smashed his lips into hers.

That man was kissing Heaven. Resentments from the past clouded Travis's judgment as he remembered another woman, another man, and another kiss. He captured his anger, caging it until it proved useful. He stepped quietly next to her ear and whispered, "You okay, Miss Wharton?"

Heaven stumbled back, lost her balance, and landed in Travis's arms.

"Nothing wrong here, mister. Just getting my welcome home kiss from my intended," Jake said.

Intended? Travis did not like the sound of that. Nor did he like the way Jake held on to his woman. Not until he saw Heaven being held by another man was he positive he would fight for her.

"So, Heaven, who is this? You should be resting that foot. Here, let me help you inside, and you can rest while I get our guests some refreshments." He snaked his arm through hers.

Jake stepped back, confusion on his face. "Jake Miles." He stuck out his hand. "Heaven's intended, unless. . ." He looked at Heaven. "Unless you got married."

Heaven shook her head no.

Travis took Jake's hand in his and gave it a good pump. "Travis Logan. No, she is not married to me—not yet. She proposed. I just haven't answered—yet."

Heaven gasped. Her eyes widened as she stared at him as if a wild animal had walked across her path.

"Well, you did ask me the night you sprained your ankle."

Angel hung out the door, "Yes you did, Heaven. You said you loved him and asked him to marry you soon."

Travis scooped her up in his arms. "Let's get the weight off that foot and get inside where it's warmer."

"Put me down, Dr. Logan."

He noticed the lack of the friendly address of Travis and the return of the proper Dr. Logan. "I will in just a moment. You'll be snug as a bug in your rocking chair. Then you can introduce me to these beautiful women who came with Mr. Miles."

"My rocker is gone; the tornado took it. Mrs. Miles is Jake's mother. And Annabelle is my best friend."

Heaven didn't put up a fight about him carrying her. He considered that a good sign. "If you all will kindly follow me to the cabin, I'll see what I can do about righting the place so you can talk."

Travis led the group to the house. With the door blown off by the tornado, the cabin stood exposed. He'd need to do a bit of work before he'd feel comfortable about Angel and Heaven sleeping in here tonight.

He stepped inside.

Heaven screamed.

He almost dropped her. Then he saw why she was upset. Mrs. Jackson had decided the most beautiful rug in the world, according to Heaven, was the perfect place to drop her kid. He didn't know whether to laugh or offer thanks to God. He decided to offer thanks, silently.

There was nothing in her mother's book that could have ever prepared her for the mortifying moment Heaven was now living. Mrs. Jackson, her all-white goat, had given birth on Heaven's rug. No, not just a rug, but the one her great-grandmother had treasured and passed down.

As if the tornado wasn't enough, God? He brought Jake back alive, and that was good, but why did he have to arrive with his etiquette expert mother when that goat had tromped up the front steps into her cabin and given birth on her carpet? She let her head rest against Travis's chest. If only she could stay here in his arms and sleep—make it all go away. She was so tired.

"Heaven?" Travis's breath whispered across her head. "Are you going to be okay?"

She tipped her head back and tried to say something.

"Too much today? You're white as a sheet." He squeezed her more tightly against him. "Cold, too."

"Why'd you stop, Dr. Logan?" Angel pushed against his back. "Why'd Heaven scream? What's in there?"

"Step back, child." Jake jerked her away.

"Ow." Angel pulled her arm out of Jake's grasp and rubbed it.

"There's no need to be rough with her," Travis growled.

Heaven was grateful he'd stepped in to correct Jake.

Angel wiggled past Travis. "What is it, sissie?"

Her sister hadn't called her that since their Ma had died. "Set me down, please, Travis."

He did, but he took his time about it and didn't let go of her completely, wrapping an arm around her shoulder.

"Angel, Mrs. Jackson had her kid." Heaven swallowed. "On Great-Grandma's rug."

"That's the problem? There's a goat in the cabin?" Jake stepped past Travis and Heaven. "Let's get it out of here and clean up this mess." He strode over to the rug and looked back, his lips curled. "Good thing this was old; it will have to be burned."

"But it belonged to. . ." Angel stepped forward. Travis grabbed her with his other hand.

"Don't move, Little Miss. It's still a mess. Nothing is the same as before the tornado. It wouldn't be a good thing to get hurt." Travis squeezed Heaven's shoulder.

He was looking out for Angel, smoothing Heaven's protective side, giving her a measure of peace.

Mrs. Miles and Annabelle piled into the cabin.

"There really is a goat in here. And a baby one. It's so sweet." Annabelle inspected the ruined rug. "It's bad, Heaven. I don't know if it we can get it clean."

Mrs. Miles nodded. "Time to get a new one and start passing it down. Although you won't need to get one, not once you and Jake get married."

Angel stomped a foot. "She ain't marrying Jake."

"Angel, now is not the time. There' a lot of discussing to be done with Jake and Travis," Heaven admonished. Her home was in shambles. What the tornado hadn't accomplished, the goat managed to take care of. Muddy hoofprints decorated the upside-down table, and even her apron had been snacked on. "As you can see, it would be best if the three of you returned to town tonight. If you could come back tomorrow for a visit, then Angel and I will have taken care of this mess and we'd be happy to serve you a nice lunch." She'd found her voice, but it sounded thread thin in her ears.

"Nonsense, child. We're going to get this place back together right now." Mrs. Miles glanced around the room. "It won't take long."

"No, no thank you!" Had she shouted those words? It didn't matter. She didn't want Mrs. Miles putting her home together piece by piece and commenting on how her life would be with

Jake. "I'm sorry, Mrs. Miles. I do appreciate your offer, but I can see that the trip has tired you. Why don't you allow Jake to take you back into town? I'm sure there will be room at the hotel."

"We've already taken care of that. We acquired rooms before we came this way." Mrs. Miles searched for a place to sit. "I don't mind getting my hands dirty, Heaven, but I can see this has been a bit too much for you already. We'll head back into Friendship. Are you sure you won't come and stay with us, where it's warm and the critters can't come in?"

Angel squared her shoulders. "She said we will be staying in our home tonight. We'll be just fine."

"Heaven, will you at least let me stay? I'd like to help. It's been so long since we've talked." Annabelle's sincerity spoke to Heaven's heart.

"It's going to be cold, and we'll have to sleep on the floor."

"I don't mind."

"Say yes, Heaven. Please," Angel pleaded.

She found it harder than ever to say no to her sister. "It will almost be like old times."

"Except you never let me stay with you and Annabelle. This time you will though, right?" Angel's face shone with eagerness.

Heaven smiled, and her shoulders relaxed. It would be good to share stories with her best friend in front of the fire. "This time you can stay."

"Guess that means you don't want me to stay either?" Jake wore a stormy look. "It looks like most of the work is women's work anyway. Where does he sleep?"

"In the barn." Travis answered before Heaven could. "You're

welcome to come back after you drop off Mrs. Miles and sleep there with me. I'm not one for gabbin' before bedtime though."

"I'll stay at the hotel with Mother. That way I'll be able to bring her back earlier." Jake stepped over to Heaven. "I'll bid you goodnight." He grasped her hand and brought it to his lips.

Her glance shot across the room and locked on Travis stoking the fire. Compared to Jake, he'd been kind and concerned for her. Jake had changed from the man she remembered.

"Perhaps we'll get a chance to speak alone tomorrow?"

Heaven shivered, and not from desire. What was wrong with her? She should be overjoyed to spend time with Jake. Maybe Annabelle could help her make sense of it all.

Travis's fingers curled into his palms. He shoved his hands in his pockets. "Let me walk you to the door."

Angel snorted. "You said there isn't a door."

"He's being polite, dear. That's how things are done." Mrs. Miles picked up the hem of her silk dress and stepped over a shattered tea cup.

"Something else you've forgotten, Angel." Heaven frowned, one more thing for Mrs. Miles to take note of—her inability to teach her sister how to behave.

As soon as the buggy noise quieted, signaling the departure of Jake and his mother, Heaven breathed. Not that she'd been holding her breath, but it seemed to be such hard work to make the air go in and out of her lungs.

"Heaven, I know this is a mess in here, but if you can wait for me, I'll take care of dragging out the rug." Travis stood in front of her.

Why wasn't it hard to breathe around him?

"Angel and I will get Mrs. Jackson and her kid settled in the barn. That is, Angel, if you don't mind helping me."

"Yes sir." Angel made her way to the door and stepped out onto the porch. "You shoo them this way."

"Will do in a minute. That's a great idea. Wait there." He started to turn the kitchen table over.

"Stop, Travis. First, I need to wash off those muddy footprints. It will be easier if the table is upside down."

"Don't move anything heavy. Once I get the goats bedded down, I want to get the canvas over these openings. Then I'll be back in to help you get your home back together."

Heaven hunted in the kitchen for two clean aprons. She handed one to Annabelle. "At least Mrs. Jackson didn't get to these."

Chapter 23

The buggy rocked and swayed down the drive. Jake mulled over his feelings about Heaven and that Dr. Logan who seemed to have claimed her. She'd even called him Travis and hadn't bothered to blush. Funny—wasn't that what he had been hoping for? That Heaven wouldn't care, and she would release him from his promise to her?

"I don't like that man staying on Heaven's farm. Jake, you should go back after you drop me off. She's your fiancée." Mrs. Miles wrapped her cloak tighter around her chin. "I would have thought you'd feel a need to stay and protect her, if not from the elements, then from the good doctor."

Jake flicked the reins. The sooner he got his mother back to the hotel the sooner he could find a place to dull his senses. His mother thought all was right with her world, now that her son was living. He supposed it was—for her.

Holding Heaven in his arms almost made him feel whole again. The quick kiss on those soft lips reminded him of who he used to be. Could he still let her go? He hadn't liked leaving Heaven with Dr. Logan sleeping in the barn either.

Maybe he couldn't let her go without making sure she

would be all right. Or was it more than that? Could she heal him, fix his hidden injuries? Could they still marry and have that life they'd talked about before he'd left for the war and become a coward? The question crawled into his mind and tangled itself around his emotions.

He'd puzzle it out tonight. He would reconsider letting her go. She was worth fighting for, and he knew that doctor would challenge him for her. It wouldn't be hard to knock Dr. Logan out of the competition. Jake knew her better, knew her secrets. He also knew winning her meant returning to Nashville with her on his arm. Could he do that? Could he face those who called him a hero? No, he'd have to convince her to head west and start a new life.

Jake Miles irritated Travis worse than an infected blister on his foot. He'd wanted to help Jake on his way the moment he'd commented about Angel. Then when the man kissed Heaven, Travis would have volunteered to stick him in a cannon and shoot him back to where he'd come from. But his mother had raised him to keep such instincts under control.

What had Heaven seen in Jake to make her fall in love with the man? Did she still see it? This was a woman he professed to love, and he was ready to ride off and leave her without a door and her belongings scattered about? Something wasn't right.

He closed the gate to the goats' pen and shook it to make sure it held.

"Do you think Heaven has to marry Jake still? Heaven didn't read anything about that to me from the book. Seems like the promise she made him wouldn't be bona fide anymore since he was supposed to be dead. Why, she could have even already married someone else by now." Angel paused, took a breath. "And why doesn't he want to help get our house fixed?"

He looked to see if she was finished talking. Her mouth was closed, and her eyebrows held a question mark. She must be done. "I don't think your sister has to marry Jake or me, but she needs to marry one of us."

"Then I pick you."

"You don't get to pick, Little Miss. It doesn't work that way." He needed to get the flour and sugar in the house. He guessed it could wait until he made the temporary repairs to the cabin.

"I don't want to live with Mrs. Miles and Jake. They aren't fun like you."

"You'd be back in Nashville with your friends." He pulled the roll of canvas from the back of the wagon.

"Don't need them now. I got new ones today at church. Cassie and I are going to be best friends. We even have the same color hair."

"Is that how you choose a best friend?" He hoisted the canvas to his shoulder.

"No. We like a lot of the same things. That's why we're going to be best friends. Now if Heaven could find a friend here, she would be happy, too. It's too bad Annabelle won't be staying. She makes Heaven smile."

"That she does, Little Miss."

Chapter 24

Annabelle and Heaven snuggled under the blankets, and it was almost like when they were younger. Except for Angel was asleep in the middle and they were on the floor, not a soft bed.

"Good-looking man, even with that scar. . . . I've been thinking, Heaven, that it's not a good idea for you to be staying out here with that man by yourself."

"What?" Annabelle had been talking while Heaven was thinking about kissing Travis again. Daydreaming could be a dangerous thing or a delicious one. She just wasn't sure which it was when it came to Travis.

"With Travis?"

"But what will people say? It's so improper." Annabelle stuck her cold feet against Heaven's leg.

"Annabelle, your feet!"

"Sorry." She pulled them back. "Have you thought about that?"

"Of course I have. No one really knows us here, and things have changed since the war."

"Not that much, Heaven. What about the people in church?"

"The preacher was okay with him staying in the barn since he's a doctor. He's been helping around here because of my ankle." Heaven squirmed, trying to get comfortable. Then she turned on her stomach and squished her straw pillow. It just was not as comfortable as the down-filled pillows she had grown up with. She flipped back on her back. "As for church, we haven't been going. It's a long walk, and with Angel not able to see. . ."

"That is just an excuse. It seems to me that Angel is handling her lack of sight just fine." She propped her head up on one hand.

"I realized that today. While we were there setting up for the lunch, Angel made some friends. She wants to be in the Sunday school play."

"As who?"

"An angel."

"Of course, that makes sense. Who else would she play?"

They giggled some more then settled as their bodies warmed and they relaxed. The fire popped and crackled.

"Angel, are you asleep?" Heaven touched her sister. No response. "We're getting out the jam and biscuits. Do you want some?"

Angel's breathing pattern didn't change.

"I think she's out." Heaven sat up. "Now, tell me why you didn't get married this summer."

"Oh, that." Annabelle waved her hand in the air as if to push the experience away from their conversation.

"Annabelle, it's a big deal, even if you make it sound like it wasn't. What happened?"

"He sent a letter. He wrote he didn't love me and he'd married a—a Yankee. I could have stood the pain, but he brought her back to Nashville."

"That's awful! How're you going to reside in the same town?"

"I'm not. Once I found out Jake was coming to see you, I figured I'd leave with him and never go back."

"Never? But your father."

"I left him a note explaining my intentions to go to Memphis and open a store. I aim to never have to answer to another man the rest of my life." Annabelle lay back on her pillow. "I'm on my own now, and that's the way it is. This world is changing, and some day getting married won't be a requirement. Instead of babies, I'll—I'll just get cats. Don't you to want to marry Jake anymore?"

"Maybe. It's just that I have thought him dead for so long. He seems different. I have to get to know the new Jake." And there was Travis and the fact that her father wanted him to have her. And the kiss.

"I think the grown-up Jake is dreamy." Annabelle sighed. "I am so tired of this place."

"Already? You just arrived." A hole in Heaven's soul opened and leaked sadness. "I had hoped you would stay for a while."

"I'll stay here for a while, at least until you get married. I meant Nashville. It isn't at all like you remember it, Heaven. There are bullet holes in some of the houses, and everyone wears clothes that are old and tattered. Food is scarce. Everyone seems angry or blank like they have no expression or they no longer live in their own bodies.

"And there are no suitors left. Either they're dead or they

came back in such a state that to marry one of them would mean nursing them forever. I've had that life with Father. That isn't how I want to be married."

"There have to be some men who weren't wounded that you could consider."

"There are, but they're engaged or married. I guess I could marry some old coot, but I want a young buck."

"How young?" Heaven said. "Surely there are some boys in town. Maybe you could wait until they grow up?"

"Heaven, be serious. The prospects of finding a decent husband in the South have dissipated. Then here in your own home you have two good candidates."

"Do you want one of them?"

"No, not really. Jake is fun, but he's from our past, and I don't think he'll ever be happy if he's not living in a big house with someone to wait on him. That's not what I want. That's supposed to be you."

"Like I said, I'm not sure about Jake, and Travis seems so much older than me."

"Pshaw, he can't be that much older than us. Why don't you ask him?" Annabelle said. "He seems to care for Angel a great deal."

"He's been very good to her. Better than me for sure. He's encouraged her to do things I was afraid to let her do."

"That has to have been frightening for you. Losing your ma, and then Angel losing her sight. I don't know how you coped afterwards. Then, with your papa taking off and dying." She reached over and patted her friend's arm. "It's too much, Heaven."

"Yes, well one good thing has happened. Jake Miles is alive, and he still intends to marry me." But it wasn't Jake's face that came to her in her dreams. Instead, it was the face of Travis Logan with his coffee-colored eyes, dark brown hair, and the scar on his cheek.

Heaven's eyes flittered open. She blew out, and her breath turned to steam. Getting out from under toasty blankets seemed daunting. Staying on the hard floor made it less so. She glanced at her sister and Annabelle. They were still asleep. From the glow through the canvas-covered door, she knew it was sunny. She hoped it would be a warm day.

She wiggled out of the blanket, attempting to keep any cold air from floating under and disturbing her sister. This would be a good time to have a few moments alone to think about what she needed to say to Jake and to Travis. Angel muttered something then rolled over, anchoring Annabelle with her arm.

Heaven dragged her fingers through her hair to loosen the tangles. She yawned and then stretched. Her back crackled and popped. Sleeping on a floor was something for children.

She should start the coffee, but if she did, the racket from tending the stove would likely wake her guest. For just a few minutes, she craved to talk to God. Then she'd get back to being a proper hostess.

She slipped on her shoes and her skirt and the gray drop-sleeved shirt over her chemise. She'd lost the ribbon she'd tied in her hair yesterday. If it was outside, by now Mr. Jackson had most likely ingested it.

She peeked over at the two curled up by the fire. Seeing no movement, she tiptoed to the makeshift door. She slipped through the edge of the canvas covering. The sun shone bright, blinding her as she tripped over something, wrenching her ankle. She popped her hand over her mouth to smother her voice, "Ow, ow, ow."

A loud groan emitted from a dirty bedroll. "What's wrong?"

She knelt and spoke low, "Travis Logan, what are you doing on my porch?"

He covered his eyes with his elbow. "It's my porch, and I'm protecting my property."

She stood. She wanted to kick him, but her ankle hurt too much. "Why are you sleeping out here?" Her hands went to her hips. She bent over and stared in his face. "Were you spying on us last night?"

He threw back the blankets and sat up. "Too many questions without coffee."

"Doesn't matter. I want an answer anyway."

He stood.

Even without his boots, he towered over her. The top two buttons on his shirt were loose, exposing chestnut hair. Quickly she lowered her eyes and noticed his suspenders rested at his waist. Realizing she'd made another mistake, she inspected the porch. Her rifle rested next to his discarded bedroll. "You have my gun?"

"Easier to shoot a predator that might try to wander in the cabin that way." He rubbed the corner of his eye.

Her head jerked up to see if he was serious. The whiskers on his chin and face intrigued Heaven, along with the way his hair was mashed flat, covering his wound. She wanted to lift it with her fingers and put it to rights. "How'd you get that scar on your cheek?"

He blinked as if he wasn't sure what she was asking about, then nodded. "That." He stroked his cheek. "Trying to helping someone that was dying. I didn't know they had a knife. I think the man thought I was trying to kill him instead of help him. He lashed out and drew the blade across my cheek."

"Did that happen often? Soldiers trying to hurt you while you saved them?"

"More often than not." He touched her arm, let his hand rest a moment, then slid his fingers down her arm. "Don't trouble yourself about it."

"I'm not sure I could sleep if I'd been to war."

"Some men don't." He bent down and bundled up his bedroll and scooped up his boots. "I'll be out of your way here in a minute. Don't worry about tending the animals. I'll take care of them this morning."

"Travis?"

He turned, with a raised eyebrow.

"About Jake. . ."

"Guess you have a dilemma on your hands now, don't you? You have to pick one of us, Heaven. Guess time will tell which one it will be." He gave her a long look, as if waiting for her to choose that moment. When she didn't answer, his shoulders slumped, and then he slowly turned away.

Travis didn't bother plunking his feet into boots. He grasped the bedroll and boots close to his chest and kept the rifle in his hands. He wouldn't even stop and put on his shoes.

He crossed the frosty ground, ignoring the sharp bits of frozen dirt nipping at his soles. Inside the barn, he tossed the bedroll into the hay where he'd been sleeping last night before Miss Simmons had pounced on him, waking him. He started thinking about the women in the house and the idea that anyone or any animal wouldn't find the canvas over the door a very big deterrent. He'd rolled over and tried to ignore the thought. He couldn't. So he'd carted his bedding and himself to the porch to sleep. And that was the thanks he got from the woman he'd been protecting. Accusing him of spying on her.

True, he'd heard them talking and giggling like schoolgirls, but he couldn't make out the words. He did hear his name and Jake's, but that's all he could understand, all he wanted to understand.

He'd told Heaven she had a dilemma on her hands, and so did he. He loved that woman, but he was man enough to step out of the way for the man she'd promised to marry.

If that's what she wanted.

He wouldn't make it easy for Jake though. He planned on quietly courting that woman, in subtle ways that would make her notice the difference between the two men. It might work, unless Jake's attitude changed from yesterday. If he didn't start treating Angel right, Heaven would have nothing to do with Jake. That would be an easy way to win Heaven, but Travis didn't work that way. Angel was already special to him, and he wouldn't use her as a pawn for marriage.

The rooster in the yard crowed, pulling him back to the

chores he said he'd take care of this morning. First, he wanted to check on Mrs. Jackson and Junior, as Angel had named him last night.

He picked up a boot and slid his foot in, stomping down on the heel to set it in place. Once he had them both on, he put feed in a bucket from the barrel in the corner. Pride and Joy nickered as Travis passed by his stall. "Be back with yours in a little bit. Yours, too, Charlie."

It occurred to him he needed to tell Jake that the farm no longer belonged to Heaven's family. After that, he planned on staying out of Jake's way. Travis would explore the woods and see if he could find any of Heaven's things that had been scattered by the tornado. That is, after he patched up the house so he didn't have to sleep on the porch again tonight.

Chapter 25

All through breakfast, Annabelle watched the interplay between Travis and Heaven. Last night she thought it was the warmth of the fire that caused the flush in her friend's face when she talked about Travis. Now that she saw the shy glances Heaven offered Travis, she knew differently. There was a spark between them. When Jake kissed Heaven yesterday, Annabelle hadn't seen that fire.

Could it be that Heaven wouldn't be heartbroken when Jake told her he wanted to be released from the betrothal?

Annabelle rested her fork on the plate. If that were true, Jake would be a free man. He didn't want to go back to Nashville, and neither did she. Maybe he'd allow her to accompany him further south. Or could it be possible she might entice him to marry her and return home? She examined the reasons for leaving, and the most important one was that she was on her way to becoming a spinster. She didn't love Jake, but that didn't matter to her. She'd been in love with William, and look where that got her. But if Jake were to marry her, she could return to Nashville and hold her head high. She wouldn't have to follow her father's directives; she'd be a Miles. She had some thinking to do.

Travis collected his emotions and stuffed them in his chest. He'd made it through breakfast with his feelings for Heaven somewhat challenged, thanks to Annabelle. It seemed she favored Jake, but at times he wondered if it was for herself rather than Heaven. He chewed on a piece of hay.

The tiny kid, Junior, appeared to be nursing well and was healthy despite being born the wrong time of year. When the cold winter settled in, they might have to move him inside to keep him warm enough. "What do you think, Mrs. Jackson? Maybe Annabelle and Jake are meant to be together." Realizing he'd spoken his thoughts, he looked over his shoulder, hoping he wouldn't spot Angel standing in the door. She wasn't. He let his breath break free from his lungs.

He rummaged around the barn until he located a hammer and a few other tools that would be useful for repairing the cabin. He wished he could get the bedroom back on the house, but working alone, he didn't think it possible.

Hoofbeats rounded the corner of the lane. Travis straightened. It sounded like more than one horse. Had Jake brought a bigger buggy back with him? Maybe, if he was bringing Annabelle's luggage.

"Dr. Logan!" A loud voice called again. "Dr. Logan!"

Someone needed him. He dropped the tools to the barn floor and rushed outside. He stopped short when he saw Mr. Shaw and another man. "What's wrong? Is it your wife or the baby?"

The man dismounted. "Neither. They're both doing fine.

My wife's sister is with her this morning. Dr. Logan, this is my brother-in-law, Harold Brown."

"Nice to meet you, Harold."

Harold nodded and climbed off his horse.

"So, if they're okay, what can I do for you?"

"My family owes their thanks to you for coming yesterday. Thought we'd ride over and help you put your house back together. There are a few others coming from town. Once word got out that there was a doctor thinking about setting up a practice here, everyone wanted to pitch in and help."

"But. . ."

"Nothing to say, Doc. A few women will be coming by later with the lunch meal, too. You might want to warn Miss Wharton. My wife said I was to tell you that. So I have."

This was sure to stir up a nest of hornets with Heaven. "I'll do that. Right now. You gentleman can tie your horses up by the barn, or put them in the pen if you like. I do appreciate your coming to help." He wasn't so sure Miss Proper would feel the same when he told her about more company coming with lunch.

Heaven met him on the porch. "What are those men doing here?"

"They've come to put your bedroom back on the cabin."

"Why?"

"Because folks around here are right nice if you give them a chance. Mr. Shaw said there are more coming to help. Some women are bringing lunch. Might want to grab some green beans to serve."

Her face went white. "Women from town? Here? By dinnertime?"

He nodded.

"But I'm not set up for company."

"No, I don't suppose anyone that's had their home ripped apart by a tornado would be, do you?"

"I guess not." She frowned. "But I can sure try and make it look better with Annabelle's help."

"How's your ankle? I saw you trying to hold that scream inside when you tripped over me."

"It's fine, a bit tender is all." She looked past him and brightened. "Looks like Jake and his mother are here. He can help, too."

He stepped down from the porch.

She brushed past him, rendering him invisible, as she rushed to the arrival of her intended.

She hadn't asked him if he'd slept well. She didn't seem to care that he'd had a miserable night sleeping out in the open watching over her. He should have known better than to believe she would ever marry him. She wasn't exactly like Mary. She wasn't betraying him outright, though it felt that way. Jake had claimed her first, and it appeared that he intended to keep his promise to Heaven, unlike Mary's to Travis. His stomach soured at the memory of finding his fiancée with Mort, his best friend. Mort's arm wrapped around her shoulders and their lips mashed together.

Heaven hoped her face wasn't flaming red as she raced past Travis. She had to get away from him and his ability to make her want to throw herself into his arms. Again the memory of him carrying her into the cabin yesterday sent tingles throughout her—and they weren't undesirable.

But there was Jake and his mother standing in front of her. She'd made a promise, and she would keep it. It was what both families had wanted since she and Jake were small. No matter that Ma and Pa could no longer make those choices for her. A promise was a promise. But what was she going to do with these feelings for Travis?

"Morning, Mrs. Miles, Jake. Glad you're here, Jake. A few men from town are here to help put the bedroom back on the cabin today." Travis stood behind her, close enough that if he were a cattle brand, he'd burn his initials into her back.

Needing less heat, she stepped forward. "Mrs. Miles, it won't take long to get some tea ready. Would you like to go inside?"

Mrs. Miles nodded. "The tea in town was dreadful, very weak. I hope yours is stronger. It has been so long since we've had good tea."

"It's passable, but not like we used to have. I pray someday soon the prices will come down and we'll be able to make it sweet and dark like before."

"I can swing a hammer, though I'm not dressed properly to be pounding nails," Jake said.

"I'm sure I can find something of Pa's for you to wear, Jake. He didn't take everything with him."

"I had hoped to spend time speaking with you, Heaven."

"There will be time for that later." She offered her best southern girl smile. "I would feel much safer having the cabin put back together." She shot a look at Travis. "Then I'd know for sure there wouldn't be any way for predators of any kind to get inside."

"Then I'll be happy to assist in what ways I can."

"Mrs. Miles, would you mind if I held your arm to help to steady myself? I reinjured my ankle this morning, not seriously, but I'd rather not take a chance on twisting it on the rough ground."

"My dear, that's understandable." She took Heaven by the arm, and they started a slow walk to the porch.

"Heaven, you're favoring that leg. Do you still have the ankle wrapped?" Travis asked.

"No, it was loose last night, so I slipped it off."

"Then that's the first thing I'll do this morning. It should be rewrapped to give you support and contain the swelling."

Her eyes locked onto his. Mercy, what was she going to do with these feelings? She was still engaged to Jake. Why didn't she have the same bacon-sizzling excitement when he looked at her? If Jake hadn't been standing there at that moment, she shamelessly would have felt disappointed if Travis didn't carry her to the cabin.

"Now, sir, you don't mean to be touching my fiancée's. . . um. . .personal—?" Jake stopped and faced Travis.

"I'm a doctor, and it needs to be done." Travis took a step closer to Jake. "Do you have any medical experience, sir?"

"No I have not. But Mother will be watching." Jake strode toward the cabin, his feet striking the ground and sending up shards of mud.

"Really, Jake, I wouldn't have it any other way. Mrs. Reynolds, the preacher's wife, was here the last time, and so was Angel."

Jake's jaw clenched. "Then I suppose it will be fine." He yanked the canvas covering to the side and waited for the women to pass through.

Heaven stopped, let go of Mrs. Miles, and glared at Jake. "Dr. Logan has done nothing improper." *Except for kiss me.* "He's treated me like a lady." *Except doctors ought not make a lady stir up embers of feelings inside.* "He was very gentle and didn't hurt me in the least." *Except he's taking my home from me.*

His eyes narrowed. "I'm glad he was here to help you, Heaven. It must have been a terrifying experience for you."

Annabelle and Angel were busy in the kitchen. "Heaven, we wondered where you took off to. I see you've found the Mileses. Good morning." Annabelle bent down and opened the oven door. "I'm reheating some biscuits. Would you like some?"

"We have tea, too," Angel said. "Why don't you have a seat, Mrs. Miles, and let us serve you this morning."

Heaven wanted to hug her sister. She was using her hospitality skills well. "Travis, would you mind asking the men outside to come in for some as well, before they get started. It will take a bit of time to apply the wrap."

Travis nodded. "I'll be right back. It might be best to do that out on the porch steps, with Mrs. Miles in attendance, while the men are inside."

"I'll get the bandage strips and meet you there."

"Mrs. Miles, would you like some tea, or maybe some milk?" Angel offered.

"I'll have mine as soon as Heaven is medically attended to. Jake will be honored to have his now." Mrs. Miles turned then stopped. "Then Jake is going to work on the cabin with Dr. Logan."

"Are we getting it put back together?" Angel slid into a chair.

"Yes Angel, isn't that wonderful? God is providing us with men to help Jake and Travis with the rebuilding. They said there'll be women coming around noon with lunch." Heaven could feel the tightness of her pasted smile. God had provided for them. But why did her free will seem to be stripped away as decisions were made without her saying a word?

"Annabelle, would you mind helping me get ready for them after Travis is finished with me?"

"Of course I will help you."

Chapter 26

Heaven surveyed the cabin, which was overflowing with the men who came to help and the women serving food. Mrs. Reynolds had brought Mrs. Tate. They hadn't come empty-handed either. There would be enough food for Heaven to feed her guests for a few days.

Mrs. Reynolds had requested a trade of green beans in exchange for canned pumpkin and orange marmalade. Heaven felt awful about her first judgment of the woman. She truly had a kind heart.

The men had finished their afternoon meal, and Heaven was collecting plates from the table. "What I don't understand is how you came to be at the Wharton's, Travis," Jake said.

"I was with Heaven's father when he died en route to Chicago. He sent me out here. Made me promise."

"Promise what?"

"Caleb wanted me to take his home, said it would be a good place to raise horses."

"Just like that? He gave you the place?" Jake stared at him. "So this is *your* cabin we've been putting back together today, not Heaven's?"

Travis sent Heaven a glance she didn't quite understand. "That, and he told me he wanted me to have Heaven." The log behind him popped.

"He what?" Jake's face was full of fire.

"I imagine he was concerned about his daughters being left alone. He shouldn't have been, since Heaven shot me before I had a chance to explain my arrival." His boot tapped loudly under the table.

Mrs. Miles gasped. "Oh Lord have mercy!"

Annabelle squealed. "You shot a man?"

"He was the first one I hit. Not the first I shot at."

Angel sat eating her warm bread with the jam Annabelle had brought. She had made herself a sandwich and hoped to enjoy the bursting blackberry flavor alone. A chair scooted out from under the table. She knew it wasn't Travis, because he took great care not to scrape the floor. She could hear her sister's voice and then Annabelle's soft laugh along with Mrs. Miles's throaty one. It had to be Jake, and he hadn't said a word to her. She hated that. He was probably staring at her, trying to look at her eyes. She lowered her head so he couldn't see them. Heaven said sometimes blind people put patches over their eyes. She didn't want to do that. Heaven said she didn't have to because her eyes were still pretty. She wondered if they would stay that way or if they would fade. Did eyes need to work for the color to stay?

Jake touched her arm as if she couldn't hear him sit down at the table like a bear in the general store. "How did you go blind, Angel?"

The bread stuck in her throat, and she coughed.

"Are you all right?" her sister called, panic in her voice.

"Fine." She cleared her throat. "I'm okay. Just went down the wrong pipe is all."

She jutted her chin toward the direction Jake's voice had come. "I got real sick the same time as Ma. Heaven saved me, but the fever made me blind. At least that is what me and Heaven think happened."

"So do you see anything, or is it just all black behind those eyes?" Jake snickered.

Angel's shoulders tightened. He was like those town boys. She could just feel it. She remembered him pulling her pigtails a time or two, and she didn't like that. He had called her pipsqueak when her sister was not around.

Once he had offered her a stick of candy to leave him and Heaven alone in the parlor, but she wouldn't take it. She didn't trust him then, and she decided she wouldn't trust him now. Dr. Logan was going to marry Heaven, so the sooner they sent Jake Miles packing, the happier Angel would be. But first she would finish this delicious jam sandwich. She wouldn't even answer his dumb question.

"So Monkey, your mama and your papa took sick and died. You Whartons don't have much luck do you?"

"We don't need luck. We have God. Our family is better off in heaven than living here. But now that Travis is here, it is much better. He brings us rabbit meat for stew." She took another bite of her sandwich. It wasn't blackberry jam but blueberry, and it was almost as good as blackberry jam. She wished Jake would go so she could enjoy her treat without his sour attitude wafting across the table at her. And she really wished he wouldn't call her Monkey like he did when she was four.

"Hmm, seems to me like God's forgotten about the Wharton family. Here you two are stranded out here. God has to know Heaven isn't worth anything in the kitchen. Why she probably never even used a stove before coming out here, much less chopped wood."

Angel stiffened her back. "My sister can do more than you know." She put her jam sandwich down on her plate. It no longer appealed to her. She knew one thing, and that was she didn't like Jake and she planned to do what she could to send him back to Nashville, away from her sister. And she decided to start right now.

She fluttered her hand in front of her as if trying to find her glass of milk. She knew where it was. Dr. Logan had placed it at two o'clock from the top of her plate. Satisfaction almost made her smile when her hand hit the side of the glass, sending it sailing across the tabletop. She could imagine the white liquid pooling in the middle.

Jake scooted his chair back. "Watch what you're doing! You almost doused me with your drink."

She heard Dr. Logan's heavy footsteps and Heaven's lighter ones. Dr. Logan reached her first. "How did that happen, Little Miss?"

"I don't really know. I thought the glass was where it always is, but maybe Jake moved it." That was a lie, and she would have to ask forgiveness for saying it, but it had snuck out across her lips before she had barely thought it. But it did help move her plan along to make Jake look bad.

She heard the towel swish the liquid across the table. Her sister said, "It's okay, Angel. It wasn't a lot of milk spilt. Did any of it get on your dress?"

Angel patted her skirt. It was dry. She hadn't even considered she might have made a mess of herself. Angel felt guilty then for making her sister clean up, especially when her ankle hurt so much. "I'm sorry, Heaven. Let me finish cleaning the table."

"You didn't finish your jam sandwich, and you were so excited about it." Dr. Logan stood next to her with his hand on her shoulder. "I'll get you another glass of milk and make sure it doesn't get moved."

"Will you sit next to me?" Angel asked. "Then I know it won't happen again."

"I didn't move the monkey's glass. Maybe she ought not be living out here, but in a home where they can take care of her and she can learn some skills." Jake sputtered. "Really, it is uncivilized to have someone who can't see try to feed themselves."

Angel hadn't considered that she might be viewed that way. She would have to be careful so Heaven didn't come to the same conclusion as Jake.

Heaven sucked in her breath, and the sound made Angel feel secure. She would never put her in a home for blind children.

"Jake Miles, her name is Angel, not Monkey. In fact, I think she is old enough to be addressed as Miss Wharton, so please do so. It seems the war has erased some of your fine gentlemanly manners."

"Pardon me, Miss Wharton. Your sister surprised me is all.

It seems that I may have misspoken."

Annabelle giggled. "Jake, you sprung up awfully fast. One would never know you've been shot at the way you were trying to skedaddle away from that river of milk."

Angel laughed. "Milk doesn't hurt anyone Jake, I promise."

It was quiet for a moment, and then Jake laughed. "I supposed when you look at it that way, it was rather funny. I do apologize, Miss Wharton. I seem to remember you being such a sport when you were younger, never minding my teasing. I've grown fond of thinking of you as my little sister."

"I accept your apology, sir. While you thought the teasing was fun, I never enjoyed it." She heard the plunk of the glass on the table and knew that Travis had refilled it for her. He whispered in her ear, "It is in its usual place; let's make sure it doesn't get moved from there." She heard the creak of his knees as he bent and lifted the chair from the end of the table and set it next to her. "I will be right beside you from now on when you eat."

"Thank you, Travis."

"My pleasure, Little Miss."

Angel took another bite of her sandwich followed by a long drink of milk. Yes, she had some work to do. Jake Miles had to go.

Jake brushed away the line of sweat on his forehead that threatened to drip into his eye. He picked up another log and gave it a whack with the ax. He'd been trying to get Heaven alone all afternoon. After that embarrassment with Angel, he wanted to assure Heaven that he cared for her sister. As his mother had pointed out to him later, Heaven and Angel had become more than sisters during these trying times. He wasn't quite sure what that meant, but he didn't have a desire to have her explain it to him. He had figured out enough to know that from the way Heaven treated Angel, she wouldn't hold his past against him.

He lifted his chin and stood taller than he had in months. Heaven would help him find his way back to being a man, not a coward. Though he didn't think he'd tell her about that until after they were married, just in case.

Choosing to chop wood rather than put Travis Logan's house back together seemed childish to him, but he couldn't see his way to putting the cabin to rights. He'd come outside and discovered the low wood pile. Chopping wood would help Heaven stay warm and cook if she refused to marry him right away. And if she decided to marry him, then Travis was welcome to the wood, because Jake would have won the prize.

On the chopping block, he set a log on the cut edge, balanced it, and then swung the ax against it. The sharp split of the wood filled him with strength. This was something he could do well while avoiding conversation with the other men about his war experience.

He reset the log and let the ax fall again. What was Heaven doing now? Earlier she'd been mixed up in the middle of the women who'd come to help. He was feeling a bit thirsty. Maybe he'd see if she was available to talk to him while he satiated his thirst.

He set the ax next to the pile of split logs and ran a hand

through his sweaty hair. Not much he could do about his mussed appearance; it wasn't what he'd ever consider a desirable courting look. But with Logan around, he didn't want to waste time preening. He had a feeling he might have already lost Heaven, but he wouldn't quit without trying. She'd meant a lot to him before the war, and someday—if he ever felt whole again—he'd want her with him.

Determined to speak to her, he headed for the cabin.

In the root cellar, the candle flickered and spat. The light cast a warm yellow over the multitude of jars of green beans. The color didn't add appeal to the vegetable. Heaven picked up another jar of canned green beans. It was the third one that had an odd color and weight about it.

She held it to the candlelight. It was more than the hue from the candlelight. The color seemed sickly. She set it to the side with the other two she'd found the day of the tornado. She'd meant to discard them. While not sure they had gone bad, the likelihood was they had. She still had plenty of beans to trade. She thanked God again and asked for forgiveness for her worry about not having food. God had certainly provided through the good women of the Baptist church.

She plucked another can from the shelf and wiped the dusty top with her apron. It didn't have the dull green look and felt the right weight, so she placed it with the others in her basket.

"Heaven, are you down there?" Jake's face appeared at the top of the ladder.

Her breath sucked in as she backed up. "Jake, I almost

dropped my basket. Good thing it was looped on my arm, or there would have been another mess to clean up. What do you need?"

"Can I come down and talk to you?"

"In the root cellar?" The man had lost his mind. Why would he want to converse with her amid rows of beans? "I'm on my way up." His face retreated, and she climbed the ladder.

Jake waited for her. "Let me take those for you." He slipped the basket from her arm and set it on the dry sink.

"I came in for a drink of water and wondered where you disappeared to."

"Just gathering a few things to trade before the women leave. Did you get your water?"

"No." He shook his head.

"Mercy, let me get you a glass then. One of the other women would have been happy to serve you." She slid a loose lock of hair behind her ear.

Jake grasped her arm. "I didn't want anyone else to serve me. Heaven, I—can, will you take a short walk with me for a moment?"

She glanced around the cabin. Most of the women were outside helping where they could. Only Mrs. Miles remained seated by the fire. "No. I can't. There's too much to do before everyone leaves."

"Just a short walk."

She didn't want to be alone with Jake. Despite her responsibility to the promise she made him, she wasn't ready for the conversation she knew he wanted to have. "I don't want to be lollygagging while the others are working on my home."

Jake grimaced.

"It's my home, as long as I'm in it, and so far Travis hasn't mentioned me moving out."

But he hadn't asked her to stay either.

"I understand. If it will ease your mind, why not help me carry some of the split wood to the porch while we converse?" He held out his arm for her.

She shifted her weight from side to side, for a moment undecided, and then she noticed him—the Jake that had returned. Gone was the quick wit that made her hold her stomach in laughter, the sureness he carried himself with, as if the world would grow a rose path for him to walk on wherever he went. She sought the memory of him in his eyes and saw a depth they'd once lacked—worry, hurt, fear? She grasped his arm and remembered the man he was, the one who made her smile, the man her mother said would give her the world. The one she should be grateful to God for, for providing such a fine specimen for her to marry.

"Let's get the wood on the porch."

Outside Heaven piled the split wood into Jake's arms and waited for him to say something. They'd made two trips to the porch with the wood, and he'd been as silent as the wind today.

"Guess you're wondering about what I wanted to say?"

"Yes I am. If you want to talk without the others, you'd better start. Angel will be looking for me soon."

"I doubt that, as she seems to have attached herself to Logan."

She slapped a piece of wood on top of the others.

"Sorry. It's just that I came up here to release you from

marrying me, but now that I've seen you, I can't let you go. I still love you, Heaven. I want to marry you, but not in Nashville."

He'd said it, what she didn't want to hear. She swallowed and tears burned. "It's been so long. I thought you were dead."

"I know, and I'm sorry about that. I should have written the moment I could. I thought it would be better this way. You could find someone whole to marry. That's not me, not right now."

"I don't know what to say, Jake. I feel like I need to get to know you again. And then there's Angel—where I go she goes. You need to find a way to get along with her."

"I understand. Do I still have a chance at winning your heart?"

She placed one more piece of wood on the stack, covering most of his face.

He let the stacked wood roll out of his arms to the ground.

She jumped back. "Why did you do that?"

"Stop. Don't stay anything else. I need you to know that I'm not going back to Nashville. I'm leaving Tennessee."

"Where are you going?"

"West, maybe to Colorado, stake out a claim at one of those gold mines. I want to start a new life with you as my wife."

"But your mother and father expect you to go back and work in their business."

"I can't do that, not anymore." He grasped her hands in his.

She never noticed before how her hand didn't seem to fit in his, not like Travis's. And now that Jake held her hand, where were the spitting sparks of fire that happened when Travis's hand touched hers?

"So will you think about it? Will you give Logan this house

your father wanted him to have and marry the man your mother wanted for you?"

She withdrew her hands and hugged her arms around her chest. "Jake, I don't—"

Annabelle ran up to them out of breath. "There you are, Heaven. Travis found something, and he's looking for you."

"Think about it. Will you, Heaven? Leave with me, next week?" Jake turned to collect the wood he'd dropped.

"Leave where?" Annabelle tugged on Heaven's shawl. "Where are you going?"

Heaven didn't reply. She just shook her head and put up her hand to stop Annabelle from asking more questions. Clutching her shawl tightly in one hand, she went to find out what Travis discovered that was so important. Meanwhile, she had so much to think about. Should she marry the boy her ma wanted her to have or the man Pa had sent for her?

Annabelle watched her friend walk away. Jake still gathered wood in his arms. "Here, let me help you." She bent down and with care picked up a wood chunk hairy with splinter offerings. "It's always easier when you have someone to help you put the last pieces together."

"Sometimes it is." Jake straightened. "Thanks."

She searched his face. "Did you tell her you weren't going to marry her?"

"The opposite. I asked her to marry me and leave next week."

"You'll go back to Nashville then?" If Heaven went back, it

could be bearable to go home to her father's house.

"No, not Nashville. Never back there. I asked her to go west, leave this life that's happened to us far behind."

"Next week? That won't work, Jake. I told you I'm not going home. You have to return with your mother. I have other plans." She let the wood she held roll back to the ground and turned away from him. Why had she thought he was adorable or would be if he could change his attitude? Her lips burned as she remembered the kiss he'd stolen from her a week after getting betrothed to her best friend. Jake didn't deserve Heaven, and she would do what she could to help her see the truth.

Chapter 27

The hammering continued as Heaven rounded the corner of the cabin. The noise echoed Jake's question: marry-him-go-west. It wasn't exactly what Ma had in mind when she orchestrated the engagement. When Heaven accepted Jake's betrothal, Ma's face had beamed as if she were the bride to be; she praised God that her daughter would be living in comfort and be a part of society. Heaven shivered. Why hadn't she been as excited? She liked Jake, thought she loved him, and when she'd lost him, she'd cried herself to sleep for months.

But now? If Travis hadn't kissed her and woke feelings inside of her she didn't even know existed, she'd be accepting Jake's offer of a new life. But Travis did kiss her. And she liked it. A lot.

The side of the cabin seemed different. The logs appeared lighter than the ones on the front. She hadn't realized how much work it would have been for Travis to repair the cabin alone. How would he have even lifted those heavy logs into place?

Her steps halted. The room they were adding on was bigger than before. She tilted her head to get a better angle. It was larger. Too big for just one room, now it would be a fancy two-bedroom cabin. Angel could have her own room if they didn't leave with Jake. *God, I need direction. You've placed two good men in my life, and I don't know who You want me to choose. I'm so tired of worrying about taking care of Angel and where the next meal might come from, and yet You keep blessing me with gifts from You. But which of these men is the gift?*

She shielded her eyes from the sun, trying to locate Travis among the men working. She didn't see his dark hair at first. Then he turned and saw her. His smile blazed across the distance, and she responded.

He scampered down a newly made ladder and trotted over to a pile of coats abandoned as the men grew warm from the sun and the work.

She hurried over, not wanting to squander any of his working time. "Annabelle said you found something?"

"I did."

Light bounced off something in his hand. She blinked.

"While we were looking for fallen trees to use, I found this. Does it belong to you?" He held it out to her.

Rubbing her arm, she stepped back. Grief hammered her heart as her mind recognized what precious memory Travis held. Could it be? Her fingers trembled as she reached for the frame. With great care, she traced the crack that ran between the people in the photo. There wasn't any water damage. Other than the broken glass, it had survived. She looked up, and her eyes melded with his. Warmth filled her, soothing the pain. "It's my ma and pa."

She couldn't look away.

He took a step closer. "Heaven, you don't have to go through this alone."

Their connection snapped. Unsettled, she hugged the picture to her chest. "We've never been alone, Dr. Logan. God has always been with us."

"That is true." He pulled a hammer from his back pocket. "I guess I'd better get back to work."

"You made it bigger."

"Is that all right with you?"

"Does it matter? This doesn't belong to me anymore, as you like to remind me as often as you can."

Travis rubbed the wooden handle. He took a breath and looked as if he were going to say something. Instead, he glanced over at the grove of cedar trees. "I'll be working out here until supper if you need anything. We should have the logs pinned by then. The chinking will have to wait."

"Heaven!" Angel called out from the porch. "Mrs. Reynolds wants to know if we have any salt. We're making pie. Never mind. She said she found it."

Heaven raised her hand in acknowledgment and then slowly lowered it as she remembered her sister couldn't see her. It didn't matter anyway, since Angel had scampered back into the cabin, not waiting for her sister's response. "I'll take this inside. Again, thank you for finding it."

Travis watched her walk away clutching that photo with her shoulders sunk lower than rock in a river. He cherished her reaction when he'd given her the photo. What would it be like to lose almost everyone you loved? Then have the things that reminded you of them swept away? He'd left home by choice, no room for him there and a strong desire to be his own man. And to get away from the painful memories of Mary. He couldn't watch her marry and raise kids that weren't his. He'd made his peace with that and forgiven the both of him, but he didn't have to stick around and watch their future unfold. It no longer mattered. What did was finishing this cabin and winning Heaven's love.

"Travis." Heaven called. "Wait."

He turned back and waited until she walked across the dead weeds to him.

"Can I ask you something? It's about doctoring."

Her face was pinched tight enough to cause him pain. Was something wrong with her? "What do you want to know?"

"You know how my ma died? The fever? And then Angel got sick but she lived but lost her sight?"

"Yes, you mentioned that."

"I know you didn't have any luck saving Pa from the same fate, but I'm wondering if I could have done anything to save Ma, and maybe Angel's sight?"

She might as well have mule-kicked him in the stomach. How did she know his most vulnerable weakness? How could he answer her, tell her there was never hope, at least when it came to him saving people who contracted a fever? He had to say something, offer her a bit of hope that the next time the ending wouldn't be the same. "Why don't you tell me how you tried to get the fever down."

Annabelle meant to go back inside and help the church women prepare the meal, but instead she found herself leaning against the railing feeling all warm and happy as she watched Heaven and Travis. They stood close to each other, a bit closer than necessary. Annabelle rubbed her hands together. Heaven surely had feelings for the handsome doctor.

She knew right then she had to keep Jake from marrying Heaven and hauling her out west somewhere. Her friend had suffered more than enough this year. To marry Jake, a ladies' man at his best and a broken man at his worst, would likely bring Heaven even more grief.

Annabelle leaned over the porch railing, trying to get a better view of her friend's face. She couldn't, but she did see Heaven's posture shrink, like her spine wasn't capable of being straight despite years of training. Then she hustled away from Travis toward the woods. What had he said to upset her? Maybe Annabelle had made a mistake, and Travis wasn't as good as she thought.

She grasped the fold of her skirt to lift her hem and took off at a quick trot to follow her friend and offer her comfort.

Heaven had numbly thanked Travis and then headed to the woods. She couldn't go inside, not right now. He hadn't said it was her fault, but when she'd said she'd kept Ma and Angel tightly covered and kept the fire stoked, his eyebrows shot heavenward. Right then, she'd known it was the wrong thing to do. They were so cold, shivering so hard their teeth were clattering. She'd made them sicker by piling on more blankets. Why hadn't her ma taught her how to nurse someone? Most likely her ma never thought Heaven would have to since she'd be married to a Miles. As Jake's wife, she'd have access to a doctor anytime one was needed.

"Heaven. . .wait." Annabelle huffed behind her. Heaven wiped her shirt sleeve across her eyes and spun around.

"I saw you. . .talking. . .to Travis." Annabelle's cheeks were pink from exertion.

"Were you running?"

"No, walking fast." She dropped the skirt fabric from her hands. "It would have been easier to run."

"It is. When we moved here, Angel and I would sneak off to the back pasture and run. We knew Ma wouldn't catch us and Pa wouldn't care." She angled the photo for Annabelle to see. "Travis found this and brought it back to me. He wasn't even sure if it belonged to me."

"He's nice. Thoughtful, too." Annabelle extended her hand. "Can I see?"

Heaven, reluctant to let it out of her grasp, held on to it a second longer then gave it to her. Annabelle wouldn't harm it, and she knew Heaven's parents. She was the only person as close as her sister was to her. "The glass is cracked. But the picture is okay." She hovered next to Annabelle. "I wonder how old they were? I never thought to ask Ma."

"You look like her. You both have that wavy hair and penetrating gaze." Annabelle handed it back.

"I'm sorry that I didn't share Ma with you more. I never

knew how hard it was without one." She'd been mean more than once to Annabelle when she'd asked if Heaven's mom would fix her hair, too, or show her how to arrange flowers. Jealousy had risen like the flooded Mississippi, causing her to say things she now regretted.

"I forgive you. We were kids." Annabelle pushed aside a branch that crossed in their path. She held it back for Heaven. "If I could have told you in words what I was missing, then you would have shared her." She let go, and the cedar branch shivered back into place. "I know your heart. Back then you probably saw me taking away from you precious time with your mother."

A broken branch crunched under Heaven's foot. "Ma was gone often, doing things for the church and the poorer families. The time she spent with me often felt limited. And when Angel came, there was even less." A small brown bird flew overhead and landed on a bare tree limb, making it sway.

"So, do you know what you're going to do? Are you going to marry Jake?"

"He asked me to marry him again this morning."

"I know. I'm sorry. I wasn't trying to eavesdrop. Travis sent me to find you, and then I overheard Jake ask if you would go out west with him. Does he have a plan for when he gets there?"

"I don't think so, other than finding gold." She tried to picture what the West might be like. She'd heard stories, and that life seemed even harder than the one she was living now. Even with Jake by her side, there would be a lot of difficult days. Not that she minded times like that. It made the good

days seem so much better. But somehow when she pictured living out west, Jake's face did not come to mind; Travis's did.

She looked up as another bird flew overhead. It came to a stop by the other one. *That's nice. They must be family.*

"You have other options. You could marry Travis." Annabelle's red curls bounced as she rose up and down on her toes in front of Heaven. "Or come with me to Memphis! And we'll open a shop together. That would be so much fun! And of course Angel can come, too. We'll teach her all the special knitting patterns, and she can help keep the shelves filled." Annabelle grabbed Heaven and pulled her into a hug. "Please, it would be delightful to be together."

Holding the photo in one hand, Heaven embraced her friend while considering the possibilities. Starting a knitting shop with Annabelle sounded like fun, but also irresponsible. She had to consider Angel in her plans. How long would it take to find a place to live? Did Annabelle even have enough money for all three of them to live and pay rent on a shop? Most of all, was she ready to say good-bye to being a wife and mother now that it was truly possible?

Chapter 28

A ngel listened to the footsteps, heel, toe, heel, toe, as Travis headed for the cabin door. "Are you going to the barn?"

"I thought I'd walk out and check on Junior. I find the little babies entertaining. Want to go with me?"

She liked the way he asked her to do things with him, just like Pa used to. She scratched at a spot behind her ear. Mosquitoes must not die off here as early as they did in Nashville, 'cause it seemed she'd wandered into a pack of them. "Yes sir." She scrambled off the floor to her feet. "Do you want me to lead you since it's getting dark?"

"I'd like to escort you, Miss Wharton, if your cute button nose wouldn't be offended by the rankness of my work shirt."

Angel coughed several times. "I'd be honored, Dr. Logan." She dipped in a mock curtsey. Her throat tickled, causing her to cough again.

"Pffft. It's not dark."

Jake. Ready retorts climbed onto her tongue, waiting for her to fire them from her mouth, but she packed them into the "proper lady basket" and shut the lid with reluctance.

Someone cracked his knuckles.

"Please don't do that, Jake." Heaven's tone was as sharp as their rooster's beak.

Step, swish, step. Heaven was wearing one of Ma's gowns. She wasn't as tall as Ma, and the skirt dragged across the floor. Whose attention was she trying to get? She hoped not Jake's. The light steps grew louder as she came near. "Are you feeling all right, Angel?"

"Peachy." She wouldn't tell Heaven her throat hurt, or she'd be tucked in bed with a warm brick before she could protest.

"Jake, I think we should see the baby goat as well. It's been a long time since I've been around farm animals, and the little ones are adorable." Mrs. Miles brushed past her, leaving behind a flower bed of roses.

Angel's fingers made their way to the itchy spot again, and she dug in. Those two were as annoying as the bug bite. She didn't want to spend time with them. She wanted Travis to herself, or at least to have only Heaven with them. "Then let's get going. Annabelle and Heaven, are you coming, too?"

"I'd love to. Thank you, Angel, for inviting me," Annabelle said.

"I think I'll stay here and heat the coffee. When you come back, it will be hot, and we'll have another piece of that pie you made this afternoon." Heaven hugged her. "It's a really good pie." She whispered in Angel's ear and sent her out the door.

Today had been a tornado of emotions for Heaven. The coffeepot clanked against the stove burner plate as she replaced it on the stove to keep warm for the others. The china cup warmed her hands as she took a sip of the dark brown brew. The silence fed her soul. Before today she'd missed the hustle and bustle of friends coming and going, having forgotten how wearying it could be to have your company face stuck in place all day like dried molasses.

The canvas-covered windows took on a reddish glow from the setting sun while the evening chill snaked through the fibers. Travis said he'd ordered shutters as glass was still too costly, but they wouldn't be in for a week, maybe longer. But with the wood Jake chopped and split, she and Angel would stay warm through the winter. She set her cup on the table and stuck her hand into her apron pocket. She pulled out her parent's daguerreotype. Someday she would get the glass fixed. For now she wanted a safe place for it where Angel wouldn't knock it over by accident. One more fall and the glass would likely crumble.

The bookcases had been righted, and there was an empty spot where books used to sit. She'd place it there until the bedroom was weathertight. She held it up for another good look. Her parents weren't smiling, but then no one did, Ma said. Back then it took so long to take a picture that smiles often drooped. But Ma's eyes seemed to sparkle, and the way Pa stood proud behind her with his hand on her shoulder, she knew they were in love. She wanted that, had begged God for it, and the only one to ask her to marry was a man she didn't love. The frame went on the newly waxed shelf. The women from church had cleaned everything. The marks on the wall she'd made to measure the passing of days since her father left were still there. They hadn't touched them. She brushed them with the hem of her apron, but they smeared. If she stayed, she'd cover them with new chinking when they did the new room.

She had to give Jake an answer soon. Angel had found a lot of motherly love in the cabin's kitchen today. The church women had treated her like one of their own—on a special day. They had her sister laughing.

Laughing. Not the laugh Angel had been offering since their ma passed. This was the belly laugh that started with a throaty chuckle and ended with tears sprinkling Angel's cheeks.

How could she take that away from her sister? Move to some unknown place where they might not even have a home? With Jake hunting gold, they'd be living in some miner's shack. She wouldn't marry him. Besides, something had changed. She liked him still. And that was the problem. She *liked* him, not *loved* him. She wanted to marry for love. She knew that now. Like Annabelle, she'd rather live as a spinster—if she could find a way to support herself. If not on this farm, maybe there would be a place in town she and Angel could afford. Maybe the Shaws would let them live on their farm and help with their baby and clean. They could bring Mr. and Mrs. Jackson and Junior and start their soap-making business.

In her heart, she knew that wouldn't happen. Times were still difficult, and it was doubtful Mr. Shaw could afford to hire her or even feed them long enough for HA to bring in enough money.

Jake was no longer a choice, but that left her staying in Friendship and marrying Travis—just because Pa said so. That rankled her, despite the knowledge she liked Travis a lot, even loved him if she weren't afraid to admit it.

And then there was Annabelle's offer to consider. Heaven

knew that was a bad idea, romantic and adventurous, but not something she should do, and neither should Annabelle. Without a husband or true means of support, it was craziness to think they could move to a new town and open a shop.

The rain-sodden door shuddered against the threshold as it was thrust open. The door had been found in the woods, and one of the men reattached it, assuring her it would work fine once it dried. Annabelle came in leading Angel by the hand. "Heaven, something is wrong with her."

The light in the cabin wasn't sufficient for an examination. Travis had Heaven light the lamps along with the candles so he could examine Angel. Red spots dotted her hairline, and now she scratched her side. He glanced away from his patient to her hovering sister. "Heaven, have you had the measles?"

"When I was five. Is that what Angel has?" Heaven placed a trembling hand on Angel's cheek. "She's burning up."

The pie in Travis's stomach soured. The spots, the fever, and the cough she'd had yesterday were clear signs that she had the dreaded disease. The town needed to be notified, quarantined. The sourness turned to acidic bubbles. People in this town would die.

"The child has the measles?" Shards of panic sliced through the cabin as Mrs. Miles backed away. "Jake, we need to leave now. Neither of us has had them."

"Mother, we need to stay and help." Jake took a step closer to his mother and away from Heaven.

Travis noticed. If the man loved Heaven, why wasn't he

offering her comfort?

"Annabelle,"—Heaven's face leached to the color of porcelain as she spun around and faced her friend—"did you have them when I did?"

Annabelle shook her head in denial. "No, Mother kept me locked in the house every time there was a threat so I wouldn't catch them. It worked, because I didn't catch them."

"Then you have to leave. With Jake and Mrs. Miles." Heaven pushed her friend toward the door. "Jake, get the buggy."

Annabelle whipped away from Heaven and backed up against the wall. "I'm not leaving. You need help. I wasn't here before, but I am now."

Angel scratched at her face.

"Don't." Travis grabbed her hand. "If you do that, you might get scars on that pretty face."

"But—I—can't—help—it. It itches." Angel whined and tried to pull her hand back.

"I'll make a plaster for you. Heaven will smear it on the spots, and it won't itch as much." Travis struggled to talk like a comforting doctor. "The rest of you all need to go back to town. Stay in your rooms. Jake, you need to find Preacher Reynolds and ask him to get the word out. Everyone should stay home. Maybe we can keep the town"—he remembered Angel's presence—"safe."

"Heaven, when you were at church the other day, did anyone mention not feeling well?"

"No, not that I remember." Her wide eyes didn't even blink at him. He knew she was thinking about what had happened the last time a fever came to this cabin. He wanted to reassure her that this was different, but he couldn't. And if he tried, she would know he was lying to her.

"Cassie was coughing. She coughed a bunch." Angel's hand went back to her scalp. Her fingers went walking.

"So it's probably making its way through town now." Travis knew he couldn't turn his back on the town. He would be called, and most likely some would die. He didn't want to look Heaven in the eye and tell her that her sister might be one of them.

Jake took Annabelle's hand. "You need to come with us, Bella. Dr. Logan knows what is best, and that's for us to be in town. It won't help Heaven if Angel gets better and then you get ill."

Bella? So now that Heaven wasn't jumping into Jake's arms, it looked as if he was setting his sights on her best friend. Annabelle seemed to be a smart woman though and would see through him.

Mrs. Miles gathered the stitching she'd brought along. "He's right, dear. Your mother protected you when you were young, and now that she's gone, I feel I should do so in her place. Get your things together. It's a good thing we didn't bring that trunk of stuff along."

"Angel, I'm going out to the barn to get what I need to mix up that plaster for you. Say your good-byes to your friends."

Travis left the cabin with Jake thumping down the porch steps behind him.

"Logan, think she'll survive?"

Travis halted. He stared at the barn and saw army tents in

his mind. "I don't know, Jake. A lot of people don't." His flesh crawled as if he'd been ordered back to the front. Devastation of families awaited him wherever he went. Beads of sweat rolled down his neck as the tents turned into Heaven sobbing over the death of Angel.

Chapter 29

Heaven pinned the last cloth on the line to dry. There had been more washing to do with Angel getting sick to her stomach. Heaven saw Travis running toward her from the woods, holding something. She smiled. He'd been out all day searching for anything belonging to them that might have been dropped in the woods by the tornado. Before lunch he'd found her rocking chair, the paint scratched and the wood dented.

What had he found this time? She met up with him by the porch. He held his treasure behind his back like a little boy. "What is it?"

He gave her a found-a-hundred-dollar-bill grin and brought his arms around front. His hands held the Wharton family Bible. "It got a little wet. Some of the pages are stuck together. Might even be few of them missing. Here." He thrust it into her hands. "I know how much you mourned the loss of it."

"Where did you find it?" She ran her hand across the dark brown leather cover. She never thought to see it again.

"I was walking and searching the ground when a mocking bird let out a screech, and I looked up and saw something catch the light up in a tall tree. The more I stared at it, the more it seemed to call to me. So I climbed and found it wedged tight between two branches. The sun was bouncing off those gilt-edged pages like a beacon so I could find it."

"You climbed the tree for me?" She hugged the Bible to her chest and wished she were brave enough to hug him, too. "For me and Angel? You saved our family history, Travis. Thank you."

A horse came barreling down the drive. Travis pushed Heaven behind him.

"Dr. Logan!" The rider called out.

"I'm here." Travis shouted back.

The man brought the horse to a stop in front of them. "Obadiah sent me. Mrs. Shaw's turned sick, real bad. He wants you to come right away."

Heaven grabbed Travis by the arm. Fear grabbed her by the throat. "You can't go. What if Angel gets worse?"

He pulled away from her, not answering her question. "Ride on back and tell them I'll be there right away."

The messenger nodded and pulled on the reins to turn his horse, giving it a nudge. It took off on a run back to the Shaw's farm.

"I'll be back as quick as I can." Travis walked toward the barn. "You know what to do for Angel. I told you, and I believe you can do this."

Being left alone with Angel sick terrified her, and her body shook with anger. "No, I can't do it." She followed him into the barn.

"I'm taking Charlie if that's okay. He's not as high strung, and I won't have time to baby him when I get there." He saddled the horse.

Heaven clutched the Bible tighter and watched Travis tighten the girth strap on Charlie's saddle. He gave it another quick tug and then buckled it.

"You can't mean to ride off and leave us here."

"She's ill, Heaven. I may be able to help."

"He didn't say she has the measles. Maybe it's just a cold."

"Maybe, or maybe it's something worse. I have to go." He slung the saddlebags over the horse's back.

In between the post and the stall gate, a spider had at one time anchored its web. Some of the threads were broken and quivered in the breeze that snaked through the barn walls. What had made that spider leave its home? She raked her fingers through her hair, stopping at a knot. When had it gotten tangled? "Angel needs you here." *I need you.*

"I took an oath, Heaven. To help people." He gripped his hat tightly in one hand. "You can take care of Angel. I've told you what I would do if I were here. None of it's difficult." He popped his hat on his head.

He was going to leave. She searched for some way to reach him. He had to understand why she couldn't be left. People she loved died or became blind when she took care of them. Guilt joined with fear and braided in anger. Her fingers curled into a fist, her thumbnail worried the top of her index fingers. "Where was that oath when you took care of Pa? Where was it when you decided to raise horses instead of helping people? Why does it have to be important to you now?" Behind her, Mrs. Jackson butted her head against the door. Heaven wanted to do the same. She might as well. The man wouldn't listen to her pleas.

Travis took a step toward her with his arms outstretched.

Did he mean to embrace her? Comfort her? She backed away. Her breath clawed the sides of her throat as it came in and back out at a rapid pace. "Didn't Pa tell you to take care of us? That's what you wanted, right—the farm, me? Well you can have it. All of it. Including me. Just don't leave me here alone to take care of my sister." *Or there is no deal.* She slid the Bible under her arm and wiped her moist hands on her apron then folded them as if in prayer. She rested her chin on her folded knuckles and refused to let him see her tears.

Travis mounted Charlie and tipped his hat. "Miss Wharton, I would never accept a woman in that manner." He kneed the horse and left the barn.

Heaven watched the twitch of Charlie's tail as Travis's back grew smaller. She waited for him to look over his shoulder, even turn around and say he was sorry. He didn't. She wouldn't call after him, beg him to come back, even though the words were tugging at her throat, begging to be said.

She could not allow herself to panic. But how could she stop the ice from taking root in her veins? *Get busy.* Yes, that's what she needed—to do something, follow the directions Travis left.

Her stomach felt pecked full of holes. She stumbled back into the cabin. She'd start supper. Maybe Mrs. Shaw wasn't that sick and Travis would return in time to eat with her. He'd apologize, and she'd forgive him, and he'd promise never to leave her like that again. She clung to the back of the chair where he'd sat since he'd arrived. Why did it seem she could never hold on to a man? Why did they always pick someone or something else instead of her?

Angel. Check on her first. She might have taken a turn for

the worse while Heaven had been in the barn pleading with Travis to no avail.

He'd said he didn't want her. Not the way she was offering herself. The disgust dripped off his lips when he said it as if she where one of those poor girls without mothers who worked in the saloons. Is that what she'd lowered her standards to? She didn't have a mother, and she had just offered herself in a most undignified way.

"Heaven?" Angel called out from the straw bed they'd put together for her yesterday.

"I'm right here." She hustled to her sister's side. "Are you ready for a drink of tea?"

"No. Will you scratch me?"

"I can't do that. I can draw a bath and wash you with lye soap. That seems to help."

Angel rolled away from her. "No. Go away."

"Ah sweetheart. You'll be better soon. Travis said in a few days the rash will all but disappear, and so will the itching."

"Go. Away."

She didn't reprimand her sister for her tone. Truth was she wanted to go away. She didn't want to take care of Angel again. What would happen to her sister this time?

Cook. Get busy. Peel the potatoes and boil them. Open some beans and spoon them into the pan. She operated from memory, not feeling. She even made a plate for Travis and set it in front of his chair. Then she made the fork go in her mouth. *Chew. Swallow. Repeat.* She listened for Charlie's hoofbeats. None came. She finished what was on her plate, scooted out of her chair, and checked on Angel.

"I said go away."

"I'll leave you alone for now. I'll be back as soon as I clean up the kitchen." She picked up Travis's full plate and set it on the stove for later. She shouldn't be angry at him. God had made it apparent that healing was His gift to Travis. But what did He give to her?

As she washed the few plates, she remembered the barn chores would need to be done. It hadn't taken her long to acclimate to Travis doing them for her. She set a dried plate on the hutch and picked up the other to wipe. How did he expect her to milk the cow and feed the horse and the goats while watching Angel every second in case her fever rose? The dishcloth in Heaven's hand whipped across the plate and then over her shoulder as she settled the last dish on top of the other. One pot remained to be cleaned.

He didn't even say he'd be back. He would come back though, wouldn't he? Even though he said he didn't want her? And now that he seemed to want to be a doctor again, did he still want her farm? A dishwater bubble sparkled in the glow of the lamp and expanded from her furious pot scrubbing. *But did that mean he really didn't want her either?* Her hands stilled, and the iridescent beauty exploded.

Travis felt the pace of the last few days. He hoped this was his last stop before getting back to Heaven. And Angel, she had to be better. If she'd turned for the worse, he wouldn't know, because Heaven wouldn't have left her sister to find him. Guilt gnawed at his stomach. He should have at least sent someone to the farm.

"You have to keep the baby away from Mrs. Shaw." Travis stared at Mr. Shaw's eyes until the man blinked.

"I'm sure it's difficult for all of you. I'll explain it to her again. Will you tell her I'm here, please?" Travis stripped off his coat and hung it over the back of a wooden chair. He turned back. "It looks like the town escaped a major epidemic. The mayor is considering lifting the quarantine."

"How many did we lose?"

"One was too many, but the five we lost could have been much higher."

"She won't quit crying for the baby." The man swayed the infant in his arms. "I don't know how much longer I can keep Etta away from her."

Instead of placing the baby in the hand-carved cradle, Mr. Shaw plunked the infant into Travis's arms. "Here, as long she's held, she won't cry. And if she's not making noise, it's easier for me to keep Etta calm."

Before Travis could protest, the anxious husband raced past him to the bedroom. The door closed with a solid clunk.

He eyed the small cabin, looking for a pitcher of water. It would have been good to have at least washed his hands before holding the baby. Perhaps he could lay her down for a second. He made soothing baby sounds and leaned over the cradle. The baby's eyelids sprang open, and her mouth formed an O. Her little chest rose as she sucked in air. Her face turned red. Travis scooped her up and cradled her in his arms before a sound could escape her tiny body. At least he'd washed his hands well before leaving the last sick family.

What was taking so long? He glanced at the door and swayed from side to side. One more look at the bedroom, and he realized he would be holding the baby a little longer. He was so tired, and that rocker by the cradle beckoned him. Maybe Mr. Shaw was having some success at convincing Mrs. Shaw to be patient. He yawned.

He decided to take a chance on the baby not liking the rocker. He'd still be holding her, so maybe she'd remain quiet. He would ease into the chair. He dropped, sinking a few inches at a time until his thighs burned. The baby didn't seem discombobulated, so he sat.

This was nice; babies were nice. Babies with Heaven would be even nicer. He rocked and relaxed. He wanted to get home and talk to Heaven. The way they had left each other sawed at him. Why couldn't she just admit she loved him and would marry him? Instead, she threw the marriage sacrament at him as if it didn't mean anything. He knew she was hurt and scared when she said it, and if he were a lesser man, he would have said, "Fine, let's get it done. Get the preacher and say the words."

But he wanted a home like his parents' home, like the Shaw family's home, and he would wait until she was ready, even if he had to spend the entire winter in the barn.

Etta Shaw's voice rose to a crescendo, and Travis heard her pleading to see the little girl. He wouldn't allow it, not when the mother was this ill. So far the baby seemed healthy. The goat's milk was keeping her body strong, and he wanted her to stay that way. But he couldn't stop Mr. Shaw from taking the baby to her mother. He hoped for the baby's sake Mr. Shaw would be strong enough to make his wife wait.

Mrs. Shaw wailed. Travis's back stiffened. He gripped the tiny baby to his chest and rocked harder. *Please God, heal her mother and protect this little one.* He'd wanted to ask for so much more, but he knew God didn't answer many of Travis's prayers, at least not when it came to healing people. The sun that had shined through the window dimmed, and its yellow fingers on the floor turned to gray.

The baby reached out a tiny hand and slid it across his chin. She was too young to have sensed his sadness and reacted to it with a caress of care, but for Travis it felt as if God had reached out and offered him hope.

Heaven wanted to get the morning chores done quickly, so she crept out of the house before the sun came out. Angel was sleeping. The poor child had worn both of them out with her whining. With a lantern to light the way and the egg basket in hand, she headed for the chicken coop. She'd start there and then feed the rest of the animals. She'd have to come back later and muck the stalls. She'd really hoped Travis would have returned by now, since that was a chore she hadn't minded handing over to him.

Angry squawks blasted from inside the coop. Something was wrong. The chickens shouldn't even be awake. She broke into a run. As the lantern swung from her hand, it cast ghostly shadows across the yard. She reached the door. It was open a crack. She'd shut it last night, hadn't she?

She yanked it the rest of the way open.

Yellow eyes glared at her, and her blood chilled as she took in the scattered feathers and a half-dead chicken clutched between sharp teeth.

A fox—and she hadn't brought the gun. She was armed with a basket and fire.

The fox growled, and she took a step back. She had to get him out of there. They needed those chickens. Without them they would surely starve. Maybe if she opened the door all the way so he'd have a clean exit, he would leave. She eased the basket to the ground but not the lantern. As long as she had that, the fox wouldn't come after her, would it? Putting all of her strength into her one arm, she dragged the lopsided door across the dirt until the opening to the coop was much wider.

Her heart thumping, she picked up the basket, and she banged it against the side of the building. "Get out!"

The stubborn fox didn't move. Just blinked at her. A red feather floated from his mouth.

She stepped to the opening and hurled the basket at him, knocking him squarely between the ears.

He shook his head and feathers flew, but he didn't release the chicken.

She yelled again, stomping her foot. This time he seemed to understand he might be in danger and ran from the building still grasping her chicken. She let him go.

The vim and vigor she had directed at the fox drained away faster than money in a gambler's hand, and hard shivers took their place. Why had she come out without her gun? She could have been attacked, and then Angel would have been all alone. She wanted to collapse onto the damp ground and have a good cry. But if she did, the fox might return.

She set the lantern on the ground and inspected the door. The fox must have tugged on the bottom of the door and worked the hinge loose from the frame. She didn't have the means to repair it or the time. She ran her hand through her hair. If she didn't fix the door, the fox would have another free meal tonight. And he might tell his friends.

She could put the chickens in the barn, but it wasn't as secure as the chicken coop had been. She slid a hank of her hair through her fingers and worried the ends. Was there something in the barn she could easily move back and forth as a temporary door? That wouldn't work, because if she could move it, then so could the fox. It would have to be heavy.

She counted the chickens in the coop. Not many were left. One seemed to be struggling for air. She plucked it off the dirt floor and wrung its neck. She could use it to make broth this morning for Angel. Maybe even have enough meat for a small meal. She took the dead chicken outside, found the bucket to stick it in, and placed it on the porch. After she finished the barn chores, she'd take care of pulling out the feathers.

As for the chickens that were still living, it seemed they would be roosting in her cabin come evening.

Chapter 30

Heaven stood at the stove, eyes burning. Sleep was something she didn't remember. She stirred the chicken broth, hoping that this time it would stay down in Angel's stomach instead of erupting all over her. She rubbed the back of her neck where the knots had settled. She took a small sip of the broth to test the flavor. She had plucked the meat off the bone earlier and set it aside on a plate. She would have some for lunch along with the dreaded green beans. And maybe, just maybe Travis would come home and she would have a meal for him.

She regretted the words she shouted at him before he left. Her embarrassment of throwing herself at him and being rejected clung like the fog clung to the cedar trees outside. She wanted to clear that fog like the sun would clear a foggy day. *Did he feel the same?* She had no way to find out until he returned. She didn't even know how Annabelle and Jake and his mother were doing. Had they come down with the measles as well?

She tasted the broth. It was the right temperature, so she dipped it into a cup and took it to Angel. "Can you sit up for me, sweetheart?"

"I don't want any." Angel rolled away from her.

"Angel, you have to try. You won't get better if you don't eat."

"Chicken broth will not cure the measles. Everybody knows that."

"Angel Claire, you sit up right now and try to drink this." Maybe if she'd barked at her like a ferocious dog, her sister would obey.

Using her elbows, Angel scooted herself up into a half-sitting position. She glared at her sister with her red-rimmed eyes. "You know what's going to happen don't you?"

"Until you drink it, we won't know, will we?" She placed the cup in her sister's hand and waited for her to take a sip. She felt her teeth move over her bottom lip as she chewed on it waiting for the results she figured would happen a moment after the broth hit her sister's stomach. But she had to try to get Angel to eat. Heaven didn't have to wait long, as Angel leaned over the edge of the bed and let the contents of her stomach flow into a pan on the floor.

"I told you so." Angel was too tired to even wipe her face before falling back onto her pillow and closing her eyes.

Heaven reached into the other bucket on the floor that held cold water and a rag. She wrung out the rag and with great care wiped her sister's face. "We had to try, sweetie. Next time I will listen to you. I hope you feel better soon, because we have a whole chicken to eat."

Angel groaned. "I don't want to talk about chicken. Or green beans either."

By afternoon Angel no longer complained, as her fever went from a slow-burning ember to a roaring fire. Heaven stroked her sister's face with a cool washcloth and prayed, begging God to save Angel, to bring her back from this rising fever that attacked her. Unlike the broken dishes–patterned quilt on the edge of the bed, if Angel died, Heaven didn't think her life could be pieced back together.

She had no hope of saving her sister. It was like before, with Ma. Only this time she was doing what Travis told her to do, and it wasn't working. She'd lost track of time between emptying sick buckets and wiping cool rags across Angel. Had it been three or four days since Annabelle had left? And Travis hadn't returned since the night he left. Heaven couldn't remember all of the days. Hours and minutes swirled together since Angel got sick.

Unidentifiable stains splashed across the bottom of her apron. She hadn't even changed her clothes for days. And when was the last time she'd combed her hair? Or even ate? None of it mattered now. She dropped the cloth back into the bucket.

Heaven stood and stretched. Washing her sister down wasn't helping, and Heaven felt blackness slipping into her soul. Maybe if she read a few chapters of the Bible, some of God's promises, she'd feel better. She fetched it from the small table next to the fireplace and brought it to the kitchen chair she'd dragged over next to Angel's bedside.

"Angel, I don't know if you can hear me, but I think reading some of God's words will make us both feel better." The weighty book offered the presence of her father and mother almost as if they sat next to her. When Travis had brought it to her, she'd cried, having thought it was lost forever. She realized he'd taken the time to look for the things that meant the most to her, the daguerreotype, the family Bible, and even that silly book on manners. He hadn't found it—Mr. Jackson did—but Travis rescued it for her. He'd been putting her home back together, not just the cabin her father had given to him. Her home.

"Angel, I'm going to read about the little girl that Jesus healed. Do you remember that story? Everyone thought she had died, and they were on the streets mourning her, but Jesus came and said she wasn't dead but merely sleeping." Her sister didn't move, not even a twitch of an eyelid.

Heaven couldn't remember exactly where to look in the Bible for the miraculous story of Jesus healing the girl before he even arrived at her father's home. As she turned the fragile pages, now water-stained and some even creased from the storm, she thought about how many people in her mother's family had turned these same pages. Had they, too, come here when all seemed lost? There weren't any papers or notes stored in it from those relatives. Perhaps they had only seen the book as something to own and not as a way to grow closer to God, as Ma had taught her and Angel.

Pa began to read from its pages only after Ma had passed on. He'd changed a lot after they moved here from Nashville. He no longer stayed away all hours of the night and came home smelling of cigars and whiskey.

She turned another thin page, and her hand stilled. She saw a passage underlined and something written in small letters next to it. She traced the inked line, Matthew 6:34, with her finger as she read. *"Take therefore no thought for the morrow: for the morrow shall take thought for the things of itself. Sufficient unto the day is the evil thereof."*

Underlined. And a note. No one ever wrote in the Holy Book. Was that her pa's handwriting? She turned the book sideways and pulled it closer to the lamplight. The print was so tiny she had to squint to read it: *This is the way I want my daughters to live.*

She closed the book. *The way he wanted her and Angel to live? Without worry?* She wanted that, too, but how was that possible when her sister could die? Her head clogged with burning tears straining for release. She swallowed them. Even though her emotions warred with her exhaustion, she wanted to think about this message.

She stood and placed the Bible back on the mantel where she'd been storing it since Travis returned it. She tugged the chair a little closer to the fire and picked up the quilt draped across the back. She sat back between the arms of the battered blue rocker and covered her lap with her grandmother's quilt.

What else didn't she know about Pa? The warmth of the fire melded with the weight of the blanket, and her eyelids shuttered. She wasn't going to fall asleep; she needed to make sure Angel's fever didn't climb higher. She rocked a little bit harder in the chair, hoping the action would help her stay awake. She entered into conversation with God, begging Him to heal Angel from the sickness and to bring Travis back to the cabin soon so they could talk. She had many things to say to him. . . .

Startled, Heaven sprung from the rocking chair. What woke her? Was Travis back? A quick glance at the mantel clock and her heartbeat jumped. She'd slept for almost three hours instead of the few minutes she'd intended.

Angel moaned and thrashed in her bed. Her hand smacked against the wall.

Heaven rubbed her eyes as she sped across the floor to her patient. She bent over and pressed the palm of her hand against her sister's rosy cheek. She yanked it back, gasped, and covered her mouth. Angel's fever was higher than ever. She had to lower it. She knew if she didn't, her sister would die. *Cold water this time, not hot, and no blankets piled to keep Angel warm.* Heaven thanked God for bringing her this knowledge through Travis as she rushed with her bucket to fill it with cold pond water. *Please, God, don't take her away from me.*

Travis wondered how Heaven could go on living after losing so many people she loved. Being a doctor at times like this made him feel inadequate. He was supposed to be a healer, and that's what he had wanted to be. When he chose to be a physician, he thought he would be saving people, making their lives better, bringing joy to the world through babies. Not this. Never this.

He straightened the sheets around the small girl, placing her little hands on top of the sheet. Carefully and artfully he arranged her golden hair and closed her eyes. *Cassie, Angel is going to miss you.* This could be Angel lying here instead of her new friend from church. The memory of Angel's face radiating happiness that day in the barn caught him off guard. He knew she would be heartsick, which meant that Heaven would be as well. Once again he would be the bearer of bad news. He was thankful this wasn't Angel, but she would be devastated. *If she lived.* He took a moment to adjust his expression before turning to the parents and saying the words they didn't want to hear. "I'm sorry. There wasn't anything I could do."

The mother's face collapsed like a melting candle, and her husband held tightly to her waist to keep her from dripping to the floor. But from where did the father pull his strength? Travis couldn't imagine being that strong if it were Angel lying there.

They knew she was dying. They'd caught him before leaving the Shaws'. He'd warned them the minute he'd seen her, but the reality that she really did die hit hard. He supposed parents hold on to hope until the bitter end. He thought about Heaven and wondered how Angel was doing. *Please, God, please let her live. Don't let the measles take her as well.* He excused himself and stumbled out of the bedroom, not wanting the parents to see the grief on his own face. Along with the fear that he might be losing someone he had come to love as a daughter.

The stillness of the room woke Heaven. It was too still. *Angel.* Ice sheathed her veins. Her own heart beat in her ears. She threw aside the quilt. It landed in a puddle on top of her feet. She took a step, but the quilt clung to her feet like lint to cotton, slowing her.

She crossed the room to the bed. Angel lay there still, her hair around her like an angel's halo. *Was she?* Heaven's hand went to her throat. *Please, God.* She bit her bottom lip to keep the cry of anguish from bolting. She laid her palm against her sister's head, expecting to feel the ice cold of the dead.

It was cool, normal cool. No fever remained, and her sister

was alive. As the joy of life expanded in her, laughter exploded. "Angel, wake up!"

Her sister stretched her legs under the quilt and then opened one eye. "What's wrong?"

"Nothing's wrong! Everything is right, wonderful! Your fever is gone! You're going to be okay!" Heaven couldn't stop the happy tears—and the snot that came with them. She tugged a hanky from her apron pocket and blew.

"Ew. That's not very proper." Angel sat up in the bed.

"I don't care. I don't care if we are ever proper again as long as you are alive." Heaven crawled into bed next to her sister and gathered her in a hug. "I love you, Angel. Don't you ever scare me with another fever as long as you live. Promise me."

"Okay, but I don't know how to keep that. I'm hungry. Can I have some green beans and taters? I don't want any chicken broth ever again."

"Yes, I'll run down into the root cellar right now."

Angel was awake, and her fever had broken. Heaven couldn't sing enough praises to God for weathering the storm of sickness with her. She'd come out stronger, and she could take care of Angel no matter the circumstances. As soon as she could, she would tell Annabelle that she and Angel would go with her. She loved Travis, but unless he loved her, she couldn't marry him. Despite his kind ways toward her sister, it wouldn't be enough for her. She wanted to be loved the way God loved her. And she had His love now and for always.

She climbed down the ladder to the root cellar. Maybe she should take what was left of the green beans with them to Memphis, because, as her uncle had said, they were life-sustaining even if they weren't appealing after so many days of eating them.

The lamplight flickered and illuminated the jars she'd set aside when the women came the day after the tornado. She might as well take those upstairs and empty them before someone ended up eating them by mistake. She slipped them into the basket she carried.

Once upstairs, she took the jar of beans she would cook and placed it on the table. "Angel, I'll be right back. I want to dump out the jars with the spoiled beans outside."

"Don't take forever. I'm really hungry."

Right now Heaven didn't mind her sister's orders. She was grateful Angel was giving them.

Mr. Jackson waited on the porch. He'd been there since Travis left. Her very own guard goat. "Stay here, and come get me if Angel calls." She laughed. "Now I'm talking to a goat as if he were a living breathing person!"

At the back of the cabin, she popped the lid of the first jar and poured it out. Something chunky landed in the middle of the beans. She held back a gag. The beans were rotten. She opened the second jar and poured. Again something fell out, only this time it clinked against the other thing in the pile. It sounded like metal on metal. What had Great-Uncle put in these beans? She scooted the pile with the edge of her boot. The sunlight streamed into the gray-green mess of beans and sent shots of light back at her. Gold? Could it be? Is that what the message her father had left her meant? What Great-Uncle joked about? She dropped to her knees and slid her hands through the slimy beans and plucked up several gold pieces. Her heart beat rapidly as she opened the other jar and more pieces fell to the ground.

Here was her answer to all of her worries. She might have the means to stay on the farm. If the gold weighed enough, she could buy back her home from Travis.

Or she could take Angel to Missouri to the school.

With the hem of her apron, she wiped the pieces one by one and dropped them into her apron pocket. Sure she had found them all, she stood. The world around her looked fuzzy, as if she were dropped into a fairy-tale land. Even the colors looked brighter to her. Is this what it was like to live in the moment free of worry? Is that what Pa had discovered at some point? It must be why he wrote that message in the Bible. He had no idea that one day she would read it. But God did.

Something nudged her behind. Mr. Jackson tilted his head to her and back to the green beans. "You're right. It's not about the money; it's about what is life-sustaining. I need to remember what I read. Worry will not change anything. God knows my troubles and my happiness."

She turned and ran into the house to tell Angel about the find in the green beans they'd grown to detest. She'd never look at green beans the same way again.

Chapter 31

Travis let Charlie have his head as they rode toward the farm. The horse was as tired as his rider and didn't race to the barn. Travis wasn't sure how he was going to tell Angel about her friend's death. He hadn't been home since the night he told Heaven he didn't want her in the manner she'd offered herself. He hoped that Angel was okay. He should have come sooner or at least sent someone to check on Heaven and Angel.

His head nodded to his chin. He jerked awake just as Charlie entered through the barn door. Pride and Joy nickered when he saw Charlie. Travis dismounted and unbuckled the saddle. He slid it from the horse's back and tossed it over his shoulder. He carried it to the vacant sawhorse next to the one holding Pride and Joy's saddle and plopped it down.

He wished there was someone else who could take care of Charlie for him tonight. As much as he loved brushing horses, it was the last thing he wanted to do. He made quick but careful work of it, put Charlie in his stall, and gave him some grain. The kitten, Miss Simmons, wove between his legs as he walked to the door of the barn. He bent down and picked her up and scratched behind her ears. "Did you miss me? I'll be back as soon as I check on Heaven and Angel, and you can sleep on my chest." He set the kitten gently down on the ground and pulled the barn door shut just far enough that he could squeeze through it when he came back to sleep.

There was one light flickering through the shutter cracks, creating dancing shadows across the porch as he walked the beaten path. At the door, he knocked gently. He waited. No one came. Scared, he flung open the door, hoping that Heaven wouldn't be aiming her father's shotgun at him.

The door shuddered against the floorboards, but he didn't hear anything. No cries of alarm. No shouts of "Get out!" Only quiet. He tiptoed inside, and by the firelight, he could see that Angel lay very still on her bed. Heaven was surrounded by chickens on the floor, and her head was resting on Angel's chest. Travis's heart lifted at the sweet scene and then plummeted. Had Angel died?

"Heaven!" His feet propelled him across the room, and he dropped to the floor next to the woman he loved. He touched her hair softly, stroking it so he wouldn't scare her as she woke. Her eyes fluttered for a second and then opened wide as she realized Travis knelt beside her.

"Travis, Angel is fine." She hastened to stand while putting her finger to her lips. He followed her to the door, and they went to the porch. "I thought she was going to die. I really did. But I remembered what you told me, and I did my best to keep her cool despite her asking for more covers. And then this morning—early this morning—she opened her eyes and she wanted to eat something. Green beans! It was a miracle, Travis. God blessed us—He let me keep Angel."

Travis pulled her into his arms, and she nestled into them. She felt like home. He hugged her tighter, wanting to tell her how much he loved her and missed her. "I am so sorry that I couldn't get back here to help you. I wanted to. Every time I tried to leave, someone else came needing me, asking me, pleading with me to help them save their family members."

"How many died?" Heaven peered at him with eyes of blue.

Could she read that in his face? "Not as many as I feared. But one death nearly broke me." The words that tried to follow clogged in his throat.

"Who was it?" Heaven brushed the side of his arm with her hand. Her touch comforted him. "You can tell me."

He shook his head and then realized she would find out anyway. "Cassie, Angel's new friend. I tried so hard to save her, but there wasn't anything I could do." He drew from his professional doctor attitude and pasted a calmness he didn't feel across his face. Right now, he didn't want to be a doctor. He was on the edge of shouting he only wanted to be the husband that held her and comforted her.

Heaven wavered like cotton in the wind in front of him, and he noticed the circles the color of eggplant under her eyes. Concerned, he reached out and steadied her. "Have you slept at all since I left?"

"Only a little. Every time I drifted off, it seemed her fever spiked higher, so I began to stay awake to make sure I didn't miss an opportunity to cool her with a washcloth. I am not sure how much longer I could have continued. At one point. . .I thought. . .I'd lost her."

"But you didn't, Heaven. You saved your sister." He took

her by the elbow and directed her toward the rocking chair. "You need to sit and rest. I'll take over watching her tonight."

"But Travis, you look as tired as I feel. You need to rest in case someone needs you."

"I'm not leaving. Not again."

"Really? I— I'm hoping you're not going to give up doctoring because of what I said before you left. I need to talk to you. Travis, some things have changed. I've changed."

"I can see that. Why are the chickens in the house?"

"The door won't close, and there was a fox inside killing the chickens. I had it trapped, but I didn't have my gun. I couldn't leave Angel alone or I would have waited for it to return so I could kill it. I decided rather than lose what little food we have left, I'd bring the critters inside." She wrinkled her nose. "It wasn't my best decision. They make a mess, and it smells in here."

"I'll fix the door tomorrow, and then I'll help you clean this up. I have some things I need to tell you as well. If you're not going to go to sleep, maybe we should make some coffee and talk." He let go of her but held on to her hand and walked her to the rocking chair. Once she was settled, he snatched up the quilt that lay on the floor and draped it over her lap.

"The stove should still be warm. I made dinner for us."

"Good, then it won't take as long to make the coffee." He headed to the stove to put on a pot. During his absence, he couldn't wait to get home to her, reinforcing the feeling of love in his heart. He was going to ask her to marry him. He touched his pocket where his great-grandmother's small gold ring rested. His mother had insisted that he bring it along with him even though Travis was reluctant. His mother was confident God would provide the perfect mate for him, and it seemed He had. But first Travis wanted to be sure Heaven no longer had feelings for Jake.

Travis knelt in front of the chair and looked into Heaven's eyes. Was this the right time ask her? No. She was exhausted. He would give her the news that he brought from town and then make sure she went to sleep upstairs in the loft while he looked after her sister. Tomorrow would be better. That's when he would ask her. Things always looked better in the light of day, and he didn't want to follow bad news with a marriage proposal.

"Heaven, I saw Jake and Annabelle in town. They didn't stay at the hotel. Jake acquired tickets for Nashville."

"But Travis, you told them to stay to make sure they didn't get sick. I need to send a telegram and see how they are." She threw back the quilt from her lap.

Travis put both hands on her arms and stared at her eyes. "Not tonight. Besides, Annabelle sent you a letter. I have it in my pocket. And Jake asked me to tell you something." He looked away from her. He didn't want to see the pain in her eyes when he told her—if there was pain.

"What did Jake say?" Heaven's voice held a hint of sorrow.

"He said. . ." Travis could feel the tension mounting across his shoulder blades as he worked for the right words to leave his lips. "He asked me to tell you that he hoped you would understand, but he was releasing you from his marriage promise. He wanted to tell you in person, but he never got the chance and didn't want to wait until it was safe to come back to the cabin." Travis thought the man a coward. He didn't like to say that about another man, but in this case, he felt justified. It wasn't right not to tell Heaven in person that he wouldn't marry her.

She didn't say anything. She sat there quiet for a moment. He looked at her, afraid he'd see tears spiraling down her face. Instead, she had no expression at all. "Heaven? Are you okay?"

She blinked. "Yes. I didn't think marrying Jake felt right anymore. He wanted me to go west with him and look for gold. And leave Angel with his mother. I couldn't do that, especially now that I almost lost her again. She will always be a part of my life and will always live with me. No man is going to take her away from me."

She stared at him as if he were the one who suggested Angel live somewhere else.

The fire crackled and sent a spark in the air. Angel rolled over in the bed, and Heaven's eyes went to her immediately. Travis jumped to his feet. "I'll check on her. Stay here and rest."

He felt her presence behind him so close he could feel her breath on his neck. He should have known she wouldn't stay, but he wouldn't send her back. He knelt down next to Angel and whispered her name. "Angel? Are you awake? I've come back to see you. How are you feeling?"

Angel rolled over and faced him. Her face was gaunt and white even with the yellow lamplight. She looked so much smaller than when he left, as if she had lost ten pounds even.

"Hi. You were gone a long time. Heaven had to bring the chickens in the house. It smells funny. Are you going to fix the chicken coop door so they can leave?" She rubbed her eyes and yawned. "I'm glad you're back. Heaven missed you, and so did I. I hope you won't leave again."

"I'm not going anywhere, Angel." He bent over and whispered in her ear so Heaven couldn't hear him. "Nothing can make me leave you two ever again."

"Heaven?" Angel's eyes fluttered open. "I'm hungry. Did you tell Travis about the green beans yet?"

Travis whipped his head around and looked at Heaven. Was Angel falling back into another fever?

"No. I'll tell him later. First I will get you something to eat. How about a little chicken broth?"

"No! Please, can't I have something else?"

"Heaven, I think that she could try a little food."

"I ate the green beans, and they stayed down, but I don't want any more of those."

"What about a piece of toast? Would you like that Angel? Does that sound good?" Travis stroked the little girl's arm.

"Can I have some jam Annabelle brought on it?"

"Of course you can," Heaven said. "I'll make it right now."

"No. You sit with your sister, and I will make it."

Angel gave a weak laugh. "Men don't cook."

"This one does." He fished in his pocket and withdrew Annabelle's letter. "You read this while I make a mess of what's left clean in your kitchen. Those chickens have made themselves at home in there."

She smiled at him. The sadness he'd experienced in the past days melted away.

"Thank you." She tore open the envelope and read aloud.

Dear Heaven and Angel,

*I hope you recover quickly. Jake has arranged for
us to leave by carriage in a few moments. He thinks I
am going back with them to Nashville. I am not. I am
going to continue on with the plans I discussed with you,
providing I can find a way to exchange my ticket for
Memphis. I'll write to you as soon as I am settled. You
and Angel are welcome to come to Memphis and live with
me. There we can be our own little family and take care
of ourselves, answering to no man. Affectionately,*

Annabelle

She folded the letter and stuck it in her apron pocket.

"I hope Jake is able to stop her." Travis feared for the young woman, thinking she could travel alone and not be accosted in these times of restless recovery.

"I'm afraid Annabelle is headstrong, and Jake doesn't seem to have much strength to fight anything right now. She may get her way unless Mrs. Miles manages to change Annabelle's mind, and that is very likely. I shall pray that is what happens."

"You wouldn't want to go with her?" Travis asked.

"We could. But I don't think it's the right thing to do for Angel."

"Is anyone going to bring me toast with jam?" Angel wrinkled her nose. "Heaven, we really need to get these chickens out of here."

"Yes, of course. I'll start making that toast right away, Little Miss. And it's good to see you feeling better and ordering us around."

"You see, Travis, Angel is back to being a sweet young lady with all the rules memorized from our book." Heaven slid a hand over her mouth. Her laugh snuck past her fingers.

Angel fell back against the pillow. "The proper Angel is gone. And she is never coming back." She struggled back up on her elbows, "Did I miss Christmas?"

Heaven turned and looked at Travis. "What day is it?"

"Tomorrow is Christmas. It's Christmas Eve." The crestfallen look on her face told him she wasn't prepared. "Don't worry, I'm pretty sure Christmas will be wonderful. We will celebrate Angel being healthy." And while they were sleeping, he planned to do a little decorating of his own to bring Christmas joy to the house. And as tired as Heaven looked, he was sure she would sleep through the entire process. He only hoped that Angel would as well, since she was downstairs. Unless now that she was feeling better he could convince her to go upstairs in the loft and sleep with her sister.

Travis had worked through the night quietly carrying out chickens and putting them back into the coop after fixing the door by lantern light. Neither Heaven nor Angel had put up much of a fight about sleeping in the loft once he said he wanted to clean up the mess made by the chickens. Angel thought it was good to sleep somewhere else besides a bed of hay, and Heaven was happy just to lie down with her sister.

Once the chickens were out of the house, he made quick work of scrubbing the floor by candlelight. Then he went outside and cut down a very small cedar to use as a Christmas tree. He set it up in the corner of the living room and wondered what he could use to decorate it. Scratching his head, he could not come up with any ideas. There might be decorations somewhere in the cabin, but he didn't know where to look and probably shouldn't. Instead, he folded up a sheet of paper and wrote Heaven's name on the back and put it under the tree. He then went to the barn to retrieve from his saddlebag the new toy he had bought for Angel for Christmas. By then it was time to do the morning chores. When he came back inside, the two of them were still sleeping, which made his plan all that much better. He banked the fire, poking it until it blazed with warmth. Then he filled the coffeepot with water and ground the beans before placing the pot on the stove.

Upstairs he could hear Heaven and Angel waking up. There were some whispers and giggles, and finally he heard feet coming down the stairs. He turned to greet them, "Merry Christmas!"

They returned the greeting, both wearing huge smiles.

Heaven looked around the room with wonder. "Angel, there's a tree. Travis put up a tree for us. And the chickens are gone."

"I thought it smelled better." Angel touched her sister's hand, "Where is the tree?"

Heaven wound her fingers through her sister's hand. "Come with me. It's in the corner." She led Angel to the tree. "Travis, this is the most special tree we've ever had."

"What does it look like? What decorations are on it? Are there candles?" Angel reached out and brushed the branches in front of her.

"I'm sorry there aren't any. I didn't want to wake you up trying to find something to decorate the tree with. I thought maybe we could do it together today." Travis stood behind the girls. "If we have it decorated by this afternoon, we could make a very special Christmas dinner with some of the things that I brought back from town."

Angel popped a hand over her open mouth and squealed. "Did you bring back good food? Like candy?"

"You will just have to wait and see."

"I have a few things I want to put under the tree to open this evening, too." Heaven's nose crinkled up as she noticed there was something under the tree with her name on it. Her hand snaked out to reach for the paper. "Is this for me?"

"Yes it is, but you have to wait." Travis loved this part of Christmas. He had missed the past few Christmases while he was away at war. Memories of teasing his sisters and his sisters teasing him about packages that were hidden and what they might contain filled him with happiness. As did this package he left under the tree. It would make Heaven smile.

Later that evening the three of them gathered around the tree. At Travis's request they sang Christmas songs.

"Can we open the gifts now?" Angel bounced on tiptoes.

He hadn't told her about her friend yet. That sad news could wait a day. "Yes Angel, let's open the presents." He reached under the tree and withdrew the doll he'd bought for her at the general store and placed it in her waiting hands.

Carefully she pulled the paper away. Her hand moved over the porcelain face and the hair. "Heaven, it's a doll! What does she look like? Are her eyes blue like mine?"

"Yes they are, and when you tip her as if you were putting her to bed, they close. Her hair is the color of sunshine on hay."

Heaven's voice seemed thick with emotion. Travis hoped he hadn't made her sad. He reached over and withdrew the paper from under the tree. "This is for you."

Her sapphire eyes gazed at him, questioning.

"Open it."

She unfolded the paper and read it. "Travis, are you sure?"

"Yes I am. This place should belong to you and Angel, not me. I don't know why your father gave it to me."

"Because he knew you, Travis. He knew you would come here and find us and make sure we were okay."

"That's not all, Heaven. There's something. . ." He gave a quick glance at Angel who seemed to be involved in figuring out how to unbutton her doll's dress. "Can you step out on the porch with me?"

She nodded, but he noticed she kept a tight grip on the deed to the farm.

Outside he grasped her hand in his. "I never wanted to marry someone because it's what people do. I wanted to fall in love and have a marriage like my parents. When your father *gave* you to me, it bothered me sorely."

She tried to pull her hand back, but he held tight.

"Wait, I'm not done."

Her hand stilled in his, and he could feel her pulse in her fingertips.

"I'm sure by now you realize how much I care for you. I love you. I love Angel as well. And while I know your father gave you to me in his will, I want you to want me." He bent down on one knee. "Miss Heaven Wharton, would you please do me the honor of becoming Mrs. Travis Logan?"

He watched her eyes widen, and tears pooled, creating a sapphire lake.

"I will."

Travis hopped to his feet and gathered her in an embrace, kissed her like a man in love, and then let out a whoop of joy.

"You must of told him about the gold," Angel said.

"Gold?"

"No, not yet, Angel. He asked me to marry him, and I said yes. Travis, I discovered why there were so many green beans. Great-Uncle used them instead of the bank to deposit his gold. So I'd like to give you some of it for Christmas. With that you can achieve your dream of raising horses on the Logan Farm."

"How about we call it the WL for Wharton and Logan?" Travis wanted to hug her again.

"I like it," Angel said from the doorway. "I'm going back inside to play with my doll so you can kiss each other again."

"Travis, don't give up being a doctor. You can do both. This town needs you. God gave you the gift of healing and teaching. You taught me how to care for Angel, and I'm sure there are other things I—as well as the people of Friendship—can learn. I'd give you all of the money, but"—she looked to see if Angel was really inside—"I'd like to send Angel to school someday to learn to read Braille."

Heaven stroked his arm, starting a fire the size of a barn. He backed away. "Honey, I'll do what you ask if you will do this one thing for me."

"What?" Her eyes narrowed as her head tilted.

"Ride into town with me right now and marry me so I don't have to spend another night without you by my side."

She smiled, and her eyes sparkled with joy. "I'd be honored. I'll get Angel, and you get the wagon."

"I'll get the wagon"—he pulled her to him—"after I kiss you one last time as Miss Wharton."

Angel stuck her head out the door. "Does that mean once she's Mrs. Logan you won't be wastin' time kissin' anymore?"

"No Little Miss, that's never going to stop. You'll have to get used to it."

Discussion Questions

1. In the story, Heaven Wharton reaches for a rifle out of fear instead of using words. Can you think of a time when out of fear you reacted in the wrong way?

2. Heaven suffers from the burden of worry. She looks to the future and finds no easy answers. Why do you think she doesn't turn to God immediately?

3. In the beginning, Heaven is overprotective of her sister, Angel. Is there someone in your life you're trying to overprotect? If yes, what steps can you take to give them freedom to grow and trust God with their future?

4. Travis Logan no longer wants to use his gift of being a doctor, and yet time after time he is called upon to help someone. What gift has God given you? Do you embrace it or fight against using it? Why?

5. Why do you think Heaven has problems believing God will take care of them?

6. What is your favorite scene in the book? What made it stand out for you?

7. Which character did you relate to the most? Why? Was this your favorite character?

8. How does Angel's story parallel Annabelle's?

9. Talk about a time you had to make a choice between two things that meant a lot to you.

10. Do you think Heaven made the right decision to tell Jake she wouldn't marry him?

11. The rocking chair is where Heaven retreats to feel safe. Where do you go?

12. Do you feel any sympathy for Jake? Would you like to know if he is able to forgive himself?

DIANA LESIRE BRANDMEYER has a background in education and psychology. Her credits include *My Devotions*, *The Metro East Family Gazette*, *Little Visits Family Devotions*, and *The Lutheran Witness*. She received her degree from Webster University. She lives in southern Illinois where the corn grows at a rapid rate behind her home. She is married and has three grown sons, all on their own now, each of them bringing someone special to join the family.